LOVE,
LIFE AND
NEW YORK

LOVE, LIFE AND NEW YORK

Part True Part Fiction

SHANTAM DHAANAK

PARTRIDGE

A Penguin Random House Company

To order additional copies of this book, contact
Partridge India
000 800 10062 62
orders.india@partridgepublishing.com

www.partridgepublishing.com/india

CONTENTS

DEDICATION

*All my creations are dedicated to the girl who asked me
to keep writing that beautiful diary for her.*

CHAPTER 1

ME? I AM JUST A REGULAR GUY

WHAT DID YOU DO AS a fifteen year old boy in 9th standard? Well, most probably, you played football with your friends, you annoyed the teachers you didn't like, and you watched wrestling shows at home or if you were a really sincere student you studied at your respective tuitions. Let me tell you what my routine was like. Oh no, wait, first, let me tell you who I am.

I am Deven Dhaanak. I am a guy that you would probably miss on a busy road. I am not flashy at all. People who know me can tell you that. I stand five feet and eight inches with a wheatish complexion, I have hair that would remind you of maggi, and I wear big glasses. This is actually the description of a really big loser. But, in real life, I had always been quiet famous, in my school I mean, not for my looks or my style precisely, but for my friendly and warm nature. I always meet people with a smile on my face and treat everybody as a friend. Maybe that is the reason why everybody calls me a friend, or to be precise, they call me 'bhai'. Now, that is a nickname that I got because of how I look or maybe how I walk. Not much of a bodybuilder though, I have always been Interested In all that stuff. It was like my passion to me. Moreover that nickname was given to me because I am a huge fan of Salman Khan. I mean, who isn't? But moving forward, this is all that I am. No special features to make me an extraordinary looking guy or not that wealthy to own a city. I am a regular guy who lives in a normal house with a normal and typical Indian drama family.

So, I was telling you about my routine when I was in the 9th standard. Well, I was not a geek. I was actually a very hyperactive teenager who wanted to do a lot in a very short period of time. I was on the school basketball team, cricket tem, quiz team, debate team and to top it all I was the bhangra captain of my school team. Now some people would be fascinated to see the word captain linked with 'bhangra'. Well, bhangra is a dance form practiced in almost every state, cIty and culture in India. But it is particularly derived from the Punjabi culture. In India, each and every function starts with this dance. Though in some marriage functions it is initiated by the drunk uncles who claim to be great at it. So, I was telling you about bhangra, a lot of energy is required to perform this dance form as the moves can be pretty tricky. But as a teenager and moreover a north Indian, I had mastered this art form. Basically, the guy with the most flexible and energetic body was designated as the leader of the group. But in some schools, like in ours, the leader of the bhangra group was designated as the 'captain'. This should give you guys a hint why I was so famous in my school. I was almost everywhere.

I had friends who were like my brothers at that time. Obviously, with age and time you loose connection, but anyway, it was all good in my life. My family was great. I came from a Haryanvi family who never really lived in Haryana. I had mostly spent all of my childhood In

Chandigarh although I was born in Haryana. Being the older child n the family is a burden and especially when you have a baby sister. You are supposed to set an example for the younger ones. Thankfully, my parents decided to stop producing more siblings for me after Tamanna.

I had a really huge clan. My father had 3 brothers and 3 sisters and all of his siblings had 2 chIldren each. So that kind of sums up to be a big total. As far as my mother's family was concerned, they were a little more population conscious. My mother was the youngest of the 3 children my grandparents had. I had a maasi and a maama and just as the ritual goes both of them had 2 children each. So you can see how huge my family actually was. But I was lucky that all of my relatives didn't live in the same city. My father and his elder brother i.e. my taauji decided to live together, and that was the reason our two families lived under the same roof. I had two brothers, Saman and Naman. Both were my taauji's sons. We loved each other. We had spent all our life together until I lost one of them. But more on that later.

So, to sum it all up, this is how my life was when I was in 9th standard. Everything was going smooth until she showed up. Who was she? You can call her my nightmare. She was an arrogant, egotistical and the most stubborn girl I had ever met in my life. Harshaali Singh Sandhu, yeah, that was her name. Isn't that too long to be a name? Seriously, there should be a law against these kinds of names that are hard to remember and even harder to pronounce.

Well, as I was saying, she was the most obnoxious girl I had ever met in my life. I don't know if it was my bad luck or somebody who hated me a lot had cursed me in a very dIfferent and cruel way. She was a typIcal Sardaarni. Everything about her was so cliche. Long brown hair, one could literally smell coconut oil standing a mile away from her, attitude like she came from a place far beyond our reach, that only she was supposed to be in. It was like she had come to the school to ruin our lives. As annoyIng as she was, she was far more intelligent than all of us. Even I was considered as a topper in my class. But that girl had a brain that made us look like 6 year olds, and I hated that so much. I hated her. I didn't want to talk to her or see her or sit around her in the class or do anything that involved her presence. But as we all know, Karma Is a bitch, and that bitch was furious at me and wanted to bite the hell out of me. Our class supervisor decided that my seat should be right behind her. I have no idea why she did that. Maybe she knew I hated her and wanted to punish me. And the worst part was that I had to sit like that for more than a month, until the class supervisor decided to change the seat format again. So, basically I was stuck with her. The guy who sat next to me was a dumb Idiot and had no idea what was my situation. So, there was nobody I could talk to except Harshaali.

It was depressing as I had to sit behind her and smell her coconut hair all day long. Sometimes, when she would get up to go somewhere in a hurry, she would turn instantaneously and her long, bulky hair which she tied in a knot would strike me in the eye. I was sick of her hair. It was a torture that I had to sit through it all and do nothing.

One day, suddenly she started talking to me. First I was a little confused as it was the first time I had heard her voice. The biggest surprise was that she was smiling.

'HI. Do you realise we have been sitting like this for the past 3 weeks and we haven't talked to each other yet?' she said. It was obvious that she didn't like talking to me either. She must have heard It from somewhere that there is this guy in the class who does not like you at all and stuff. Girls are like that. They like to transfer the information along as they get it.

'Yes, I know we have been sitting like this for more than 3 weeks, and I also know that I don't have anything to talk to you about.' I said.

'Well, we can always start by knowing about each other. Let's start by discussing what we already know. You go first. What do you know about me?' she asked with a little smile on her face.

I couldn't tell her how much I hated her because that would have been inappropriate. So I thought about what I knew about her and my answer was as dumb as it gets.

'I know you are from a Punjabi family.' I said. I can bet she could literally see a question mark hanging on my head as I had no idea who she really was.

'Hmm.. Don't you think that's pretty obvious?' she said, barely able to keep herself from laughing on my face.

'I know It's obvious, but that all I know about you. We haven't talked to each other, ever. This is probably the longest conversation we have ever had, keeping aside that argument that we had in our science class.' I said In an Irritated voice.

'Ok ok. It's not the end of the world Deven. Ok let's start now only. I will tell you something about me and you have to tell me the same about you, ok?' she sounded cheerful today. Or maybe I thought so because it was the first time I was talking to her.

'Alright, we can do that. There's nothing else that we have to do.' I said, trying to sound uninterested.

'Ok, so where should I start from? Got it. I live In Panchkula only. I am from a Punjabi family that you already know. I have a younger brother in the same school in class 5. You go. 'She said and pointed her Index finger at me.

'Hmm I am from Haryana but I have never lived there. I have always been In Chandigarh and yes, I also have a sister studying in our school. She is in 6th standard right now.' I said. It was strange but I was smiling. I had no Idea why.

'See. That was a good start. Ok, my parents are both working and my best friend's name Is Radhika Sharma who lives the same neighbourhood as mine.' She said. The conversation was now getting interesting.

'Ok. My father is a businessman and my mother's a housewife and she is a great cook by the way, I just like telling this. 'I said with a childish smile on my face.

'Hey. How come we have never tried anything that your mom sends in your Tiffin box? If she's such a nice cook you must ask her to make something for us.' She said.

'Ok I will surely ask her to make something for you. What do you like In food?" I asked as If I was going to make that for her.

'Ammm.. I guess rajma rice would be my choice.' She said.

'You like rajma rice?' I asked. There was actually something common between us. I was crazy about rajma rice since I could pronounce rajma rice.

'Yes. Don't you?' she said It like I had committed a crime.

'No.' I said.

'How the hell can a north Indian Haryanvi boy not like rajma rice?' she asked me like It was a sin not liking rajma rice.

'I love rajma rice. I don't just like them.' And then we both started laughing looking at each other's expressions.

'Would you really ask her to make some for me?' she asked with a cute puppy face.

'Of course. I would bring that for you tomorrow.' I said and the teacher entered the class.

Our first conversation was a nice one. We learned some Interesting facts about each other and established that we both loved rajma chawal. It was nice talking to her. It was the first time, after her joining the school that I didn't hate her that much.

After that we started talking almost every day and sometimes we would just talk about random stuff like what shows I liked on TV, what malls we went to, what movies we liked. I knew a lot more about her now. She would talk to me about everything now. Like what happened with her last the previous evening, what she thinks about a random guy in the class, which girl she thinks was a bitch and so on. Eventually we became friends and all the hatred I had for her disappeared. It was hard for me to understand too until I finally got the answer to my confusion.

'Yaar we guys never do anything fun here. We just sit idle and do nothing but talk. Talking is not fun.' She said. She sounded irky.

'Talking can be fun too sometimes.' I said, not looking at her.

'Shut up Dev. Talking Is boring now. I have an Idea. Let's play truth or dare. What' say?' she said, with that Instinctive grin on her face. Sometimes that grin on her face gave a picture of evil in her. But as usual I agreed to what she said.

'Ok, I am assuming that everybody here knows the rules.' she said, pointing towards me, Abhilasha and Sooraj. Abhilasha was her best friend and Sooraj was, well, he sat next to me.

'Yeah we all know the rules. Start the game now.' I said as I spin the pen. The pen stopped and it was Harshaali's turn first

We were in the 9th standard and that means we were teenagers, all of us. So we only had a few questions in our minds for each one of us. Sooraj was supposed to ask the question.

'Truth or dare?' He asked. I could see he was ready with his question if she chose truth.

'Truth.' She said.

'I was hoping you chose that. Ok, so tell me, do you have a crush on anyone?'

I wanted to know this too. Not that I liked her or anything. Just for my own knowledge.

'No yaar. I mean there is nobody in the class, or in the school. If that's what you are asking.' She said, very confidently. You see that's the first rule when you lie to someone in their face. You have to make sure that he believes you, and In order to do that you should be able to believe yourself first. So whenever you are in a situation where you don't want the truth to be out in the open, lie confidently.

'Hmmm... that's diplomatic. But it's ok.' Abhilasha said, smiling at her.

The pen was rolled again and this time it was my turn. Harshaali was supposed to ask the question from me.

'Truth or dare Dev?'

'Truth.'

'Alright. I have a very serious question for you.'

'Go on and ask anything. I have nothing to hide from anyone.' I said.

'Do you like any girl from the class?' she prompted and looked at Abhilasha.

'Ammmm... I don't really have any fondness for any particular girl in the class. I do have good friends, like you. We have been good friends for almost 2 months now. But no, I don't really like anyone in the class.' I said and took a long breath.

'You are so boring Deven. I wish you had said some girl's name so that we could have made fun of you and teased you the whole day.' Harshaali said.

'Yeah well maybe that's the reason I didn't take a name' I said and winked at her.

She smiled.

The teacher from the next classroom interrupted our game. She came in to calm the class down as our class was making a hell lot of noise. The school peon had complained about us.

I went back home thinking why would Harshaali want to know about who I like. I was in my room lying down and still thinking about Harshaali. Maybe I liked her, maybe I didn't. But I was not sure If she liked me or not.

The same evening I was walking outside my house when I saw Abhilasha. We lived across the street since we were both little kids. Our families knew each other from a long time. But this was the first time she stopped to talk to me. I mean we had talked before. But this was different. This time it was a little serious.

'Dev, I think we need to talk.' She said in a very serious manner.

'What is it that you want to talk about?' I said. I was surprised that she wanted to talk to me suddenly.

'You remember we were playing that game today?'

'Yeah obviously I remember. What about It?'

'You need to know something. Harshaali really likes you.'

I was out of words at that moment. I didn't know how to respond to that. What could I possibly ay to this?

'Are you serious? I mean why? And since when?' another stupid question.

'What do you mean why? Why does someone like somebody? Do we really need a reason?'

'No we don't need a reason. But I still don't think that's true. She should have told me if this was the case.'

'She is dumb just as you are. We had to tell her that she likes you. She is talking to you all day long. We only see her in the lunch break. You guys are always smiling at each other. Don't you guys get the signs?'

'The signs, ok now I am confused and I need to think.' I said and walked back to my house.

'She likes me. Oh my god Harshaali likes me. That good news I guess. But wait, do I like her?'

All this was running in my mind as I paced up and down my room. Some things had changed in the past month. I did not hate Harshaali at all now, Infect I liked her. I didn't have any problem with her hair; I started liking its smell. I loved her voice. I often told her to audition for an RJ In a radio station. I also liked the way she talked. I even liked her attitude now. At first I hated her because I didn't know much about her. But after becoming friends with her I realise that she was a great girl, she was fun to hang around with. And I also noticed that she was quiet pretty. But I never saw myself with her like that.

The next morning was a Sunday. Normally I used to be happy about it, but this time it was different. I missed her. I missed talking to her and watching her in the class all day. That was strange. I had never felt like that for anyone. I was fifteen years old and this was my first crush. I liked this girl and I realised it today. I knew I was thinking too much. I did not have anyone to talk about this. She had Abhilasha and her other friends to discuss this with. But I had nobody. Then suddenly I found someone to talk to about all this. It was Naman, my older brother. He was always the cool brother and I could discuss anything with him. And he was also quiet experienced in this matter if you know what I mean.

'Bhai.. I think I have a problem.' I said. We were sitting in his room watching a movie called Wanted. It was a Salman Khan starrer. We were both huge fans of that guy.

'Girl problem? Like someone?' he asked. I had one of those looks that you get when you are about to say something and the other person says the same thing first. I just kept staring.

'Yeah... but how the hell do you know?' I asked. I had no idea how he guessed that so easily.

'Experience brother...' he said, closing the laptop screen.

'Tell me the whole thing...' he said

'Well, it all started a month ago. There's this girl in my class. A sardaarnI. I didn't like her at first. I actually hated her. But then we started talking and now I guess she has become the first girl that I have had a crush on this bad. I am only thinking about her. I am not being able to get her voice out of my head. I guess this is a problem. What do you think?' I said and took a long breath.

'Hmmm.. Does she like you?'

'Well her friends tell me that she does.'

'Did you ask her out yet?'

'That is actually what I am asking here. Should I ask her out?'

'If she likes you and you like her then what is the problem? Does she have a boyfriend already? 'He asked.

'No, I don't think so.' I said

'then you should go for It. 'he said

That was the end of our conversation. Now I knew that I definitely like her. But the problem was that I did not have any Idea how to tell her.. the same night I was planning some stuff. I was actually trying to find out ways to tell her about how I felt about her. But there was nothing that I could do except one thing.

Chapter 2

How we started

I WAS GETTING READY FOR SCHOOL. A little more than I used to. I wanted to look extremely good today. I was going to tell her that I like her and I wanted to ask her out. I was so nervous. This was my first crush and I was not sure how It would go because I had no Idea how she would respond to this. Would she get mad? Would she be flattered? Would she just simply Ignore me? I was afraid because I was putting my newly formed friendship with her on the line. But I had to take that risk. I had to know If something could happen between us. So I was pretty sure that today was the day, the judgement day.

I entered the class and went straight towards Harshaali. She turned to me and I saw something in her eyes. She was wearing kaajal today. Her almond eyes looked so pretty. I was left speechless then and there.

'Hi Dev, How are you?' she said with a smile that made me smile now.

'I am good. I need to talk to you about something.' I said.

'Hmmm. You sound so serIous. Is everythimg ok?' she asked.

'I wish it was...'I said.

We walked out of the class. I was still carrying my school bag. We walked through the corridors towards the canteen. She wanted to know what I was thinking.

'What's wrong Dev. Speak up now you are scaring me?' She said, worried.

'There's nothing to be scared about. It's just that, I need to know something from you. I will talk to you in last class ok. It's free today.' I said. I knew she didn't want to hear it at that time. So I changed the topic.

'Did you prepare for the mathematics test today?' I asked

'Can you ever prepare for a mathematics test Dev? She said.

'Well you are a genius, so maybe you did.' I said and instantly got smacked in the head.

'Don't ever call me that again.' She said

'Call you what? Genius?'

'Yeah... I hate that word. I am not a genius. You of all people should know that' she smiled at me.

'I think we should go to the class now. We are already late ten minutes.' I said

She looked at her watch and started running towards the class. I was always a lazy kind of a guy. So I just walked.

It was 1:30pm already. Our school ended at 2:30. She remembered that I said I would talk to her in the last lecture. As soon as the bell rang for the last lecture she turned around, and again, her hair flew in the air like a boomerang and hit me in the eye.

'Harshaali, I am really sorry to say this, but I hate this. This happens at least twice a day.' I said in a very rude tone. She apologised and looked the other way instantly. I was rubbing my eye when I noticed she wasn't even looking at me. I understood that I had made a mistake. I didn't realise but I guess I was yelling at her when I said all that stuff. I knew I had to apologize.

'Hey... Harshaali.'

'What? I already said sorry. What do you want now?' she was mad, the way I said whatever I said, it was normal.

'I am sorry yaar. I didn't mean to yell. I am really sorry.' She gave me a stare before replying.

'It's ok. What did you want to tell me in the morning? Do you want to tell me or not? It's almost 2'o clock and we are leaving in another half an hour now.' She said

'Let's play truth or dare. But just you and me. Nobody else. What say?' I said. I had no Idea myself what I was about to do.

'Are you mad? Why do you want to do that?' she said. She was confused, obviously. She had no Idea what I had in my mind.

'Just take out a pen and spin It.' I said and she did exactly the same.'

The pen stopped at me. It was all I wanted.

'Truth' I didn't even wait for her to ask.

'Deven? Do you want to say something?' she asked

'Hmmm.... Harshaali. Last time when we played it was two days ago. You guys asked me who my crush was. I said there was no one. I lied. I didn't actually lie. I just realised it that day. I like you a lot. I realised it when I was not with you. I knew I was missing you. I knew I wanted to talk to you. I knew I had to spend some time with you. But I couldn't. For the past two days, all I have been thinking is you. Your name has not escaped my mind for a single second. It is difficult to think about something else. I guess I like you. Do you think so? And yes, I talked to Abhilasha.

She told me you like me too. I know you are going to be mad at her for telling me but I guess she did the right thing. So, what do you think?'

She was speechless. I could tell that by her expression. Her mouth was half open; her cheeks were red as an apple. I still remember that she had a Social studies guide book in her hand and she covered her face with it. I snatched the book from her hand and I saw a little tear was about to drop from her eye. She was emotional. I don't know why, but just by looking at her I knew this was also new for her as it was for me. I wanted her to say something at least. But she turned away.

'Harshaali. I am sorry if I said something wrong. That was not my intention. I don't want our friendship to be ruined. I just wanted to....' I didn't even complete my 'I am sorry' speech when she interrupted me.

'Dev. Do you realise that this has made me so happy. I was actually waiting when I would hear these words from you. Obviously I like you. I want to spend more time with you. I know you haven't proposed to me or anything. But I am assuming that you did. And I also have an answer for your proposal. YES...!' she said with a big smile on her face.

I was so relieved. I almost thought that by saying all those things I had ruined my friendship with her. But the way she responded was amazing. She wanted me to say this. Man, girls are like that I guess. They never want to be the first ones to say the right things at the right time. They always want the guy to start the topic first. But anyway, I was really happy. The second she said all that stuff to me she went straight to Abhilasha and hugged her and told her everything. I could see how happy she was.

I was happy too. Everything was so beautiful suddenly. I was in a very good mood after that. I was singing romantic songs. When I came home I walked directly into my room and started dancing. I was so excited. This was the first time I was in a relationship. I was enjoying every single moment of this. The level of excitement was unbelievable. I told everything to Naman the same night. He was happy for me too.

The next morning was even more exciting. All that was going through my mind was that today I was going to meet my girlfriend for the first time. Before that day I never wanted to dress up perfectly. But that day was so much different from the others. I was ready on time. Even before Tamanna. I just wanted to see her.

I reached school before time that day but she wasn't there. I sat in the staircase waiting for her. I just wanted to see her face once. It didn't even matter that she was going to sit In front of me the whole day. I could not wait to see her. She took a bus to school every day. I was waiting for her bus to arrive so that we could walk together to the class. But that day her bus was late. Damn that driver. He had to be late that day. Couldn't he just choose some other day to be late?

Her bus finally showed up went I was about to go upstairs to my classroom. I stood there waiting for her to step out of the bus. Finally, I saw her. Just like me I guess she also wanted to look better today. She might also have the same thing in her mind that she was going to meet her boyfriend for the first time today. She looked perfect. Her hairstyle was a little different today. She had a puff on her head that I had seen for the first time, and a pony tail. It was all so adorable. She was as fair as milk and had a mole near her left eye. I could see it so clearly that day. That moment for me, a fifteen year old boy, was the first realisation of how much I liked this girl. She came up to me with a smile on her face.

'Would you just keep staring or are we attending classes today?' she said and winked at me. I didn't realise that I had been staring at her since she got off that bus.

'oh sorry, yeah, let's go.' I said.

'You look really pretty today.' I said.

'Normally I don't look pretty?' she was laughing at me. She sensed that I was nervous.

'No that's not what I meant. I mean you look prettier than usual. You look pretty always.' I was actually trying not to say anything stupid or to sound nervous. But it was written all over my face. I didn't even have to say anything and anyone could understand my situation at that moment.

'I wish we could sit together today.' She said with a sad voice.

'No problem' I said and looked at her.

'What? What are you thinking Dev?'

'Nothing. Let's go.' I said as we entered the class together. Usually I sat right behind her. But today she was sitting alone. So I took advantage of this situation.

'Dev..!! Get the hell out of my seat...!' she was whispering that. I could see she was shy.

'I don't think I have to. Your partner isn't coming today. So why can't I sit here with you?' I had a permanent grin on my face. It was like I was proud of sitting there.

'Still Dev, what If some teacher sees us sits like this. You know I was just kidding when I said I wanted to sit with you for the day.' As soon as these words came out of her mouth I got up and went back to my original seat. This must have given her the Idea that she had made me upset by saying that. She did actually. I thought she wanted to sit with. But she was only kidding.

Later on she passed me a note. There was a big sorry written on It. The note said...

'Dev, I am really sorry yaar. I know you are upset so please don't even try and deny it. I know I made a stupid statement there when I said I was kidding and didn't actually want to sit with you. It's not true. I do want to sit with you but it's just that I don't want every single person in the school to know about us already. It's hardly been a day you see. And you know this better than me that there are people in this class who love to talk in front of the teachers. I don't want to be famous for having a boyfriend in the class. I hope you understand. If you do, please forgive me. Just write something on this paper and pass it back.

Sorry again.'

I knew she didn't mean what she said. For a minute I thought I acted childishly there. I should have thought of all this before I almost announced our relationship in the class. So I passed the paper back to her after completing my apology.

'I am sorry too. I shouldn't have done that. I understand everything and don't want you to be in any kind of trouble because of me.' I put a little smile after what I wrote.

She turned around to look at me and give me a lovely smile.

The rest of the day went pretty usual. We had just started as a couple so there was no romance or anything. Moreover we were just a couple of fifteen year olds. So there wasn't going to be any romance either.

But one thing was sure; it was now easier for us to open up. We would just sit in our respective seats (not anywhere else) and talk all day. We would even help each other with different subjects. Actually she helped me with all the subjects. I was good at studies but as I have already mentioned she was a genius, although I always got smacked whenever I called her that. But she was. She used to teach me almost everything about mathematics and social studies. Both of which she was brilliant in. Science, English, Hindi and any other subject whatsoever was easy for me. I hated both mathematics as well as social studies.

Several days passed by in the same routine. We would come to the class and sit in our seats. As soon as the teacher left the class we would be talking like we had been away for a year, during lunch break we would meet behind the canteen so that we could have some alone time together, the back In the class we would play footsie all day long. This was all really exciting and adorable at the same time. We were like little love birds who didn't want to do anything but stay together and look into each other's eyes all day. But that went on for just another month until we had our examination datasheets in our hands.

'First Is English. That is going to be easy.' I said.

'Dev. Second is mathematics. Have you been preparing?' she asked. She was obviously worried.

She knew I wasn't good at mathematics and she wanted me to prepare. But call it my stupidity or whatever, I hadn't been preparing at all. But also I didn't want her to get mad or stressed out for me. So I lied.

'Obviously babe, I am preparing. Don't you worry about me, OK? I will do well, I promise.' I said. I knew I had to start preparing now.

She was always ahead of me in everything. Even when it came to preparing notes, Harshaali had the best class notes ever. She had them all copied for me so that I could read from them. She had a magnificent handwriting, and the notes were great as well, all those details in one place, that had to help me in the examinations.

With the exams approaching there was fewer crowds in the school. Students were on leaves for their preparation. But there were two students who were always present in the class. I and Harshaali always made sure that we were there. It was simple, fewer crowds meant less classes, which meant less teachers around, which meant that we could spend a whole lot of time together. It was like we were on a date every day. We had our lunch together, we had all our classes together, we were in the canteen together, and we were always together. That was the time that brought us closer to a point where she could really start sharing her Intimate stuff with me. She never told me about the problems she had in her childhood. Or the problems she had in her family. Sometimes she would be sad and quiet alone when I would ask if everything was ok, and her reply was always the same. She always said that if I was with her there would not be any problem in her life. This always made me think about our future together.

There was a time when I thought about her just as my girlfriend and nothing more. But that thinking of mine changed completely one day.

Now we were at a point in our relationship where meeting only in the school and talking only in the school was not sufficient for us. So I had to do something. I had to ask my parents for a phone. Actually, I had to beg In front of my parents for a mobile phone so that we could talk. I obviously couldn't tell them the real reason so I had to make false excuses like, having a phone would help me stay connected with you all the time, I am at my tuitions all day, it would be easier for you people to contact me If I had a phone and a number of my own. They were really against the idea but then my dad thought that it wouldn't hurt even if I had a phone. Having a phone would rather help me. So my dad decided to give me his old mobile phone.

I still remember my first mobile phone. It was a Motorola L6. Motorola was really famous at that time. It was a small handset which was only good for calling and texting. And that was all I needed actually so I took it. Dad gave me my own new number. Now that I had my own cell phone and number I could talk to her anytime I wanted. Although, she could not get a cell phone that easily. Her parents didn't want her to have a cell phone so early. They thought it would be a waste of time and a distraction for her in her studies. Well, they were right, but we had to talk right? So she decided that she would use the landline In her room to talk to me at night when everyone went to theIr bed. She used to have a separate room so it was easy. We just had to wait for everyone to sleep.

With the new phone thing we got even closer. We used to talk all night. Almost every night we slept around 4 am. That was a long time on phone if you imagine. We would talk about everything. I would praise her voice by telling her how much I loved it when she whispered something. She would ask me to sing something for her. She loved listening to my song, although I was not a good singer. We would talk about the day at school, we would make fun of everyone Including our own friends and teachers. I just loved talking to her that way.

Although, however fun it was talking the whole night it was also risky, as there no telling when somebody from our respective families would hear us talking. But we were just too young to care about that. And that is what brought us to our first breakup.

It was her birthday the next morning. I had told her to stay by the phone that night because I wanted to be the first one to wish my doll. I wanted to call her exactly at 12 am to wish her Happy Birthday but something else happened. Something that I never realised could happen at that time. Again, we were just too young.

I called her number. She didn't answer. I called again. No answer. Then I called again. No answer. I decided to wait for some time and then call her. So I waited for 5 minutes and called her again. And again there was no answer. So I decided to wait a little longer. I waited for 7 minutes this time. This time she picked up, and instantly I started singing the happy birthday song.

'Happy birthday to you, happy birthday to you, happy birthday dear harsha....' I stopped, as a manly voice from the other was cursing me as hell. The man was shouting and cursing me in Punjabi. I could not understand even half of it, but I did get the "Teri maa ki" and "Teri behan kI" part really well. That was the time it struck me. Oh fuck, that's Harshaali's dad. OH MY GOD..!

I was scared to death. I was literally shaking so much that I could not even hold the phone properly and it slipped through my hand and fall down on the floor. The battery came out. I was just about to put the battery back on when I thought that it was better to keep the phone switched off. So I kept it on my study table and tried really hard to sleep.

That night was the hardest night of my life. I was scared. Not for me. Her father could not do anything about me I knew. But I was scared only for her. What her father would do if he suspected her of having a boyfriend. She came from a very conservative family. She would always tell me about the consequences, that what could happen if someone in her family ever knew about her relationship. She was always scared and now I was scared for her. Awful things popped up in my mind every second. I could not have even one minute of sound sleep. I knew I had made a huge mistake and I also knew that I would have to deal with it the next day.

As I thought, her father was furious at her for whatever happened last night. He blamed her for everything. He told her to stay away from me, and every other guy in the class. What was I supposed to do in this kind of a situation? I knew I could not fight with her father for her right now. WE WERE TOO YOUNG. That day Harshaali didn't talk to me the whole time. I had approached her many times; I wanted her to speak up about what had happened. But she didn't respond to anything.

She was crying. A lot, almost the whole day passed by and she hadn't stopped crying. The day was about to end when I decided to talk to her again. I knew she had to go by bus. So I stood waiting for her in the staircase. I was standing right there and she walked passed by me. I followed her and caught up to her.

'Harshaali, please talk to me. I am really sorry for what happened. It was my fault entirely. But at least tell me what happened. How are we supposed to get of this situation together if we don't talk? Please Harshaali, stop.' I put my hand on her shoulder and she threw it away. She turned to me and said...

'What do you want me to say Dev? Don't you see it's all over? We cannot be together. We were not supposed to be together. I don't know why I said yes to this stupid relationship and a stupid guy like you. I am really sorry Dev. But it's over. We are over.' She said and walked away.

She left me there. I was standing still. My eyes wet, my body shivering, I had no idea what I was supposed to do. We were so close the day before and now we were over? This could not be the end of our relationship. I gathered up my strength and started walking towards my car again. Dad was waiting outside and I was extremely late. He asked me where I had been so late. I said that I was exchanging some notes with a friend for exam purposes.

CHAPTER 3

THE FIRST BREAKUP

I TOLD EVERYTHING TO MY BROTHER, Naman, the same day. He said that I should wait. He wanted me to wait at least till the exams were over. But it was too hard. By the time all this happened, I had gotten so used to being around Harshaali that even a single second without her was hurting me. I had to talk to her. I had to find a way of reaching her. Then I remembered that she had mentioned about a friend once, some girl who lived nearby her house. So I looked her up on face book and sent her a friend request immediately. I knew it was her because her address was exactly the same. I waited for a whole day before she accepted my friend request.

I got the notification that she, Radhika Sharma, had accepted my friend request, I texted her on facebook.

'Radhika?'

'Yes, Deven. What 'sup?'

'Do you know who I am? I mean, has Harshaali told you about me?'

'Obviously, I know all about you. All she talks about is you only. Man, I want to meet you. I want to meet the guy that has got my friend so crazy.' She said.

'The guy who GOT your friend crazy. Tell me, does she still talk about me?' I asked. Although the conversation clearly indicated that Harshaali hadn't told her anything about the breakup.

'What do you mean?! Did something happen? I have not seen her since we last hung out together. It was almost a week ago. Please tell me, is everything okay between you two?' now she panicked.

'Nothing is okay between us. I have messed up everything so bad yaar. I have done such stupid things. Can you please go and see her today? But please don't tell her that I contacted you. She would kill me. I just want to know If she's fine or not.' I said.

'Sure, I will see her today. Give me your number. I will text you with the details.'

We exchanged our numbers and she promised me she would talk to her. I didn't want Harshaali to know about this because at that she was really upset. I didn't want her to think that I was a creep, that I was stalking her or something. But this was all I could do at that time. I could not call her or text her. She wouldn't talk to me face to face, so this seemed the only option.

I had been waiting for Radhika's text all night, when I heard a beep on my phone. It was her. I had saved her number on my phone.

'Deven?' she said

'Yes. I am here. Did you meet her? Did she say anything?'

Then Radhika told me everything. Harshaali told her about what happened that night after the call got disconnected. Her father blamed her for everything. He accused her of having a boyfriend. He was so mad that he even tried to hit her but Harshaali's mother Intervened and he had to stop. She also said that her father was furious at me and wanted to talk to my parents or whatever authority he could talk to about this.

This was actually what I had done. This was what my Harshaali had to go through. I could not stop myself from crying after this.

'It was my fault Radhika. I did all this and she had to pay the price. I wish I had never called her up that night.' I was crying and texting at the same time.

'Deven, it wasn't anybody's fault. It just happened out of bad luck. But seriously tell me, what do you want to do now?' she meant what she said. She didn't think I was responsible for any of this crap in our life. She was like a friend to me too.

'What do I do now, Radhika? I am all alone in this. Even Harshaali isn't with me now and god only knows what she must be going through. I have no Idea.'

She called me up. She wanted to talk me through this.

'Hello?' I knew my voice was cracking up, although I tried to sound normal.

'Deven? Are you ok?' she said.

'No Radhika. How am I supposed to be ok when she is in such pain? I can't stop blaming myself for whatever happened.' I said.

'Deven, it wasn't your fault yaar. It could have happened with anyone. And you had no idea that her dad would pick up.'

'I just want her back Radhika. I don't know how or why. But I want her back. She is the one I want to be with. I cannot do anything without her. Being with her makes me so happy. And I know it made her happy too. I know this because I have seen it in her eyes. I know she is hurting too. And I know that it's because of me. But I promise that it won't happen again, never again.' I said and started crying again.

'Deven... Please stop crying and listen to me ok? I know I have no right to judge you. I don't know you. But all I know is that I have seen her happy with you. I have seen her talking about you. And when I saw her today, I knew she was missing you too, so here's what we are going to do.' She said.

The she explained everything to me. She was willing to help me. She wanted me to keep talking to her in school. Her "plan" was to ultimately get me and Harshaali talking so that we could work things out between us. She said that she would meet her whenever she could, just to know her side of the story a little better, she would talk to her about me and make her realise how much Harshaali wanted to be with me.

The next day I started with Radhika's plan. It wasn't just plan; it was a mission for me. I had to get Harshaali back at any cost. So, the next day I went up to her to atleast have a conversatIon.

'Harshaali...' I said.

She looked at me with no expressions on her face. She actually had no smile this time. Usually when I called out her name she would smile and say 'Yes Dev'. But today I just got a 'yes Dev' without a smile.

'I think we should talk.' I said.

'What do you want to talk about?'

'Can we go and sit on some other seat please?' I said. I didn't want others to know about the situation we were in.

'No Dev. Talk to me here, whatever it is that you want to talk about.' She said. She was stern on the decision of not moving from her seat.

'Ok. I will talk here. I just want to know how you are. I mean, after everything that happened, are you ok?' I asked.

'Why wouldn't I be ok? I am good Dev. I just don't want any more complications in my life.' She said.

'That almost all I wanted to know.' I said and walked away. This wasn't the conversation I had in my mind. It was like I walked up to a girl just to get rejected.

The same day Radhika met her in the park close to their house. Radhika was trying really hard for Harshaali to see that she still had feelings for me. But Harshaali wasn't going to be so easy.

I still remember the number of days I had to go through to talk to her once. There were total nineteen days. Those nineteen days of torture made my life a living hell. I could not eat, sleep or do anything that I liked. HarshaalI was all I thought about. She was the one I prayed for. One day suddenly I saw my phone, and there was a missed call from Radhika on It. I called her back. Harshaali had her phone. It was Harshaali that called me from Radhika's number.

'Dev?' she said, her voice still as pretty as it was 20 days ago.

'Yes, Harshaali. Are you ok?' I asked. I knew she wasn't ok.

'What do you want from me Dev? She said. I could tell by her voice that she had been crying.

'It's not that I want something from you Harshaali. It's you that I want. It's you only. I want you back in my life coz frankly speaking; I seriously have nobody else to talk to, that day when you asked me to stop talking to you. I was broken in half. I almost thought that I had literally lost the most precious thing in my life. Harshaali, my life is a waste without you. Please come back to me. I am begging for you to come back in my life. Please.' This was all I had in my mind. I said it all.

'I don't want you to get hurt yaar. Why don't you get that? If we are together and my folks find that out next time, they will kill me. And then they will kill you. I have seen a lot of stuff in my life Dev, but I won't be able to handle this. You getting hurt because of me, I won't be able to handle that. Please try and understand. Please.' She said and gave the phone to Radhika.

'Dev, I guess you should call later. Let me talk to her first.' Radhika said.

'No Radhika, wait, give her the phone. I want to say something.'

She gave the phone back to Harshaali.

'Listen to me you sardaarni. I know you don't want any trouble in your life, so I promise that I won't be a trouble, but the thing that you have just said, that you can't see me hurt. I am telling you, that these words have made me fall in love with you now. Yes..! I love you Harshaali. I really do. In these few days I have learnt that without you I can't think of anything else. Without you there is nothing, no joy, no festivities, and no nothing. But with you I stay strong. I am happy. It's you who has turned my life this way and I refuse to let go of the best thing has ever happened to me. I won't let you go away Harshaali, ever. I promise.' That was all I had to say. In these words I had realised the only way I could see her now. In a matter of a few months, Harshaali had become so much more than just a friend to me. I was crazy about her. But now it was time for her answer.

'Before you say anything. There is one more thing I want to be cleared out today, if the problem is your father, if you are scared of what he might do to me, then I guess you have no idea who I am or what my family is capable of. Your father or your brothers can't even touch me.' I said. I was mad at her family. They didn't want her to love anyone. But I knew she loved me. I was just waiting for the words.

'Deven Dhaanak… I love you too. And if you ever fall in any trouble again, I will kill you myself. I just don't want you to get hurt in any way. That is all I want from you. Just be safe. You can give me this one thing, right?' she said. I could hear her voice cracking up a little.

'I will do anything for you Harshaali. And I promise that you won't be hurt because of me ever.' I said. Now I was smiling because of what I was going to say next.

'So Harshaali, Is It a yes or a no this time?' I said as I wiped off my tears.

'It's always a yes for you Dev. Always.' She said. And we hung up the line.

It was like a dream come true for me. Harshaali was back in my life. She was with me once again. And this wasn't just a mere dream. It was all possible because of one person, Radhika. I called her up later that night just to thank her and tell her how much I value what she had done for us, for me particularly.

I was a total stranger for her and she helped me like a friend. She stood by me; maybe her aim was to see her best friend happy once again. But she had definitely made a new friend in all this.

After that breakup with Harshaali there wasn't a single day when I didn't regret calling her that night. I cried whole nights blaming myself and praying that she would come back to me. When she did, I promised myself something. I still remember what I said to myself looking into the mirror.

'God, I know I don't talk to you much. I know I don't pray much either. I only call you when I want something.

But today there is something that I want to promise you and to myself. This girl, Harshaali, she Is one strong girl, or maybe that what she wants us all to think. But I have seen her, I know her now. I know she pretends to be strong but she is still a teenage girl. She is sensitive. She is not that strong. I know her, and I want to be with her. Not just for some crazy teenage years, or for just fun. I want to be with for life. I want her to stay with me and I promise I will not hurt her or let her be hurt by anything ever again. And there is one more thing that I want to promise to myself. I will never leave her alone.'

The feelings for this girl were truly from the heart now. I saw her in a totally different way now. I respected her for everything she had to go through because of me. I was responsible for everything but all she wanted was me to be safe. If that wasn't love then I don't know what is.

Finally, our exams started around mid March. We were all prepared. I and Harshaali knew we were going to score well and so we did. Harshaali aced the exams and scored the highest in each and every subject. There was no competition for her. There were other girls who scored great but could not reach her level. Well as I have told you before. She was a mastermind and unbeatable I must say.

I scored pretty well too. My folks never expected that I could score that much in mathematics and social studies. It was all because of Harshaali and her efforts with me. She wanted me to score well.

Now, the hard part of the session was I front of us. We had to say goodbye to the 9th standard. We all had been promoted to class 10th. But there was a problem. VACATIONS. There was a month of vacations that we actually didn't want. Well, all the other students wanted it.

But I and Harshaali didn't want to get separated again. We had just sorted out things between us and now again we were going to be separated. I wasn't ready to deal with that.

It was our last meeting of that month. We were now going to see each other after a month now. That was hard for both of us.

She was standing in the staircase waiting for me. She had asked me to meet her there. She wanted to say something. I had almost made up my mind that we had to deal with this separation somehow. But maybe she hadn't. She looked sad. I could tell that by her eyes.

'Dev...' she called out my name as I approached her in the stairs.

'You wanted to say something. I am here now, say it.' I said.

'I know we are going to be apart for a month or may be more than that. But please stay safe. And don't contact me until and unless I ask you to. Ok?' she said. She was holding my hand and that felt good. I was also a little emotional by then. This was the first we were going to be apart for this long.

'Harshaali, you don't worry about me babe, I will take care of myself. You just promise me that you will take care of yourself and stay healthy. I will talk to you and see you soon ok?' I said and gave her a smile. She pressed my hand between her hands.

'I think we should go now' I said.

'Hmmm...' she replied slowly.

I gently tried to pull my hand away from her. But she didn't let go. Instead she pulled me closer and took me into the corner. She wasn't emotional now. There was something else. Her eyes were wide open; I could actually hear her heartbeat. She didn't want to leave me just like that. Before I could say anything, she pulled me closer and all of a sudden her lips were touching my lips. I could feel her hand shifting from my shoulders to my waist as she pulled me closer. I didn't realise that my own hands were out of my control and so were my lips and my tongue. I could feel the heat in that moment. I could feel the romance. I could feel her soft lips pressed against mine and her tongue playing with my tongue. This was all so abrupt that I could not react. I couldn't say or do anything but just go with the flow.

That was our first kiss. To be frank there could not have been a better situation for that kiss. There could not have been a better place either. We were both lost in the moment. It was real. It was a feeling that can never be explained.

She let go of me, her head resting on my shoulders now, her eyes were still closed, her arms wrapped around my waist.

'I know It's stupid, but I just don't want you to go.' She whispered.

'You know you have to let me go before someone sees us like this Harshaali. It's risky standing here like this babe. 'I said. She pushed me away. She was still upset.

'Harshaali, I love you babe. And I promise you wouldn't even realise how fast these days would pass.' I said.

She smiled at me again. Her smile was the only thing that could make me happy now. It was like my source of strength.

We headed in different ways so that nobody could spot us together. She was one hell of a kisser by the way. I didn't know. I guess she didn't know that either.

We left the school with sadness in our hearts. We both knew it was a long time to wait to see each other's faces again. We could not go out on dates randomly. We won't be allowed to do that.

This problem has always been a killer for love stories. In India, if you are in love you have to hide it from everyone. Not because they won't like, but to make sure that your parents don't get the wind of it. That a shame really. We should also be able to share our feelings with our elders. Atleast someone. So that we can at least make a point.

I have seen In Hollywood shows and movies that kids of our age, If fall in love, are able to speak about that freely. But that not the case here. And I don't think it ever will be, because of the simple fact that people of our country don't learn that fast.

But anyway, it was clear that we were not meeting anytime soon. So the only option was to distract ourselves. So I decided to go on a trip to Jammu and Kashmir with my family and Harshaali went for a trip to Goa with hers.

We had decided that I would not try to talk to her myself. She would call me whenever she could and she often did. Sometimes she would call form the reception of their resort where they were staying In Goa, sometimes it would be from a local P.C.O and sometimes she would call me up from Radica's number. She used to tell me funny stories and stuff like what happened on the road and on the beach and I would tell her how my days were going. Everything was good, not great but good enough. The holidays were not that bad as we thought they would. That was because we kept ourselves busy.

Harshaali always loved to hear me sing. So I decided that I would give her a surprise after vacations, when the new session started.

I always had a thing for Music. People used to tell me that I could sing well. But I never took that seriously until I wanted something else from Music. I wanted to tell Harshaali how much I love her by the essence of Music. I always wanted to learn how to play guitar. I could never learn because I really didn't have any purpose for it. But now I had the motivation for it and I also found a teacher who was really famous In Chandigarh. His name was Pranav Kumar. He was the best guitar Instructor in Chandigarh. But also he was really great at singing.

He agreed to give me home tuitions. He gave me an hour every day. And I learned that instrument with its basic chords within a month and I was singing songs on it. Now all I had to do was wait until the session started again.

I kept practicing romantic songs on the guitar just for Harshaali. I didn't want to show it off. People didn't know that I could sing or anything, they never expected maybe. But this wasn't for people, this was for my love. I didn't want her to know that I was doing this for her. So I kept this to myself.

I wanted this to be my surprise to Harshaali. She loved Music and she loved watching and hearing me sing. Before learning how to play guitar, my singing was not that good. But after getting knowledge about different things like high notes and low notes, scales, rhythms etc I got better at singing. My voice was better now. Or so my mother thought. She used to ask me to practice In front of her. My mother had become my biggest fan already. But there was still a question in my heart. Would Harshaali like It?

CHAPTER 4

NEW CLASS NEW US

'FINALLY, WE ARE BACK HERE.' I said, as I stood behind the canteen holding her hand. Harshaali was with me. It was our first day back to school. We were in 10th standard now. The school had been redecorated. The paint was new, the benches were new, there was lot of new glass work and It all looked really clean an tidy. Everything was kind of new.

'Yeah, Dev, you have no Idea how much I missed you.' She said and hugged me instantly. She was looking beautiful. She was just the perfect blend of height, weight, figure and colour. She was the perfect girl. And I had her with me, loving me like she had never loved before. That was an accomplishment for me.

'Hey, I hear that there is going to be some function. What's that about?'

'How can you not know about that Dev, its mother's day this week. We are making preparations for a function and all our mothers are going to be invited.' She said.

She was appointed as the host for this show. We all had to participate. We had to do something we liked. It could be anything like dance, Music, plays or any other entertainment stuff. So I decided to reveal my surprise on that day.

We had 3-4 days to prepare and I had not even selected any of the songs I was going to perform. The same day I went to the event head and got myself enlisted as a performer under the category 'Music and Singing'.

So now I had a problem. I was tensed as it was going to be my first live performance. The second and the most horrifying thing was that I had a big audience. My classmates, juniors, our mothers, teachers, staff etc. So I wanted this to be a something really nice. I didn't care about the other people though. I only cared about what Harshaali would think about this.

We were really busy those 3-4 days as we were the senior most class and we had to make all the preparations. Parents were going to be there so our school wanted to make the best Impression. Our social studies teacher who was unfortunately our class teacher too, made sure that every single student helped in the preparations.

The day finally came and I was not at all prepared. I knew I could sing. But I also knew that this was going to be the first time I was going to perform In front of a live audience. I was nervous. I had never felt this way ever before.

The function was supposed to take place in the basement of our school. I had been sitting in an empty room for 2 hours now. I was waiting for the Music performances to start. I was already tensed and a classmate of mine came and told me that my performance was going to be the first performance. Now this was just unfair. They should not have done that. How can I be the first performer? I had to go down to the basement. My name was just about to be announced.

'And our next performer is Dev...' she didn't even finish the name and the crowd; mainly my fellow classmates started hooting for me.

All I could hear was 'Dev bhai, Dev bhai, Dev bhai...'

Out of more than two hundred people my friends were the ones who created that blast at my entrance. I swear, my face was actually red and my temperature and blood pressure levels were really high.

All of the performers were supposed to give an Introduction before their performance. But I was so nervous that I just started without it. The first stroke that I hit on the guitar made that crowd go crazy. It was like they had never seen a guy with a guitar ever.

My first song was dedicated to all my friends and all the students sitting in the crowd. I started with the song "Give me some sunshine" from the movie 3 Idiots. People were actually enjoying. They were singing with me. The song was really popular and almost everyone knew the lyrics. All my teachers were cheering me on, all my friends were singing with me. And then there was Harshaali.

I looked at her during my performance. I could see her smiling with pride. Sitting there with her friends she was just listening and clapping for me. She had all her attention in my song. I looked at her for just 4-5 seconds and we exchanged a smile.

The first song went really amazing. Everyone was cheering for me. The guys, the girls, teachers, mothers and my girlfriend. I could hear her screaming my name. She looked so happy. Everyone was shouting and they all wanted me to sing another song. I looked at her again. She nodded her head. That was like my signal. I started another song. I could not say It In front of that crowd but this one was dedicated to her. "Mein tenu samjhawan ki, na tere baajon laggda jib" the lines depicted my feelings for her perfectly. She was sitting in the front row. I sang the whole song looking into her eyes. She was left spellbound; I could make that out by her face, a little tinge of pink on her cheeks, little drops of tears pouring down her eyes. In that moment she knew what she meant for me.

My performance became a huge hit. People came up to me and congratulated me. My mother who was sitting in the audience applauded with all her heart and cheered for me when my performance was over. She was proud, I could see that. And so was Harshaali. She couldn't meet me right after my performance as she was the host and she had to be there till the function ended. Fortunately the function only went on till 1 p.m. I was excited to meet her. I wanted to see her reaction on learning that her boyfriend is a singer and a guitarist now.

She entered the class looking for me. I was playing songs for some of my friends in the class. She came to me and I stopped playing.

'No don't you dare stop. Keep playing I am here to listen. Please.' She said this with such cuteness that I dedicated all my songs to her, for life.

After everyone cleared out, there were just me and Harshaali sitting there. There was no teacher or staff member in the classes today because of the occasion. Everyone was busy somewhere. We spent time together that day. She held my hand and said

'Dev, why didn't you tell me that you played?'

'To be honest, I didn't play before. I wanted to do something for you. I knew you liked hear me sing, so I thought this was my only option. I did this for you in these holidays. Did you like it? Did you like my voice?' I said. I wanted her approval. I don't know why but she now had an unknown authority over me.

'I loved it Dev. I just can't stop thinking about this. My boyfriend is such a talented guy. I love you Deven Dhaanak.' She said and smiled.

I was so happy that she liked it. My dad used to pick me and my sister up from school. My father asked me how my day was. And all I could say was, "Dad, it was just perfect."

This was the best experience of my life yet. I had more confidence in myself than I ever did. I made my mother proud with my performance, and made my girlfriend love me a little more. That was quite an accomplishment. So I was happy. I continued training and got better with it.

After that function, my life at school was even better. People recognized me as they never did before. I was the actual school rockstar. A number of students even asked me to teach them how to play guitar. I was still a beginner, I could not teach anyone. So I politely declined.

Our seats remained the same even in the new session. Well, only I and Harshaali sat in our regular seats. That was just because we wanted to stay close all the time. Now that we had had our first kiss, it wasn't awkward at all. We would sneak out of the class for our kissing sessions. We would go into the basement when nobody was there and we knew that nobody was going to be there for a while. Sometimes we would take teacher's jobs together just so that we could spend some more time alone.

It was my birthday. I had invited all my friends to my house for a party. Harshaali came to my place for the first time that day. I introduced all my friends to my parents. And my parents gave me a good amount of money to spend at the party. We had planned to watch a movie and have lunch at the food court in the nearest multiplex. We were getting ready to leave when Harshaali took my hand and pulled me out the room where all of our friends were sitting and having snacks that my mother had made for them.

'I want to give you your present right now.' She said.

'What? You could not give that in there?' I said.

'OH god, Dev. How dumb are you actually?' she said and kissed me. But she stopped. 'Lock the door first. Go…!'

I did as she instructed.

She made me sit on the bed. I could already feel a tent in my denims. But I was so shy. I tried to hide it. She sat beside me and we kissed again. This time it was from both of us. We were doing this in my brother's room. He was out of town for some reason. But his room was at good use.

I was not able to control my hands and suddenly I found them under her shirt. Her soft and warm skin, her waist, her stomach, her back, every part of her body was in perfect shape. I felt her heartbeat rising again. My hands were working on their own. Soon they reached a point where I could feel her bra. I unhooked It Instantly.

'Good work soldier. Trained or what?' she said and winked at me.

I took off her shirt still kissing her. Then I took off her sphegettI and then her bra and made her lie down on the bed. I lied beside her and we started kissing again. This was my 15th birthday and this was by far the best gift I had ever received from anybody. She didn't move at all. As if she wanted me to take control of her bare body. And I did just as she expected. Her breasts were soft but still firm. I was allowed to do anything I wanted to do with them. It was my birthday after all. I kissed her neck and slowly reached down to her hard nipples. It was a hot day. I could see droplet's of seat all over her body. I kissed her nipples. She moaned with pleasure. I kept kissing them till she stopped me.

'That's all for today my tiger. We have to go. Quick get dressed. 'She said and kissed me on the cheek before she wore her clothes back.

'Oh yes, happy birthday again dear.' She said and winked at me again with a grin on her face.

Well, my 15th birthday was hot as hell. That whole we talked about what we did In Saman's room. She was so hot with all this stuff. It was like she knew everything. She knew how to ace the moves, how to get me into the mood. She was great and with her I felt great.

'Open your textbooks children.' Our science teacher said.

Even In the class, we used to keep on talking and laughing. We played 'footsie' all day long. It was always fun sIttIng close to her. I was thrown out of class a lot because the teachers always thought that I was disturbing Harshaali. But what could I even do. My Image was like that only.

One day, we were sitting at the last benches and there was no teacher around, I started rolling my fingers up and down her spine. It tickled her; she tried to get away from me. But I didn't let her go. I held on to her waist and pulled her closer to me and kissed her neck. She turned around.

'Why so romantic today Dev?'She said.

'I just look at you and I feel like I should kiss you. But there is not always the right moment or the right situation. So I just did it now as nobody else could see us.' I said. I used to act all childish around her. There is a phenomenon very popular around teenage boys. They always act stupid around their crushes. This phenomenon is called NAC, Nervous around Crush phenomenon.

'You should be careful you know. Wait, let me show you.' She said.

'Oh baby please don't show me anything here.' I said. She gave me a horrible expression.

'Ha ha, very funny Dev. Shut up and come closer.' She said. She gave me a little peck on my lips. 'See, this is how you take advantage of the situation.' And saying that, she winked at me. I loved this daredevil side of her. It turned me on, on so many different levels.

But there was one more side of her that I just loved. Sometimes she used to be all about fun and stuff, but there were times that she was really serious. She was a lot more mature than I was. She knew what consequences each and every action of ours had on our future. And that was the best part. She was always so mindful about the future. She cared about me a lot and never wanted to see me hurt.

As a teenager, I was really dumb. My mother always told me that I cared about my friends too much. She was right. I did care about my friends a lot just because they cared about me and respected me.

There was a friend of mine named Vinay, he was fair looking, tall and well, people could say that he was smart. Otherwise having 3 girlfriends in 10th standard wasn't an easy job. He was such a stud, he had a girlfriend in our class, he had a girlfriend at his tuitions and he had girlfriend who lived just across the street where he lived. How he handled every one of them, I never got that. I still don't understand. But as they say, all good things come to an end. So did his three relationships. Believe It or not, all of his relationships ended at the same time. This is how it happened.

I got a call from his "tuition" girlfriend, Aisha Thaapar. I was talking to Harshaali at that moment when our call got interrupted.

'Hello?' I said. It was an unknown number.

'Deven? It's Aisha here. Do you have any Idea where Vinay is? He is not picking up my call since last night. Please if you have any Idea let me know.' She sounded worried on the phone.

'Hmmm. Ok Aisha. I will talk to him ASAP.' I said and disconnected the call.

Then I called up Vinay. He was kind of my closest friend in the class. After getting in a relationship with Harshaali, he was the only guy I talked to. I knew all about his "routine".

'Where are you, scumbag?' I said, disappointed as hell.

'What's wrong now dude? I am with Yashika here at Elante mall. What happened?' he said. I could hear loud screams in the background. I wonder what they were doing at the mall that made Yashika scream like that.

'Your girlfriend called. 'I was trying to say something but I got interrupted by him again.

'Shut up Dev, you mad or what? My girlfriend is right here with me. What are you talking about?' he said. As stupid as he was, I had to tell him everything.

'STFU Vinay and listen to me, Aisha called me up. She wanted to know where you were so I told her that I would talk to you and let you know that she is worried. So please for god's sake talk to her and keep me out of this.'

There was a moment of silence, before I heard crying noises.

OH MY GOD….

Vinay was so screwed. That idiot had put my phone on speaker so he could hear what I wanted to say clearly. That dumb fellow did not realise that his girlfriend was standing right behind him.

'Hello? Who is this?' Yashika had snatched the phone from Vinay's hand and was talking to me now.

'Ammmm. This is Deven, you are Yashika right?' I said. I didn't know what else to say.

'Yes. I am your best friend's girlfriend. Well, I was.' I heard everything Vinay told Yashika to stop her from going. But Yashika didn't stop.

'Deven, you bastard. She was the hottest of them all. Why the hell did you do that to me?' he was yelling at me. Well, it wasn't my fault. He should have known that these were the circumstances of having so many relationships at once.

But this wasn't over yet. I got another call for Aisha.

'Deven? I think Vinay is cheating on me.' She said. She was crying.

'Now why would you think so Aisha. He is not cheating on you.' However gross my friend was, I had to protect him, right?

'I just got a call from my friend. He said that he has seen Vinay at Elante, with a girl. Now tell me what I should believe.' Ok. So this girl had contacts. I disconnected the call again. And again called up that bastard.

'Where the hell is you now? I am going to meet Aisha now. And don't you dare stop me Dev.' He said and hung up. Well, as I said before, Karma is a batch.

Later on I got a call from him. He told me the whole story of his second breakup of the day. He went to Aisha's place directly after Elante. And the guy that Aisha had talked to about Vinay, had followed him to her house. There was a big fight and Vinay did beat up that guy. But he got slapped by his girlfriend, oops; ex-girlfriend in the middle of the street, and that was enough to break them up.

'Dude, why didn't you tell me that Aisha already knows? I would have never showed up at her place. You Idiot, you broke me up with two girls today. Do you realise that? And they were both hot. Do you get it, Dev?' he said. I could literally hear him cry. Man that was a bad day for him.

Then I told him that he has to do one more thing. I told him to break it off with his third girlfriend too.

'Dev, you bastard. What have I ever done to you to deserve this?' he said. Now he was angry.

'You have done nothing, but think about it. People will talk about this. And this will get to her too. So before she breaks it off with you, have some shame and save your dignity for once, you crap-head.' I said and hung up.

He did exactly as I told him. He was a dear friend of mine. Although, he was a little cheap. But then, he did have some other qualities. He was one of the best looking guys in the school. He was more of a stud type guy and was always in style. I wasn't like him at all. I was just a fine looking guy with a nice hair style. I used to look fit and I looked really bad with glasses. The thing with our friendship was that we respected each other a lot. He knew me from class 7th and we became good friends the day we met. He was the only person in the class who knew all the history between me and Harshaali.

He knew everything about the little fights, huge fights, the bad breakup we had, the words that her father and I had exchanged, everything about everything in my life was known to him. He was the best friend I had and that was the reason I was so open with him, although he never wanted me to have a serious girlfriend. He always said that there are plenty a fish in the sea, why settle for one. Yes, these things made him cheap.

I always liked writing a diary. So Harshaali gave me one as a present. It carried a letter in it. The letter was scented and it said something that brought tears in my eyes.

> *"Dear Deven,*
>
> *Everyday I catch myself smiling for no reason, but then I realise, it's all because of you...*
>
> *We have been through a lot together, and all I have learnt from those situations is that if we are together, we can fight anything that comes in our way. I don't know if I will be there to read this diary in the future or not, but you have to promise me that you will keep on writing, you will not stop, this way I will atleast know that there is someone out there who cares for me more than I care for myself. I am always with you and you are always with me in my heart. I love you.*
>
> *Always yours,*
> *Harshaali"*

After reading this all I could think of was calling her up and telling her how much I loved her. But I couldn't as she didn't have her own cell phone.

CHAPTER 5

WHEN THINGS GOT BETTER

WE USED TO BE SCARED whenever we talked on the phone. I was not allowed to call her because she could only talk on the landline number. It was getting difficult as I could not stand a single minute without talking to her. She was always busy with her parents and her family. The only time she called me was when her parents were not around, and that wasn't a lot. They didn't trust her now as we had already been caught once. The only way that we could talk now was if she got a mobile phone somehow. I couldn't get her one because it was risky and if she was caught again her parents could easily make out where the mobile phone came from.

Our summer vacations were about to start and we were going to be away again for a long time.

'You have to get a phone Harshaali. We cannot talk otherwise. You just call me for like 10 minutes a day. And even that is risky. You must do something.'I said, frustrated.

'I am trying Dev. It's not like I don't want to talk to you. It's just that my parents don't think that it's the right time to get me a phone. What can I do about it?' she was obviously sad too. She knew what a risky game we were playing. No father would approve of his daughter being in a relationship at such a young age. But what could we do. We were in love for the first time.

'Let's see what happens now. We will find out a way I know. It's not going to be easy but we will.' I said. I just wanted to make her happy by saying that. She did smile.

That day I went home regretting that I said all that stuff to Harshaali. She must have been so upset. It wasn't her fault that she couldn't talk to me. I should have understood her situation.

Our vacations had started and as expected we were not talking now. Somewhere in my mind I thought that she was upset with me because of the stuff I had said to her the last day we were in the school together.

The same evening, I got a call from an unknown number. I usually didn't pick up unknown numbers, but that day I did.

'Hello…' I said.

'Hello. Is Deven Dhaanak there?' a female voice asked for me. I could recognize that voice from miles away. It was her. It was my love.

'Harshaali…!' I literally screamed out her name. I was surprised to hear from her.

'How did you know it was me Dev? I was going to play a "call center" prank on you. 'She said, barely able to keep herself from laughing.

'Do you really think I would not recognize your voice? You could have at least tried to change it a bit if you wanted to play a prank on me. So dumb you are Harshaali. So dumb my girlfriend is.' I said. I was laughing. It was almost a week we had not talked to each other. Then she explained why.

'Actually Dev, I didn't talk to you because I felt responsible for us not being able to communicate properly.

I was really passed off at myself actually. So, after we had our discussion, I talked to my dad and explained to him how Important It was for me to have a phone now. I told him that I needed it for tuitions and stuff. And…' she said before I Interrupted her.

'And??' I said.

'This is my new number Dev.' she said and I was suddenly so happy inside.

'I can't even explain how happy I am Harshaali.' I said.

'I know Devi know.' She said. I could not have been happier. One of our biggest problems was solved. Now we could talk all day and night if we wanted to. Nobody was going to stop us.

This was the best news I had heard since a very long time. After Harshaali got her new number, we talked all day. We had our holidays but it never seemed like she was away from me. We downloaded a new online chatting application called Whatsapp. It was even easier to stay connected now. It was like we were always together. She would send me pictures of everything she did during her day, I would record my songs and send them to her, and we would just chat and talk all day. It was great. This schedule went on for the rest of the vacations. But on the last night we had to plan out some stuff.

'We would only talk till 2 am in the morning.

We will get up early and chat for some time.

We would not be careless about our phones.

We will always delete our chats and pictures from the gallery of the phone before leaving for school.

We will always keep our phones password protected.

And YOU will never call me by yourself. We talk when I call. Do you get that?'

These were her instructions on how we must use our phones without getting caught. I agreed on each and every one of them. I loved her and I never wanted her to be in any kind of trouble because of me. And her thoughts were the same for me.

Our vacations were really great. We had a really good time talking to each other every night. Our schedule became something like this- wake up, talk, have food, talk, and sleep, wake up, talk, do anything, talk. It was like we were always talking. I knew everything she did during her day and she knew exactly what I was doing. A few days before our school started again, we decided that we would start sleeping early, as we had to build up a habit to sleep because we had to go to the school. So we started our routine, we would talk till 12 a.m. and then we would go to sleep. Sometimes when it didn't work we would call each other up again just to talk. But ultimately it worked and we were back on track.

Our summer vacations ended somewhere around mid July and we were fully prepared to see each other again. We had not been around each other for more than a month and we wanted to see each other so badly. We were just waiting for the time to come.

Our school timings were the same as before. I entered the class and she was sitting right there, on her regular seat. There was an empty seat behind her. I ran towards the seat and sat down before anybody else could.

'I have missed you so much, Harshaali. Even though we were talking all the time, I think I have never been so happy in my life. I am so happy to see you baby.' I said. I was really excited to see her.

'I know...! I have been waiting for this moment for so long. I wanted to see you so badly Dev, you can't even imagine.' I was glad to see that she was also excited to see me. All we did that day was talk. We didn't attend any lectures, we didn't go for the lunch break, and we didn't even care about the teachers that day. So be it, if anyone saw us talking, what could they even do? They could not keep classmates from talking to each other. And most importantly they couldn't stop me from talking to my girlfriend.

'Dev, why are we so excited? We have been talking on the phone.' she said.

'I don't know Harshaali; it's like, I am really happy to see you. I know I am just repeating myself her but this is the truth. Everything I am saying right now is the truth. Whenever I am away from you it makes me feel like there is a part of me missing. I don't know why this happens, but being around you makes me feel a lot better.' I said this with all my heart. She knew this was true. She knew me and she knew the strength of out relationship.

'Oh Deven, such a romantic you are.' She said and pulled my cheeks.

Her laughter was the sweetest sound there ever was. It used to sound better than my guitar. I was so much in love with this girl that I couldn't talk about anything else. All my conversations with Naman or Vinay would start with 'I just love Harshaali yaar.'

I never thought that I could be that serious for any relationship. I never knew I had It In me. I always thought that this love thing is not going to be for me. I wanted to stay away but I couldn't, this girl changed me in ways that I couldn't even imagine. I felt complete with her.

Being with the one you love the most is the greatest blessing ever. I knew I was blessed whenever I saw her smiling at me. One day after school I was lying on the bed in my parent's room, my head rested upon my mother's legs.

'Maa how did you and dad get married?' I asked. It was a random question that popped into my mind.

'Why are you asking this son?' she asked.

'I just want to know. Did you guys have an arrange marriage?' I asked. I was pretty sure that they had an arrange marriage. I never talked to my parents about this before.

'No Dev, your father and I had a love marriage actually.' She said. She was smiling as If she was reliving those days. Then she told me everything about how they got married.

Both sets of my grandparents were politicians. My grandfather was a P.W.D (Public Works Department) minister for 10 consecutive years; he was a Cabinet minister for 10 more years.

And from my mother's family, my grandfather was an MLA in Delhi. So both my grandparents knew each other on work basis. They became good friends and decided that they would continue this friendship by getting their elder children married. Therefore, my taauji and maasi got married.

But soon after their marriage, a new affair was started, yes, my mother and father. They were still in their teens when they started dating. Dad used to visit her In Delhi. He used to go alone by car or a motorcycle, but there they used to roam around on a bicycle. They would go for street food and stuff. My mother told me everything. She told me how much she enjoyed being with him.

But just like every other teenage couple In India, my parents also had to face some problems. My parents were not exclusive that way. There were problems that took more than two years to solve. They cried they got punished for their so called "mistake"; so many people were against their relationship that at one point they decided to give it up. But then, you cannot change what god has already written for you.

My dad was outraged by the fact that he was not getting what he truly wanted. He loved my mother so much that he decided to take some steps by himself.

An unfortunate incident took place in my mother's family that dat. Her grandfather had died after he suffered a major heart attack and could not survive. All of my mother's family members were present on his funeral. My dad could have found a better opportunity than a funeral, but h decided not to wait. He went in there with a VAT69 bottle in his hand and a "mangal-sutra" In the other.

'I am here to marry you Anju. Come with me. Nobody can stop us now.' He said. He was under the alcohol effects. What he didn't know was that his father i.e. my grandfather was also present there. Moments later my dad was being dragged outside.

That was by far the craziest thing I had heard about my father. My mother told me that my father wasn't much of a drinker ever and he didn't drink now at all. He stopped drinking after I was born. That was just because he didn't want me to have a lower opinion about my father.

But the most amazing thing was that after all the problems and bad situations, finally, love came through. My parents ended up marrying each other. They got what they had wished for. Listening to my mother that day, my faith in love increased. I knew that I loved Harshaali. But was I so much in love that I could think about getting married to that girl?

I thought of discussing this with her. But I didn't want to scare her either. So I decided to control my feelings and see where things were headed with her. I obviously wanted a bright future with her, and so did she. She always said that I was her first and she wanted me to be her last love forever.

That night I was astonishingly romantic with her on the phone. All I talked about was how much she meant to me and what my life would have been without her. She knew something had happened that day. She even tried asking twice but I didn't want to say anything. All I wanted to say that night was, 'I love you, Harshaali.'

The next morning as I was gettIng ready for school, my phone beeped. It was Harshaali.

'Won't be able to come to school today jaan. Not well. You take care and I love you. And don't reply. Phone won't be with me.' She had just sent me an Incomplete message. If she wasn't well she should have told me what was wrong. She was alrIght the night before.

I had the worst day In the school that day. I was worried all day about Harshaali as I had no Idea what went wrong In six hours. We had talked till one In the night. Six hours later I get a message that she was sIck. I just wanted to see her for once and make sure that she was alrIgt. I knew her family was with her but I could not stop thinking about her. I asked Abhilasha to call her as soon as she reached home. I couldn't call her because she had asked me not to call or text her.

I got a call from Abhilasha an hour after we got home. She told me that Harshaali was fine and she had just got a mInor skIn InfectIon. Abhilasha called me to gIve me a message from Harshaali that she won't be able to talk to me as she didn't have her phone with her. There was some problem In her phone and her father had taken It to with him to get It checked. This was still ok. I felt better once I was sure that she was fine.

Naman came Into my room lookIng for something. I was lyIng on my bed tryIng to catch some sleep when he started askIng questIons.

'What's wrong?' he asked. I don't know why but he looked at me as if I was sick.

'Nothing. Why?'

'You don't look so good. Everything alright?' he asked.

'Yeah, Harshaali is not well, and I am just a little bummed out because of that.' I said.

'Anything serious? Or just a cold and cough problem?' he said that and started laughing. I don't why it was so funny to him. He was never in a relationship, or maybe that's what he wanted me to think. But I had never seen him in a serious relationship. I didn't know if he understood what it was like caring for someone.

'Nothing serious. She will be fine soon.' I said and went back to trying to sleep.

I slept for almost three hours and when I got up I looked at my phone. I was shocked the moment I unlocked my phone. There were thirteen missed calls and twenty two unread messages, all from Harshaali's number. I knew I was going to get yelled at now.

I was waiting for her message that night when I got a random call from Vinay.

'Dev, where are you bro?' he screamed through the other side. It was already 11 p.m. and he was asking where I was.

'I am at a bar sipping whisky. Where are you? And what's all that noise?' I also had scream as he wasn't able to listen clearly.

'You are at a bar? So am I brother. Which bar? Tell me. I will pick you up and we can have a crazy night out. What 'say bro?' I disconnected the call instantly.

That idiot knew that I wasn't allowed to get out of my house for late night parties and all. Still he called me up to invIte me. Such a dumbass fellow I had as a friend. But I wanted to go. I had this feeling that she wasn't going to call now. I mean, I had been waiting for a whole day now. I wanted to have some fun too. All I did that was worry about Harshaali. So to make my night better, I took permission from my parents for a night stay at Vinay's house. Although we had other plans.

As soon as I called him up he got so excited that he was literally singing happy songs on the phone. He came to pick me up in his white Ford FIgo. I insisted on driving as I knew he had been drinking the whole night. We went to the closest and the cheapest bar in town. We were two very broke teenagers who had to lie about where they were every time their parents called them up. We ordered a bottle of green apple vodka. We took the bottle and got out of the bar to sit in the car and drink peacefully.

As soon as the first three glasses went down our throats, our mind and tongue coordination started to break out. We were stammering after we finished our fourth glass.

I want to tell you all that I have a strange condition, in which when I have had a lot to drink; I get emotional and very chatty. I wanted to talk to her, but I couldn't. So I thought If can't talk to her, I can at least talk about her. So I started talking about her with Vinay. Nobody else was there so I could speak freely. I knew I was talking to a friend. I opened up to him. I wanted to let go of the stuff I had in mind. I told him about what happened with her, how I fall in love with her, how madly I was in love with Harshaali. But I was not sure if he was even listening. All he kept saying was, 'dude let her go, you will be happier.' I mean, it was like he didn't even listen to a word I had said. But it was still ok; I had to tell someone about this, so I did.

We went to his place and I found out that his parents weren't actually home. That was the reason he was out at that hour. Otherwise, he would have been in his bed at nine in the evening. His parents were also very strict, just like mine.

We slept around 3 a.m. In the morning. It was a Sunday next morning so we didn't have to worry about school. I woke up at around ten in the morning. I checked my phone and there were 12 missed calls from dad. He wanted me to get back home as soon as possible. It seemed like there was a big emergency or something like that. So I got up and brushed and took a shower to terminate any possible signs that I had been drunk the night before. This was the first time I had been out for a night and I had been drinking. I didn't drink ever, that day was just really stressful. I went back home with Vinay and went straight into my father's room to talk to him. As it turned out, they just wanted me to be home. There was no emergency of any kind.

My Sunday was also ruined because I wasn't able to talk to Harshaali. I just wanted to hear her voice so badly. I wanted to ask her myself if she was ok. But all I could do was waiting until tomorrow.

The next day I got up hoping that I would see her. I got ready as fast as I could. I reached school on my regular time, sat on my regular seat and was eagerly waiting for her to enter the class.

When she did, I could not see any signs of a skin infection anywhere. In our school the girl's uniform was pretty revealing (and we never had any problem with that by the way). I noticed that her face wasn't red nor were her hands or legs. But there was something that was unusual. I saw a boy standing right behind her. He had come to drop her to school. Normally she arrived in the school bus. What was different today? She sat in a different seat, not In front of me. I tried to go and talk to her but Abhu stopped me on my way. The guy standing outside the class gave me a spiteful stare. I was confused. I wanted answers. Then I saw her face again. Her right cheek had some red marks. Those marks told me half of the story then and there.

As soon as that guy walked away from our class, she got up and walked towards her seat, In front of me. I knew something was wrong. I had so many questions; I started with the easy one.

'Harshaali?' I said.

'Hmmm…' she replied in a sound so low that I didn't even hear it the first time.

'Harshaali? Is everything ok?' I asked.

'No Deven. Does everything seem ok to you? Nothing is ok.' She said. She was crying and I didn't even know why. I hated that.

'But what went wrong? We were totally alert this time. We didn't make any mistakes. I know I didn't. I am pretty sure of that.' I said. I was annoyed at these silly things coming between us. We were not being able to enjoy the only good thing going in our lives at that moment.

'Tell me what happened?'

'I made a mistake Dev. I am so sorry. I told you that we would be conscious all the time about our phones. I was not. It happened three days ago. The guy who came with me today was my elder cousin. He is the son of my father's sister. He was visiting us for some time and was living at our place. When we were talking that night, he was sleeping in the next room only. He heard that I was talking to you and stood outside my room and heard everything. As soon as we disconnected the call, he came in and started yelling at me. His yelling woke up my parents and he told them everything. They wanted me to give them your address. He forced me to open my phone and show him the chats we have had.'

'You showed him our chats?' I said, scared about the chats we had. If those chats were read by any of her family members they would have killed me.

'No Dev, luckily I had deleted all the chats before we hung up. There was no history of the chats either. I had saved your number in my phone with Abhilasha's name on it. I kept saying that I was only talking to Abhu but they just wouldn't believe me. He kept saying random stuff to me In front of my parents. He was threatening me by saying that he would find out who I was talking to and he would beat him till he was left half dead. I got so angry that I started yelling back at him.'

'Did he touch you Harshaali? Did he try to hit you?' now I was angry. She sensed it.

'No Dev. He didn't.' she answered. I obviously didn't believe her.

'Then how did you get this mark on your face? Tell me the truth Harshaali. I need to know.' she was scared. She knew me, she knew what I could do If I got angry. Although her brother was taller than me and older. I couldn't do anything myself. I knew that. She must have thought the same when she told me.

'He did Dev. This scar you see on my face is from his bracelet when he was slapping me.' She said and started crying. She was crying her eyes out. I asked Abhilasha to take her to the girl's washroom and calm her down.

I thought that day was going to be a good one as I supposed I was going to see my baby, my girlfriend, Harshaali. Instead, I met a girl who was scared of her brother. That made me angry. And I knew what I had to do.

She returned to the class and I told her that I would make everything right. The good thing was that her parents didn't think it was a big deal then. They thought that after slapping her a few times, the matter was settled. They had no Idea what was coming.

I took all the details of her brother and noted them down on a piece of paper and kept it in my pocket. I didn't say much for the rest of the day. I just wanted to make her feel better. I was just waiting for the school to be over ASAP.

When I came back home, I called up Naman. I am not proud of what I did next. Wait, no, somewhere deep down inside, I am proud that I did what I did in that rage of mine. I told everything to my brother, every single thing. I told him that he had threatened to "beat" me to death. Well, I had exaggerated a little. I told him that he had laid hands on my girlfriend and I was not going to sit quietly now. I told him to pick me up as soon as he could. He came home and I was already waiting for him outside. We didn't waste any time. I had that piece of paper in my hand that had his Information in It. I knew where we could find him.

Now, I didn't tell you the whole thing about my brother Naman, he was quite famous too. But he was famous in a different way. He was famous as the actual 'hitman' of our city. I am not saying that he was a "gunda", but he was not anything less than that either. Every single guy in our city knew who Naman was. He had been in fights before, whenever he had a fight, he didn't go alone. My friends and known ones, If put together, were just a regiment. But the number of people Naman could gather with only one phone call, his friends, If put together, they were an army. There wasn't even one single guy who would say no to a fight If Naman was involved in it. And by being his little brother, I got the same privileges.

We tracked down Harshaali's brother. He was sitting in a bar having drinks with his friends. I had his mobile number. Naman called him out of that bar and I am pretty sure that when he came out of that door, he wet his pants at the sight. There were more than thirty five guys who were waiting for him outside that bar with hockey sticks and chains in their hands. We picked up some empty beer bottles too.

'Which one of you is Harsimran Singh?' Naman asked the four drunken guys who came out of the bar.

'I am.' Naman looked at me for confirmation. I nodded like a good boy. I was enjoying this.

'You want to beat my brother to death? Didn't you say that in front of your sister? The same girl that is in a relationship with my brother?' Naman and his voice. He was talking like the actual terminator that day. He was angry too. Obviously, you threaten a boy and his brother will retaliate with whatever he has. And my brother, well he had a lot.

'Tell him to stay away from my sister. Otherwise I will do what I have said. I will kill your punk ass brother.' He said that, and he was regretting that a minute later.

That guy was so hammered that he could barely stand straight; in that condition he threatened me in front of my brother. Naman didn't think for once before punching that guy in his face. Not once, Naman scored seven huge blows to his face. If it was a boxing match, Naman was the clear winner there. The rest of the three guys were also really drunk. The guys that came along us took care of the rest of them. Naman and I were more concentrated on Mr. Hardeep Singh. I had to beat him. He gave a scar to my girl. How dare he even touch her?!

'You stay away from my brother now, and you also stay away from your sister. The next time you lay a hand on his girlfriend, think about this beating and stop. Because if you don't, I will stop you myself.' Naman and I sat in our car and drove back home. Nobody had any Idea where we had been. We didn't think it was necessary to tell our parents. This was another secret between me and Naman.

The same night Harshaali called me up.

'Deven, what did you do?' she asked.

'How is your face now baby?' I asked.

'My face is alright. Did you do this?' she asked again.

'You remember when I said that you really don't know what my family is capable of? You really don't have any Idea. Ask your brother who did that. And then ask him to slap you again. I bet he won't.' I made my statement and disconnected. The next second I got a text from her saying

'I love you. My hero ;)'

I simply smiled and went to sleep. I was satisfied that day. That brother of hers, he never visited them again.

The next few days were a little difficult. Obviously her parents took her phone. They believed that she was still with me, which she was. But they also knew that they couldn't do anything about it. She wasn't going to listen to anything now. She was madly in love with me too. The moment her brother threatened me, she got furious. I can swear on god, if her brother wasn't older than her, she could have slapped him back.

But she wasn't that kind of a girl. She was quiet and composed. She always knew how to react to any situation. And she knew what that situation demanded. We were not talking on the phone but now we were talking a lot more in the class. Maybe because we knew that would be the only time we could talk.

After a while, we became the class couple. There is always one couple in the class that makes all the other couples jealous of them. We became that couple when everyone understood that nothing was going to break up apart, and believe me, if her parents and brothers couldn't do that. Nobody in this world could.

Even Vinay understood that I was really serious about Harshaali. One day he came up to me to discuss something.

'Dev, I want to ask something.' He said.

'Since when did you start taking permission to say something man? What is it? Tell me.' I said. I was talking to Harshaali at that time; she got up and started walking away so that we could talk.

'Harshaali wait, I need to talk to both of you. Please sit. Dev, when that thing happened with her brother and you, where you went off to kick her brother's ass with your brother, why didn't you give me a call?' he sounded serious. I knew this was going to upset him, but I had my reasons for not calling him. Although I told him everything the next day.

'Vinay, I know you don't like Harshaali that much. You just talk to her because I am in a relationship with her, which also depresses you I know. But dude, the thing is....' he Interrupted me.

'Listen to me you bastard. I know you are crazy for this girl, and I know she loves you too. Or else she wouldn't keep taking chances for you like this. I just want you to know that I am there for you always. And that is something that you cannot take away from me. I love you like a brother and that means I have a right to fight for you ok? Do you get that?' he said. I was happy that I had a friend like that.

'I understand buddy. Don't get mad now, calm down. The fight is over.' I said. After that he apologized to Harshaali for not being more supportive of our relationship. Harshaali was a sweetheart with everyone. She just smiled at him and said that he didn't have to worry about anything now.

'He cares a great deal about you Dev. A great friend you have made. Never let him go, ok?' Harshaali said.

'I am not letting either one of you go anywhere anytime soon. Trust me on that my baby.' I said that and kissed her hand.

'You just say stuff like that and make me fall in love with you more and more every single time Dev. What you did for me, getting into a fight with my brother for me. That was amazing. I can't even tell you how scared I was. But you took care of everything.' She said, I knew she meant every single word.

'I love you Harshaali. I will do whatever it takes to keep you safe. And I am not going to let anyone touch you again, ever. 'I said and clutched her hand tight.

She knew I wasn't lying. I knew I was going to do anything for this girl, now and forever. My parents had a love story that got successful. I had the privilege to know that story. I wanted to tell her everything about it.

'Did I ever tell you how my parents got married?' I said. I repeated the whole story in front of her. I told her every detail. She sat there and listened to me blab about "Love story 1970". I knew it would excite her, and I was right.

'Dev, that is so amazing. Did uncle really propose your mom in front of her whole clan?' she asked.

'Yeah, he still remembers how badly he was beaten up that day by tau ji and daadu. It was a sad story. But it had a great climax.' I said. I had a proud smile on my face as if I was telling her the tale of love that my parents had written. I was proud of them. They had given me something to look up to.

For a child, his father is his hero. For me, my father was a living legend. He had the courage to tell everyone how he felt about my mom and that too in front of more than a hundred people. That's the kind of courage I needed to step up and propose to my girlfriend In front of her family. Yes, I was thinking of doing that. Not soon obviously. We were just teenagers then. But I wanted to spend my life with this incredible girl who had no boundaries when it came to loving me.

Harshaali was totally in love with me too. She would text me whenever she was free or didn't have her parents around. She would call me every single night. Sure, we had our problems, but what couple doesn't face problems in their relationship. But being young and stupid, we did not take care of those problems ideally.

I don't know why, but when it came to keeping her phone safe from her parents, she was really irresponsible. We were having a really smooth time till her father read all our text messages. Yes, again, her father came to know about me and Harshaali.

'Are you going to stop seeing this boy or not? Have you seen your age? Do you even know anything about this boy?' he threw all these questions at her like she was a criminal.

'Dad I am not seeing him. I am not with him. How many times do I have to tell you that? These chats are not new. These are from last year most probably.' She tried to get out of it. But this time it was more difficult as the chat had dates on it. He knew the chats were not old. They were from last night only.

'Do you take me for an idiot? I can see the date and time stamp on the messages. You just don't realise how bad and irresponsible this makes you look, Harshaali. You were not like this. What happened to you? What has this boy filled your mind with? Tell me. I am your father. If this guy is bothering you I will take care of it tomorrow myself. You won't even have to say or do anything.' He said. He was serious as hell. He was going to kill me this time. Although I wasn't afraid. But this thought that her father would try to hurt me scared the hell out of Harshaali.

'I will never talk to him again. Not on the phone, not in the class. Never. I will stay away from him, I promise. Just please don't do anything crazy dad.' She begged in front of him. She had to do that just because she loved me so much.

CHAPTER 6

THE SECOND BREAKUP.
BIGGER THAN THE FIRST

I KNEW WE HAD BEEN IN trouble again. Her phone was switched off; she wasn't talking to anyone, not even her besties Abhilasha and Radhika. So I couldn't even ask Radhika to do something.

The next day when we were in the canteen, she came up to me to talk.

'It's over Dev. And this time, don't even try to come back. I cannot take this anymore. Every time we get into trouble my family starts threatening you. And I know my father Dev. This time he won't forgive us. So please, if you love me even a little bit, just don't come back into my life.' She said. Tears rolled down from my eyes as I saw her walk away from me.

I still had the whole day in front of me. I couldn't cry in front of my friends or talk to them about this. Even Vinay, I could not tell him right there. I needed time to figure this out myself first. I wasn't even sure if that was it, if this was the end of our story. It was surely a breakup. This was the second time she did that. She broke up with me the last time for the same reason that her dad was against me and this whole relationship. I don't know why she thought that breaking up would solve anything. All breaking up with me did was take her sadness and loneliness to a whole new level.

She wasn't the kind of girl who could easily show her emotions in front of just anyone. She needed time and I am pretty sure everyone wasn't ready to give her time. That was probably the reason she had a limited number of friends. I felt responsible again; responsible for her sorrow, for everything she had to go through, again.

'It happened again. We broke up again. Her parents found out again. Why does this keep happening to us? Why can't we just have a normal fun filled relationship like everyone else?' Radhika and I were chatting almost every day now and became the best of friends. I had to tell someone about it and I knew she was the only person I could talk to.

'Dev, you want me to talk to her again?' she always wanted to help us. She wanted our relationship to work.

'No Radhika, not this time. I know she loves me, but as soon as we are facing a problem she runs away. She has to know what she wants. This time I will not try to get her back. This time she has to come back herself. If she does, we can work things out easily. But if she doesn't, we are through.' I said it with a heavy heart. I was not going to talk to her this time because it wasn't my mistake. You may call it my ego or my self-respect, but I stopped texting her or calling her after that. I even started ignoring her in the class. I changed my seat, I stopped talking to her friends, and I blocked her number on my phone so she couldn't call me. I was trying to make he feel that this time it was her fault. She was careless and she shouldn't have broken up with me.

As I was moving on my path of ignorance, I hurt her many times. Any time she would come to me to talk I would just ignore her and walk away. I didn't reply to her texts even though I wanted to. It was so obvious that I wanted to talk to her but for the sake of my ego, I didn't.

Our fight/breakup was still on when my Mama Ji and his kids visited us. They were on their way to Shimla and decided to visit us and stay for a night. He had two kids, both girls, and I loved both of them. The elder sister was Sakshi, she was older to me by 4 years and the younger one, Lakshita, and she was younger to me by ten years. Yeah, that's how long it took my Mama Ji to get the idea of having another kid. But it was ok because Lakshita was cute as hell and she loved me a lot. I was the second person who held her in the birthing room. I was present there when she was born. Mama Ji made me sit on the bed and kept that sleeping little baby in my lap. She was the most beautiful creature I had ever seen in my life. I loved her more than anything and she loved me too.

Sakshi and I were really close. She knew about Harshaali and she had seen a picture of her on Yahoo Messenger. She liked her and she also said that we looked really cute together. She sensed that I was sad. She wanted to know the reason, but before I could say anything, she guessed it herself.

'Harshaali? What happened between you two? What did you do now?' she asked me smacking my head

'Owwww, I did nothing, don't hit me for no reason. I wasn't responsible for our breakup this time. I didn't even have any idea that we were going to breakup.' I said.

'Then what was the reason?' She asked.

'Her stupid father, he is always the reason. I mean, if you don't want your daughters to get into relationships with random haryanvi guys, then stop creating such beautiful daughters. Either do that or stop stopping them from having these relationships.' I said. We had a pretty good laugh after the idiotic comment I had made on Sardaar community. But seriously, Sardaarnis are really cute. At that particular moment, when I was talking to Sakshi, I realised how much I missed her.

That night I spent three hours explaining everything to my cousin, Naman was also sitting there, although he wasn't interested in our story. He was just sitting there so that he could hear me talk about my stupid girlfriend who broke up with me everytime we were in a tough spot and mock me. I still wanted to tell them everything because these were the people who knew me to the core. They asked me all sorts of questions.

'What is her problem? I mean, what does she actually want?' Sakshi asked. She was angry because Harshaali broke up with me.

'I have no idea. That's the reason I haven't called her yet. I want her to know what she actually wants.' As soon as I said this, I got two slaps from Sakshi and one very "bad word" from Naman.

'You say that you love this girl, and yet you are sitting here testing her? You want her know what she wants, and you find this stupid ignoring move the correct way for it? How dumb are you exactly?' as it turns out, Sakshi just wanted to know what I was doing. I knew my sister was a bitch and will never be on my side.

But whatever she said made a very prominent impression in my mind. I was up all night thinking about what I wanted. I wanted her, and I wanted her to be with me for the rest of my life. That's exactly what I wanted, but I could never get that with this behavIour of mIne.

'I swear the next time she texts me I will reply.' I said.

'Text? You guys don't talk on the phone?' Sakshi asked.

And that's when I realised,

'Damn it…!! I have her number on block since the day we broke up.' I said. Soon after these words left my mouth, Sakshi was running after me with a bat.

'Call her right now or I will kill you.!' She screamed.

'I will, I will, calm down you idiot. It's not the right time, I will talk to her tomorrow morning I promise.' I screamed back at her, while running away from her obviously.

The next morning, I woke up with the hope to see her messages on my phone screen. But there were none. She must have forgotten to send a 'Good morning' message. She always sent me a good morning message. But sInce the breakup I had not been replying to any of her messages.

I entered my class and I saw her. After a really long time, I looked at her directly and gave her a smile. But she didn't respond. She looked away and took her seat instead. First I thought she didn't notice me smiling at her, but then I saw her looking at me and she looked pretty angry. I just walked past her and took my seat as well. A few minutes later I called Abhilasha to my seat.

'What's wrong with your bestie today?' I said.

'What do you think? You have not replied to her messages or her calls. You blocked her on your phone. What do you expect?' she said. Now I had another problem.

I didn't realise that ignoring her would get me these results. I thought she would talk to me herself. Maybe she tried and I ignored that too. Man, such a dumb guy I was.

'Tell her that I am really sorry. Please, would you?' I asked her for another favour.

'I can't do that Dev. You have to do it yourself.' She said and walked away.

I was feeling like the most stupid person on this earth. I had the most loving girl and I dIsappoInted her. But I still thought that it wasn't my fault. She broke up with me because of her dad, twice. I was hurt because of the fact that she was so afraid of her family. I knew I was being selfish, but I couldn't help it. I was selfish when it was about her. That's how much I loved her and I wasn't afraid of anyone.

'Dev...' I heard her voice.

'Harshaali, I know I have been rude these past few days. But you also need to understand my situation here. I am not going to let anyone decide what goes on between us. You want to breakup, ok, fine by me. I don't even care now.' I said. She came up to me to say something. But after listening to what I had to say, she just couldn't say anything.

'What the hell did I just do? I wasn't supposed to say that; I wasn't going to say that. Damn you Deven Dhaanak, why did you open your mouth at all...!' This question kept running in my mind for the whole day.

Our terminals were approaching and we were still broken apart. I could not concentrate on anything but Harshaali. I wanted to talk to her but after what I said that day, she wasn't ready to talk to me at all. She was right in her mind and I was right in mine. Although I knew that I would end up apologizing to her, but still, I had my ego which I knew was creating problems.

My tuitions were still going on and there used to be tests almost everyday, and I flunk each and every one of them. My teacher contacted my parents and told them everything. Bloody mathematics teacher. My mother was always concerned about my studies. She wanted to talk to me; she didn't scold me on bad grades and didn't even ask why I scored badly. She knew I was bad at mathematics, but still as a mother she wanted me to do well. All mothers want their child to be the best and my mother knew that I had the potential, so that created a whole new problem for me that night.

'Deven. Do you have any problem in your life, beta? Do you have something that you would like to share?' my mother asked me, all concerned.

I couldn't say that my problem was my relatIonship with a girl and I was going through a bad breakup. That would have scored me a lifetime of a beating from my parents and not their sympathy.

'No maa, I just find mathematics a little difficult. All the theorums and equations, I just don't get it.' I said with a sad face, I had to act a lIttle.

'Listen to me son; I know you can do it. You have always been good at studies and I know you will do it this time too. Just keep practicing and concentrate on your studies.' She said with a smile on her face. She bought what I said about my problem with mathematics. I was just about to leave the room when she called me back.

'Deven beta, keep your phone in my room. I think this is the reason you are not able to concentrate properly. I see you on the phone almost all the time, just keep it in my almirah for some time and take it back once your exams are over.' She said. That suggestion of my mom's blasted in my ears as if a bomb blast had taken place right in front of my eyes. I couldn't keep my phone aside for that long.

What if Harshaali wanted to talk to me and called me late at night? What if she texted me something that my maa thought was inappropriate? I couldn't take that chance.

'Maa, it's fine, I will handle it now, and there is no need of keeping my phone. It's ok.' I said with as much confidence as I could gather.

'Just keeep it here at once. I won't say it again, son.' She said with a stern voice now. I just had to follow her instructions. I was doomed now, I broke up with the love of my life, I had no source to contact her, and I couldn't even take her calls now. I was screwed till the exams.

My only way out from this situation was to start scoring in my mathematics tests. If my parents and my teachers saw any improvement in my scores I could get my phone back. But it wasn't that easy as well. In 9th standard, Harshaali used to teach me how to solve an equation or do something else in mathematics. But now I had to do it all by myself because she wasn't helping me now.

So I started at the basic level. Our NCERT books had a few math problems; I started attempting them one after the other. I got some of them right, the others, I just marked them for my teachers to explain. I started taking mathematics and science tuitions very seriously. I kept checking my facebook account for any messages from Harshaali. But I guess she was also busy with studies now so she didn't have time for any of this. But I was anxious to talk to her and bring her back into my life.

That road to a good score wasn't easy at all. But I started scoring well in both mathematics and science. I gained my self confidence back. And I saw Harshaali every day, she was doing well too. The one thing different during this breakup was that we were not distracted. Maybe that wasn't good. I mean I knew I was being egotistical at so many levels, but still I was happy to see her ok. And the good thing was that I convinced my mother that I could handle everything now and I needed my phone back.

I got my phone back in the evening and I was happy. Until I discovered that something had gone wrong. Just as I turned on my phone, I received 120 messages, all from Radhika's number. They were all from last night and today, from morning till one hour before. I didn't have the time to see the messages so I called her up.

She had not talked to me since Harshaali and I broke up. Well actually I didn't talk to her after my breakup with Harshaali. I really didn't want Harshaali to think that I sucked at relationship stuff and needed Radhika's help every time we had a fight or an argument or even worse, a breakup. But today she sounded really worried on the phone.

'Dev, where have you been?! I have been texting you all day. Harshaali is not well Dev, she is in the hospital. Something happened last night. You must come here. Please, I beg u, please leave this stupid fight of yours and come to the General Hospital right now.' she said. I took the car keys and my wallet and ran towards the car. I didn't even stop to answer my mother's questions.

As I approached the OPD at General Hospital I saw Radhika standing outside.

'What happened? Is she ok?' I asked, I was scared.

'She Is In room number 109. Go fast, she has been asking for you all day.' She said.

I ran towards room number 109 and saw a man leaving the room. It was probably her father. Well obviously he was. He was a middle aged Sardaar Ji and had medicines in his hand. I made sure he didn't see me standing there. I didn't want any drama there. There was already so much going on in our lives, I didn't want to create a scene in the hospital.

I entered the room and I saw her. I saw her every day in the school but I had never noticed how weak she had gotten. I could never imagine seeing my baby like that.

'What happened?' I asked, I was barely able to control myself from crying in front of her.

'Thank god, I thought you would never come. I have been waiting for you the whole day.' She said. Her voice so shaky. And I could tell by her eyes that she didn't get much sleep last night.

'Radhika told me that you wanted me here. See, I am here now, I am with you, please tell me what happened.' I said.

Radhika entered the room with some medicines. She helped Harshaali while she tried to get up.

'Dev, you guys are real idiots, do you know that?' she said. She meant both me and Harshaali.

'Will anybody please tell me what happened to her?' I was practically shouting now. I needed to know what went wrong with her and nobody was telling me anything.

'She has not eaten since last four days. All she wanted to do was talk to you but your number was switched off. She wasn't able to contact you; she didn't have the guts to talk to you at the school. You were being a jerk and ignoring her completely.' She said. She was angry with me now, man I didn't know I could pass off so many people at once.

'I didn't have my phone Harshaali. I swear I didn't, my mom took it away from me because I wasn't scoring in the mathematics tests. I didn't do this on purpose. I wanted to talk to you baby, I just couldn't. And I also thought that you were angry and didn't want to talk to me, so I didn't call. I am so sorry Harshaali. I really am. I am sorry for everything that I have done. I am sorry that I ignored you, I am sorry that I didn't talk to you, I am sorry that I yelled at you that day. But I never thought this would happen. I was so scared. Please *jaan*, please eat something.' I said, it was not getting easier to stand there and look at her and not cry.

'You are so stupid Deven Dhaanak. But I love you with all my heart. I love you so much. I can't even explain why, but I know that I do. It's just doesn't feel right when you are not talking to me, when we had that breakup, It broke me in half too. I never wanted that. I never want to be away from you. But I had to do that. Please understand and forgive me for breaking up with you like that.' She said. She had tears in her eyes and I really couldn't stop myself anymore. I was crying too.

I sat down beside her and took her hand in mine.

'I swear I will never stop talking to you. Even if we have a huge fight and you stop talking to me, I will keep on bugging you till you talk to me. I will keep on irritating you my whole life. I just can't see you like this baby. I am really sorry. And if you want to apologize for something, apologize for doing this to my girlfriend. If you were a boy, I would have punched all your teeth in, I swear.' I said, I was relieved to see a smile on her face.

'I think you should leave now Dev, uncle will be here any minute.' Radhika said. She had a point.

'Radhika, can you give us a minute? Please stay close to the door and keep an eye out for that Sardaar. Please, would you do that for me?' I requested one of my, oh sorry, one of our best friends to do me that favour.

I just wanted that minute to feed her something. She had not eaten in four days; I wanted to make sure that she did. There were some fruits on her side table, I pIcked up an orange an gave Harshaali a slice from it.

'Eat properly now, if I get another complaint from my girlfriend, I swear I will breakup with you this time and I will never come back.' I said as she ate that slice from my hand.

I was about to leave when I realised that I had forgotten something. So I went back into her room and Radhika was sitting beside her.

'What? Did you forget something Dev?' Radhika said.

'Yes Radhika, I did forget something.' I looked at Harshaali and she looked at me, it was almost like she already knew why I was back.

I went up to her bed and stood beside her for a moment. I leaned in and kissed her forehead first, then her cheeks, then her nose and then a little peck on her lips.

'That was what I forgot.' Harshaali had the biggest of smiles on her face and I loved it. That smile made my day, although I made a fool out of myself. Radhika couldn't stop giggling seeing me and Harshaali like that. But even I couldn't help it. The moment I saw her lying there on that hospItal bed, I knew I was going to cry and apologize. And that's exactly what happened. I just couldn't see that girl sad.

And just like that, we were back together. The breakup that I thought was going to be a really long one turned out to be just a little fight. I had missed her a lot in the past few weeks, and when I was told that she wasn't well, all I wanted to do was to be with her. But I couldn't. I never visited her again. Although she was discharged two days later. Radhika told me everything about how she got sick and how she ended up on a hospital bed. She was starved to the point that her body lost all its energy and then she got unconscious.

Her parents were not at home that day, when they came back they found her lying on the floor in her bedroom. The doctors prescribed her some bed rest and suggested her that she should take a week off from school. So her father got a Medical Certificate made from the hospital and submitted it in the school the next day. I saw her father. He looked sad, even though I never liked that guy, I could see that he was worried about his daughter.

Harshaali got better quite soon, but her parents didn't let her join the school again until after her Medical leave was over. So certainly I was missing her in school. I had a habit of looking at her in the free time at school, but whenever she wasn't there I would just put my head down on the desk and try and picture her in my head. I would pray that I get to see her soon and she gets better.

For that whole week, I talked to her every night. She had her phone back, but we never called each other. We would just chat all night and talk about what was going on in the school, I would tell her every single detail about how Vinay got screwed again, she would tell me how she was really stressed about the terminal exams as she didn't get time to study that much, I always told her that she was amazing at all the subjects and she would still top the class. We had our romantic moments even on the phone. Some nights we would just repeat the same thing over and over, she would tell me how much she loves me and how much she regrets doing what she did, and I would tell her that what she did made me angry but still I loved her more than anything else.

We had to stay away for another week, but it was worth it. She was always worth the wait. Moreover, it gave us time to reconnect. We had time to discuss how to manage our future fights and how to get to a solution as fast as possible.

But this wasn't the only problem; I was also worried about Harshaali's studies. She had missed on a lot of new stuff that went on in our classes and she had to cover it all up before exams. That was going to be difficult. But I somehow knew that she would do it, she always did.

She was returning back to the routine school life today. I was so excited that I almost felt nauseated, not in a bad way though, just because of the excitement. I was walking in the corridors from where she entered the school. I was surrounded by a bunch of juniors asking me how I was and practically kissing my ass, just because I was on the Bhangra selection team.

'Hey dude, I am really good and you know that. Please get my name on the list man, I really want to participate.' He said. I wasn't even listening. I was actually practically ignoring everyone standing there. All I wanted to see was my baby's face after a week.

'Ya ya, I will see to It that you get selected in the singing team. Don't you worry boy, you will sing with the school band.' I said. The guy gave me a dirty stare and left. Soon after that another guy from my class came up to me to discuss something about the team. He was a fellow team member and I couldn't actually ignore him because it was some serious matter. It was related to some of the props used in our performances, and they were missing.

'Where would they go *yaar*, they were in the school storage room. How can they just disappear like that? You go talk to the floor manager of the school, maybe they decided to change the location or something.' I said. I only wanted him to go away and let me wait for my girlfriend in peace. But my fate wasn't with me that day either. After that guy left, I waited for almost twenty minutes in that corridor.

Her bus had already arrived, all the students went to their respective classes and I was still standing right there like a complete idiot.

I walked back to the class completely disappointed and angry at myself for standing there like a fool for almost half an hour, but as soon as I entered the class, I saw her. She was standing right there in her cute uniform, all dressed and ready to get back on with the school life after a mini-pause. She saw me standing across the room, looking right at her, she gave me a trademark Harshaali smile that I thought I had a copyright on. That smile was only meant for me and nobody else in this world. I had never been so happy before in my life, seeing that beautiful girl smiling at me gave me the best feeling ever.

She was surrounded by her friends; they probably wanted to know what had happened and why she skipped so many days from school. She was busy so I took my regular seat, right behind her.

'You had to choose a different route to class today haan? I was waiting for you downstairs. I wanted to walk with you to the class today; it was your first day after you got sick.' I said, I was disappointed as hell.

'Dev, I didn't pick a dIfferent route. I saw you standing near the staircase.' She said.

'Then why the hell didn't you come up to me?' I asked her out of surprise. This had never happened before. Whenever she saw me in the morning waiting for her, she would always approach me with the same smile that made each and every day of mine special.

'I would have, but you were talking to Harman, so I thought I shouldn't dIsturb you both and I walked right to the class. I didn't know you were waiting for me, I thought that you guys were just standing there and talking. I am sorry baby.' She said. I wasn't disappointed anymore. I was angry, sure, but my anger was more towards the idiot that drew my attention away from the door I had been staring at for fifteen minutes, looking for my girl.

'I was waiting for you.' I said with a sad face. She pulled my cheeks and called me her baby. I loved it when she did that.

'So tell me, how do you feel gettIng back to the school after such a long time?' I asked.

'I love the fact that I will be seeing you everyday again, but I am also much tensed, Dev. I have not touched a single book in like twelve days and we have our exams now. I just hope I am well prepared before exams.' She said, she was always concerned about these things. Me on the other hand, I was not that concerned about these exams. I always had a theory about exams. We had three sets every year, in each class, so I was able to create a system for myself that always worked for me. I would have fun the whole year and I would not care about these terminal exams. We had two sets of terminals and one final exam set. I always studied for the finals, but not a day before we got the final datesheet. I know that method was as dumb as it sounds, but you see, I had other stuff to do as well. I already mentioned that my schedule was pretty tight when I was in school.

I participated in every event that took place in the school. May It be dance, Music, sports day, annual functions etc etc etc, I was literally everywhere. At that very time our school was under construction and the ground had turned into the main construction site. Everything even remotely related to construction was dumped into the basketball ground. We didn't even have a decent place to play our game and practice for sports day. So I initiated something that became school's tradition after that.

'DUDE..!! Where are we supposed to play if the ground is all messed up like this? We have to take this matter to our principal ASAP.' One of my basketball teammates suggested.

'What is she going to say? She would just ask us to stop playing for sometime instead, Rohan that is the dumbest idea ever man.' Another one of my teammates said.

'I think we have to do something about these ourselves.' I intervened their discussion.

'Oh really, what are YOU going to do mister? Are you suggesting that we should start cleaning this dump ourselves?' Rohan said.

'How hard can it be guys? It's just some bricks and marbles that we have to get rid of, right?' I said.

'I am not with you on this one man. I am not going to pick up this mess.' Almost every single boy from my class said the same thing, but I saw this as a challenge. I was always waiting for situations where I could prove that I was more than just a brat with a loaded father.

I started with picking up the bricks myself as the others just stood there and ridiculed me. I didn't give a damn about these people and kept on working. I created a system of my own here too. I started picking up the bricks and kept them at a corner close to the canteen window. I kept on doing the loading alone for some time, but soon almost all the boys in my class, present in the basketball court started following my lead. We were doing a pretty great job too, we didn't even realise when the lunch break started and we were joined by some juniors who helped voluntarily. Soon, the movement I started became the movement for three classes and more than sixty guys. We were done with the court within three hours. Someone must have told the principal about the efforts we all had put together, so she came out into the court and gathered us all.

'I am really impressed boys. You have made your teachers and your principal proud today. We had absolutely no Idea that our boys had this in them, truly, we had underestimated you all. But the thing I really want to know is, whose Idea was this and who started doing all this? I mean, there must be one leader, right?' our principal questioned all the boys standing around her. Half on these guys didn't have any idea that I was the one who started this motion; the other half was my own class. I was pretty tired from all the work we had done, so I was standing a little far away, when I heard my name being announced for something.

'What did I do now? I didn't do anything guys. I just started the whole thing because we didn't have a place to play basketball and our own basketball court was trashed. 'I was alarmed at the rare announcement of my name. I thought that we were doing a good thing, but at that moment I was pretty sure that I had done something that the Principal didn't like.

She came closer to me with a stern look, well I guess that was the only look she knew, I thought she was going to slap me as hard as she could, so I closed my eyes and looked at the clean basketball court floor. But something miraculous happened; she came towards me and said the most amazing words any teacher had ever said about me.

'Deven Dhaanak, the naughtiest creature in our school. Who could have imagined that you of all people would take a step so wonderful? When did you become so responsible my boy? You have actually made me proud today. I see actual leadership qualities in you. Congratulations.' This was all she said, but her words made me so proud of myself at that moment that I almost cried. But the best part was, when our principal gathered all the children around, the rest of our class came to the ground as well, and so did Harshaali. I could see her face when Princi was saying those lovely words to me, and I could see the sparkle in her eyes, her smile clearly told me how proud she was feeling at that moment.

'Why did you do that Dev? The cleaning and stuff outside?' she asked me when we finally entered the class after a very long day.

'Well, it was pretty simple; we didn't have a place to play; now we do. But moreover, I did this for a better purpose, have you ever heard of *SHRAMDAAN*?' I said. I had heard about *SHRAMDAAN* being practiced in some schools in bigger cities like Delhi and Banglore etc, but I had never heard of it in or around Chandigarh. It was something that all the students had to do, including girls. The practice contained of jobs like gardening, sweeping, cleaning, dusting and many others, that were normally carried out by the schools hired staff. The children had to do all this just for one day; they didn't have any classes that day. I just wanted our school to be the first one in the tricity to be known for performing shramdaan activities.

When I told Harshaali my actual motive behind cleaning of the basketball court, she hugged me, even though we were in the class.

'People are looking baby.' I whispered in her ear.

'Let them stare if they want to, they know about us already.' She just stood there holding me like that for a long time, and I just enjoyed the moment.

After that day I became the 'good boy' of the school. The Principal told every teacher about what I had done and almost all the teachers were praising me now. I liked being in the spotlight.

Soon, our exams started and as always, Harshaali aced all the subjects and I also did almost well, but the good news was I scored well in both mathematics and science. I don't know how that happened, but it did. We were both really happy for each other. Even after a breakup, a hospital visit, bad health and everything, this girl topped the class again. She had something special in her, and I was always very happy when she got her marks because they were always really good and made her pretty happy.

CHAPTER 7

CONCENTRATION

THE THING ABOUT CONCENTRATION IS that, you never have it in the right place at the right time, it was like, God himself didn't want me to pick up the books. All I did during my day was wake up, go to school, talk to my Harshaali, come back home, talk to my Harshaali, go for tuitions, come back home and then again talk to my Harshaali, and still I sometimes thought that I wasn't giving her much of my time.

Vinay saw this, and he knew that this wasn't good for me, so he confronted me.

'Bro, what is wrong with you?' he was sitting in my room, sipping coffee. It was actually very rare that he visited me at my place. Usually we would meet somewhere else, but he must have thought that my room would be a more comfortable place to talk to me.

'What is wrong with me? I am fine. Why?' I was still chatting with her on Whatsapp.

'Will you please put that phone down for a minute? I need to talk to you man.' He said. I knew I had to talk to him because I knew that if I don't, he wasn't gonna leave me alone.

'OK, I don't have the phone now, what do you want to talk about? Shoot.' I said.

'Are you ok? You are on the phone almost all the time, you don't even talk to anyone else in the entire school now, I mean, call me selfish man, but I think you should think about this. You might be loosing some friends.' He said in a very serious tone. This was a problem for me, whenever he was serious, I had an urge to abuse him and ask him to fuck off, but I guess he was right.

'OK, I don't see any problem if I want to talk to my girlfriend. I mean most of the people I know that Harshaali is with me. If they still think that I will spend time with them and leave Harshaali alone for even one second, then they are mistaken. And by the way, when did you start caring about all this stuff man? You have been dating from like, class 7th practically; this shouldn't be something new for you to see.' I said, his allegations passed me off and even he knew that it always got ugly whenever I got angry.

'Dev, I am not saying that you shouldn't talk to Harshaali. I am just saying that you should give some time to others too, like for example, the last time we hung out together was like a month ago, and even then you were on your phone for most of the time. I know you love Harshaali, and believe me dude, I am really happy for you, but all I am saying is stop acting like a '*Majnu*' all the time. It seriously doesn't look nice.' He said this and left.

This was the first time Vinay had said something this meaningful in his whole life, and I know that because I had been his friend for a very long time now and I knew the kind of guy he was. He never said anything about me and Harshaali, but today he left me thinking about stuff that I had never thought about.

I called up Harshaali the moment he left.

'I need to ask something, can I?' I said.

'Do you really need permission Dev? As whatever you want to my baby.' She answered in the same casual manner. Well, obviously she was. Her best friend didn't just walk out on her questioning her behavior.

'Tell me, do you think that we are always together these days? I mean, are we like the *'CHIPKU COUPLE'* people hate and don't even want to look at?' my question must have startled her. She got into her serious mode as soon as I asked her this question.

'Did something happen, Dev? Is everything alright? Why are you asking this?' she gave me questions for my question.

'Just answer my question first. I need to know this. Do you also feel this way?'

'I have never even thought about it. I mean, I love you so much; I always want to talk to you. There is not even a second of the day that I think that we shouldn't talk. Maybe we talk a lot, but how does that even matter, don't you like talking to me?' she asked. I don't know how she did that, but whenever I was confused about something, she said something that made total sense and cleared out everything for me.

'I love talking to you, I love spending my days with you baby. It's just that, Vinay and I just had a big fight, he says that I have stopped hanging out with him now and all I care about is you.' I wasn't going to tell her about my fight with Vinay, but I had to.

'Baby, you know what, from now on start making time for your friends too because they are every bit as Important as I am, and trust me, If Vinay said this to you, then maybe It's true. He wouldn't just blame you for something that you have not done. Maybe he feels left out, because even you know, he doesn't have much friends. So please, spend some time with that guy. He loves you.' She said.

'You know what? I am amazed by the fact that an Idiot like me is with a girl like you, I seriously feel sometimes that I don't even deserve you. But I am truly in love with you because of this reason, you understand everything. You know everything, how is that possible?' I said, she laughed and then we talked for almost an hour after discussing the same topic.

The next day at school, I changed my seat. I went up to Vinay and apologized for my behavior the previous day. He just smiled and asked me to bunk a class with him. And as an obedient friend, I did. We had fun; we ate hot dogs from the canteen and spent half the lecture hiding in the balcony next to the boy's washroom. It was nice spending time with that idiot. I realised that I was behaving like a jerk. But I didn't blame myself for It, I blamed God, It was his fault he brought Harshaali into my life.

After that I started taking Interest In other stuff again. These were all Harshaali's Instructions that Instead of sitting in the class all the time, I should continue with the dance practices and other stuff.

The Times of India was a very well known newspaper that covered almost each and every city of India. They were Introducing a new cultural program that would include all the schools in the trinity i.e. Chandigarh, Panchkula and Mohali respectively. All the schools were invited to participate in the 'EXTRAVAGANZA 2010'. There were dance and singing competitions at different levels. Our school was participating in three different events, and I was part of two of them. The three teams were Boys Bhangra team, Girls Gidda team an solo singing. It was pretty obvious that I was still the captain of our Bhangra team, but people were not happy with this decision as I had not been very active with the team lately. So I had to make some amends, I started practicing seriously, for the selection round our performance was pretty simple, it hardly took me two days to learn the steps and another day to perfect them. Our performance was ready in less than five days, the remaining time, we kept for practice. Whenever we were going into a Bhangra competition, my energy level was super-high, I was always very excited. But there was one thing that I didn't actually like about Bhangra. We had to put on makeup every time we had a performance. I knew I looked really cute in makeup, but seriously, we had to do that every time. but I also had a problem, I had my singing performance just after my Bhangra performance, so I had to be quick with removing all the makeup from my face and getting ready for my singing.

There were a lot of schools participating in the competition, but only five were going to be selected for the finals. I knew we had a chance. What I didn't know was that we had a gap in our performance.

I didn't realise that our performance wasn't totally ready. Our performance had a flaw that the judges were not going to miss. We had accidentally left a whole minute of the song without any choreography, the ending of our song was uncertain without that part. I had just noticed the flaw and told our dance teacher about it. Our performance was just about to start and we had new problem here.

'What can we do now; we can only do the part that we have practiced. What's the big deal Deven?' a classmate of mine said this. The look that he got from me after saying this shut him up for the rest of the afternoon.

'I have a plan.' I said.

'Tell us captain.' One of the guys standing behind me said.

'We will keep the ending just as we had practiced, the one extra minute that we have on our hands now, we will add some stunts on the stage.' I suggested. Our dance teacher had no other option.

'Ok boys, do as he says. What stunts are you talking about? Do you have any in mind right now?' he asked.

'Yes, we could assign two Chakras on each side of the stage, whoever is comfortable with doing it, I just need volunteer guys, and this is going to be kind of an experiment.'

I had two guys who were going to perform a random Chakra on the floor now, now the problem was that those guys could not carry on the chakra for much long, so I had to come up with an all new plan.

Our performance was announced and we all got on the stage looking like Sardaars, some of us were actually Sardaars. The Music was played and we started the performance. The whole performance went really great, but we were now approaching the ending. The two guys who were going to perform the chakras were waiting for my signal. The moment they caught my signal they kneeled on the floor and started their chakras. I was about to leave the stage with them when I realised that one of them was losing his pace, I don't know why I did what I did next, but I jumped back on the stage and started doing random steps with everything I had left in me, all my energy, all my spirit came out in that mere half a minute. I was dancing alone on the stage for half minute and I didn't even know that. As soon as the song ended, I heard a really huge round of applause for our performance. My teammates came back on the stage and picked me up on their shoulders. My team was pretty sure that after that one spurt of energy that I showed on stage had given us the victory.

Finally the announcements for the five selected teams were made. Four names were already taken; our school wasn't in the top five that's what I thought.

'And today's best bhangra performance was, Shishu Niketan Public School.' As soon as we heard the judges announce our name as the best performers, we all ran to the stage just to show our faces to our opponent teams.

We were now the top five contenders of the dance competition. But there was still one thing that I had to do. I was also scheduled to participate in the solo singing competition. But what I didn't know was that my school's Principal had made a terrible mistake, she had registered my name under the wrong category. I was supposed to perform in the solo singing category, but I was registered in the solo Instrumentals category.

That mix-up cost me my chance at both the solo singing and solo Instrumental categories. I got disqualified and was asked to go home. But then there I was, In front of a stage and all I wanted to do was sing my heart out. I wanted people to know that I was a good singer and I could perform. So I went up to the show host and asked him for a favor.

'Sir, I know the solo singing category has ended and the participants have already been selected for the next round. But can I please sing something on the stage? I really wanted to perform but there was a mix-up during the registration. 'I said. I was expecting a big NO, but to my surprise, the guy immediately made some changes in the schedule card and gave me my performance slot.

'Here, this is your performance number. It's really close so stay right here, I will call out your name, ok?' he said with a smile on his face.

'Thank you so much sir.' I said and returned to my seat.

Some other performances took place and I sat there waiting for my turn. This was my first live performance, outside the school. I wanted to grade myself as an artist and I already knew my high points. I just wanted to know how I would do in front of a big, live audience.

'Deven Dhaanak, please come on the stage.' My name was finally announced.

The host had to clear out the confusion in front of the judges and I was allowed to perform after that.

Well, now, I was on the stage, all confused and scare and nervous at the same time, I was sitting on the chair because I didn't have a strap for my guitar.

I was ready now. I was going to sing a song from the album Jal Pari by Atif Aslam, he was pretty famous at that time and I was a fan. The moment I started my song, there was pure silence in the hall. It was really cool, me performing and people actually enjoying it. Well, my eyes were closed during the performance as I was too scared to look in the eyes of the people who were going to judge my performance.

As soon as my performance ended, I stood up and thanked everyone in the audience (still not looking) and started walking down the stage.

'Wait wait wait, I need to ask some questions from this young man here. Please give him the microphone somebody.' A guy from the staff handed me a microphone.

'Why didn't you perform in the singing section? Were you not Informed or something?' one of the judges said.

'Sir, actually I was sitting here for the same reason. I was supposed to be a participant in the singing section, but there was a confusion related to my registration form, so I couldn't. 'I said.

'You most certainly have the talent, boy. I want you to be in the competition. Call the event manager please.' That judge had a very long conversation with the Event manager and after that the conclusion was the same.

'I am really sorry young man, but right now I have no other option. But please know that you are a really good singer and your voice has something in it. Just keep on practicing.' He said and I left the building.

I was still sad that I wasn't the part of the competition now, but more than sad, I was angry at my Principal. All she had to do was mark the right option in the registration form, couldn't even get that right. Man, I was passed. The next morning, even though the whole school was happy for our selection in the top five teams, I was still upset. I decided to confront the Principal about it, so I walked up to her office. There was our class teacher in the office before me and they were in the middle of a conversation, the seemed really happy.

'May I please come in teachers?' I said.

Till that very moment I was pretty sure that my class teacher hated me, but she did something that I would never forget In my whole life, she ran towards me and hugged me, and I know this sounds weird, but I did not like the smell of that woman. I hated her even more now, she was actually one of the worst teachers and human beings of all time, but I am getting ahead of myself right now, I will tell you guys more about that teacher later.

Well, my class teacher hugging me and my principal being all happy and smiley had a reason. That day newspaper was in, it had the children's column and that particular newspaper, had a full sized image of me singing on stage at the event. Supposedly, there was a photographer present when I was performing, now I don't know if he liked my performance that much or whatever, but he did take a picture and print it on the front page.

That moment was a real achievement in my life too, although I got disqualified from the competition but I still had something that even the selected top five didn't have. They didn't have their picture on the front page of a newspaper, I did. I was so proud at that moment.

But the best thing was that the newspaper was distributed in the entire school before I reached my class from the Principal's office.

As soon as I entered, there was hooting and name chanting all over, and I was the reason. It felt awesome being the center of attraction. I saw people clapping and cheering for me even though they knew I was disqualified, and amongst my admirers, there she stood, my biggest and craziest fan, my girlfriend, cheering and hooting for me, I could see how happy she was. All I wanted to do in that moment was to run through the class and hold her tight close to me and kiss her. The look she had on her face at that moment, it was for me, it showed how proud it made her, that look made me fall in love with her even more.

'You must have been really good on that stage, it doesn't even matter that you got disqualified, right?' Harshaali said.

'Of course it matters babe, I mean, my main focus was the competition. This big picture in the newspaper, this just a consolation prize, that's all It Is. But you know what, this is going to make my parents really happy, so that means it makes me happy too.' I said.

'I am proud of you baby.' She said.

'Well, I know.' I said and we both just continued with the classes for the rest of the day.

My life was certainly going on the right path now; with Harshaali by my side everything seemed so beautiful. When you are in love with someone, you don't even see the flaws they have, you just love the way they are, even if they are wrong, they are right for you, even if people talk shit about them, you believe in them, even when you know they have made a mistake, you refuse to accept that and just keep on loving them with everything you have got, this is what love does to you. For me, these feelings had just gone real. I loved the way that girl looked at me, any time of the day when I was sad; one look at her would solve all my problems in one second. She always said that I had the heart and mind of a kid, that there was always something childish about me, what she didn't realise was that I had always been that way, she just noticed it now because now she was a part of my life and she was a part of mine, I was allowed to act childish around her, so I did.

Everyone has that one friend in front of whom you are free to be yourself, you are free to say anything, you can judge people, you can bitch about the people you don't like etc etc. For me that person was Harshaali, and even she used to the same. Whenever we were on the phone she would talk about stuff she wouldn't even think of discussing with anyone else. I was her best friend and she was mine. It was a period of sheer romance and love, love was actually in the air that season. But so was stupidity.

It had been two months since that hospital episode of Harshaali, and we had a really smooth time since then, until I somehow turned into a jealous son of a bitch. Ya, a guy like me was jealous of someone. Well, that someone got a little too close to my girl, that was the reason I acted the way I did. I mean, what would anybody do if people come up to you and tell you that some guy was hitting on your girlfriend in the bus. Obviously, my kind of people would get mad, and so was my reaction to this. First I slapped the guy who came up to me to tell me that a guy was hitting on my girlfriend and my girlfriend was flirting back. Then I took a whole round of the school trying to find that guy, and I did.

'Hey, you got a minute bro?' I said.

'Hey Deven, What 'sup bro?' he replied. I really don't think he knew what was about to happen.

'See Ajay, I know you are a really good friend of Harshaali, and I really don't care what you people talk about, but if I hear from one more person that you were flirting with my girlfriend, I promise I will break you In half. So watch It.' I was not the kind of a guy, who would just go up to someone and threaten them, but something happened that day, I just wasn't myself. Or maybe it was the fact that I really didn't like other guys talking to my girlfriend, man, I didn't want to be that guy.

The same evenIng HarshaaliI called me.

'Dev, what happened today? What did you do?' no hello, no hi, directly the questions, just Indicated that the dumbass Ajay, has done or said something to Harshaali.

'Me? What did I do? I didn't do anything? Why?' I tried to save myself from a really bad scolding; I was actually the kind of boyfriend who was scared of his girlfriend.

'Really??!!

Because Ajay came up to me in the bus today and said that he never wanted to talk to me ever again. What was that about? Can you please explain?' she said.

'Well, then It's Ajay who should explain this to you, right?' yeah, like she was going to fall for that. Come on Dev, you Idiot, she knows you a lot better than that. Humor was a defense mechanism that I used when I was in a problem with the people I cared about.

'Dev, this is really not funny. You know, Ajay was my only friend in the bus; he was the only person that would talk to me. And now I have lost a friend because of you. And I know it's you, you have scared the crap out of that guy. What the fuck did you do and why did you do that?' she started crying over this stupid thing, or maybe it was stupid for me because I was at fault here.

'Hey baby, listen, I am really sorry for whatever happened today. I was just passed because some random guy from your bus came up to me and said that Ajay was hitting on you in the bus. So I just warned the guy and asked him to stay away. I didn't know you guys were close friends, you should have told me sooner.' I said.

'I don't know Dev, you just have to apologize to him, make sure he is not scared of you the next time I see him.' She said and disconnected the phone.

I tried to call her, but she switched off her phone. So I tried calling Ajay the Idiot. He picked up almost instantly.

'Yeah, Ajay?' I didn't know how to say what I was about to say next.

'Listen, dude, I don't what I did today was even right or not. But you don't have to stop being friends with Harshaali. You are her friend, I should have understood. So please man, don't just stop talking to her like that. It would hurt her feelings and she will stay mad at me, and If she stays mad at me because of you I will do exactly what I was going to do before, break you In half, ok?' I said and disconnected.

Then I realised I didn't say the magic word that would do the trick. So I called him again.

'Yeah bro, anything else?' he said as soon as he picked up.

'Yeah, I forgot to tell you something. Don't take it personally though, it's just my magic word, I forgot to say that. I want to tell you, that you my friend are the biggest *BEHANCHOD* ever. Now I am truly done. Talk to her in the bus tomorrow or I will beat you to death. Now bye.'

Yeah, I was really bad at sorries.

The next day Harshaali entered the class with Ajay, I know she did that just to see me jealous once again, but I didn't get jealous at all. I wasn't jealous of that guy; I don't know how or why I got jealous the first time. I mean, I don't want to sound racist but that guy could not be any girl's boyfriend. He didn't have the looks, he didn't have the skill, and he didn't even have the guts to say that he liked someone. Let alone tell my girlfriend that he had feelings for her. Damn, I should have seen that before threatening him.

'Well? Is everything OK now?' I had to ask this question. I just knew I had to.

'Why did you do that Dev? Why did even feel the need to do that? Do you not trust me?' her reply was disturbing.

'I trust you baby, but I really don't trust other guys, and I shouldn't. I have a hot girlfriend Ok, and I just know that you are going to get better with age, and I cannot take chances, even with guys like that dumbass. I will never take any chances with you, NEVER.' I said and she smiled a little.

'Hey, I am sorry. I know it was stupid, but at that time it seemed right to me somehow. Now that I think about It, I can see how dumb I was to threaten him.' I added.

'Can you at least tell me what you said? How you threatened him? I just want to know.' She said.

'Harshaali, it's really better if I don't, ok? He didn't say anything about the phone call, did he?'

'No, why? Now what did you say to him on the phone?' she asked.

'Nothing, If he didn't say anything, why should I? I don't want anything to bother you babe. Just know that I will protect you at each and every step of my life.' I said.

'You know what, we need to discuss this. We'll talk about this on the phone tonight.' She said as the worst teacher of the school entered, our class teacher.

I was sure that night was going to be a long one because whenever we discussed something serious on the phone, we would fight and call each other names and we would just try to prove ourselves right. But I don't know how she always won the argument. I guess she was good at arguments or maybe I just never wanted to win in front of her.

'Hello….' Her voice on the other end.

'Hey baby, how are you mera baccha?' I replied with as much love and affectIon in my voIce as possible. I just wanted to avoid the "discussion".

'Don't be all lovey dovey tonight; you know we have to discuss that. It's bothering me now.' she said with a really stern voice.

'Yeah, ok. You won't be gettIng any goodnight kisses from me tonight.' I said. I knew she wasn't going to let this go.

'What was the need Dev? Tell me.' she said.

'See Harshaali, I don't know if there was a need or not, but all I know is when that a guy came up to me and said that some guy was flirting with you on the bus, I just couldn't stop myself.' I said.

'But you should have at least talked to me first. I would have told you the truth, that guy Is like a brother to me, how could you even think he would flirt with me?' she said.

'Well, as I said before, you should have told me that he was a friend of yours. How was I supposed to know that the guy was your friend?' I said.

'OK, so you mean that I have to tell you about every guy I am friends with?' yeah, I knew this was a rhetorical question.

'I am not saying that, babe. I am just saying that you should at least tell me about the friends you are close with, would it hurt you to tell me?' It was my turn to ask a rhetorical question now.

'I didn't say that it's bad, Ok, I will always keep you aware of people I am friends with. As long as you keep telling me all about the girls that hit on you or the girls you are friends with.' She said, it sounded like more of a deal.

'First of all, girls don't hit on me at all.' I said.

'Oh really? What about that Malini Sharma at your tuition? Didn't she like, literally propose to you over the phone?' damn, this girl knew everything, no wait, I told her myself about Malini.

Malini was a friend of mine at my math's tuition. She was really close and I used to share a lot with her. She lived near my house so I even used to meet her a lot. She once told me that she liked me a lot, at that time I was on a break with Harshaali and I told Malini about that. She said that she had feelings for me from a long time but she could never tell me about them as I was in a relationship with Harshaali. So when she saw that I was single again, she told me everything on the phone and proposed to me. I obviously had to turn her proposal down because I was madly in love with Harshaali.

Malini took it really hard and stopped talking to me for a while, but she understood that later and we became friends again in a short while.

'Hey, Malini was just a friend ok, and she only said all that stuff because she thought I was single, because someone had recently broken up with me.' I said.

'OK Dev, my poInt is, you are a popular guy and girls do like you, so it would be better if I know about these girls ok?' she said.

'OK baba, I will tell about each and every female friend I ever have, ok?' I said.

'That's like a good boyfriend. I love you sooo much.' She said, and everything was normal after that.

This was the thing that I loved the most about this girl, she got me. I mean, she got what kind of a guy I was, she knew how much I loved her, she never had any doubts on me, she knew I loved her from the bottom of my heart, and that was all I ever wanted. The girl I loved was in my life, now everything had to go in the right direction from here on.

But as usual, it didn't.

We were sitting in our class and a sudden announcement was made that there was going to be a Parent Teacher Meeting the next day. This was random, all our PTMs were held on a Saturday, but it wasn't a Saturday.

CHAPTER 8

FOR THE LOVE OF GOD, LEAVE US ALONE!

EVERYTHING WAS GOING REALLY WELL with me and Harshaali, our relationship was in that phase where you don't care what happens in the entire world, where you just want the attention of that one special person who matters the most. We were living high on love, until that stupid class teacher of ours Intervened.

'Harshaali, what are you doing?' she called Harshaali out of the class to talk to her about what was going on between me and her.

'What are you saying teacher, I don't understand.' She replied, she actually had no idea why she was called out by the class teacher during an ongoing class.

'I am talking about you and Deven, I have been noticing you two from a long time, and I just didn't want to embarrass you in front of the whole class. Tell me the truth Harshaali, what is going on between you two?' she was sure that something was going on between us; she must have seen the signs. Me and Harshaali were always seen together almost everywhere, we had our seats arranged in a manner that we were always seen talking, we were just not aware that the class teacher was keeping a close eye on us both.

'Maam, I don't know where you got that idea that there is something going on between me and Deven, we are just really good friends, that's all.' She tried to get out of it all she could, but she wasn't convincing enough.

'OK, you won't tell me anything, it's alright. Go to your class now.' she sent Harshaali back to the class without saying another word.

Harshaali came back with a worried look on her face and sat on her seat, thinking.

'What happened? Why did she call you out between the class?' I asked, I was unaware of the situation till then.

'Dev, I think we should change our seats, the teachers are starting to suspect that something is going on between us. I really can't go through all this again, we have already been caught so many times, if this happens again, I will be shattered. They will call my parents Dev.' she spoke with such a pace that I couldn't even understand the half of it.

'Wait wait wait, slow down baby, what is going on? What did that stupid bitch call you out for?' I asked.

Then Harshaali told me everything that our class teacher had said, she knew about us and Harshaali was worried that she was going to spill the beans In front of all the other teachers and maybe even the Princi, she was also more frightened because our class teacher had direct contact with her parents and she could call them anytime.

Now this was not fair, we were having such a great time and that bitch had to screw it all again. For the next few days all we talked about was that how to get out of this mess. We were having so many problems that we ourselves had lost count. Sometimes it was her dad, if not her dad then her cousin and if not her stupid cousin then our clown ass class teacher. We just couldn't stay happy for long.

Because of what Mrs. Meena Sharma i.e. our class teacher had said, we had to change our seats, we would sit as far as we could in the class, we made sure that no one ever saw us together as we had no idea which one of our own classmates was our class teacher's personal detective that she had appointed for only one reason, me and Harshaali. She was such a bitch, she always hated me, even if I was good at something, she never appreciated me, I was always the spoiled brat for her, and didn't know what I had to do to change that image of mine.

'What do you think baby, is she settled now, or are you still scared that she would call up your parents and complain about us?' we were talking late night on the phone, her parents had been sleeping for a while and she had called me up just because she wanted to talk.

'Dev, I really want to be with you baba, but you have to stop this anyhow. Do this for your baby please.' She said this with so much fear that I couldn't say anything but "OK baby" to that.

For this girl I meant a lot, she could not see me getting hurt, and the feelings were the same for her in my heart, anything that could or would hurt her, I would stop it from happening. I loved this girl, but I loved her more when she was happy, and right now she wasn't happy at all.

The next day at school, Harshaali was called by the Principal Into her office.

'Your class teacher has told me everything Harshaali, you are a really bright student and we don't want your grades to fall down because of a guy like Deven, he is nothing in comparison to you and deep down your heart you know that yourself, you can do a lot better than that guy, just wait for that to happen and stop rushing things. This is all I want to say to you; the rest is on you, if I get one more complaint about you two, I will call up your parents. And believe me Harshaali, you don't know these type of guys, they are just after one thing, he will dump you as soon as he gets into your pants, so stay away and save yourself and your future.' This was what our respected Principal had to say to Harshaali, this is what she thought of me, my image was even worse than I had ever imagined.

Harshaali told me everything that happened In the Principal's office, she was crying on the phone and so was I, although we had different reasons. Harshaali was crying because she didn't want to hear anything like that about me, she trusted me with all her soul and loved me, she was devastated when our Principal said all that stuff about me, on the other hand, I was shocked to hear that I was being pictured as the guy who wants to get In Harshaali's pants. I mean, in my mind I had never thought of doing that to Harshaali, she was the love of my life, she was the one person I could rely on if the whole world went against me, and people thinking that about our relationship, that broke my heart.

'Harshaali, tell me something, when she was saying all this to you, did you, in your mind, even for a second think that whatever she was saying could be true?' my questIon broke her heart, she cried even harder than she was crying before.

'Dev, I love you yaar, how can you even say such a thing? If I had any doubts about you na, I would not have been with you for such a long time now. I would have left the moment I thought that any of this was true. I swear I have never pictured you as that guy, I have always seen you for what you are, and trust me Dev, I know you love Me.' her answer was reassurIng; I gained faith in myself again.

'I don't give a fuck what those people think about me, I don't give a fuck what my teachers and my principal thinks about me, all I care about is you baby, If you have decided to stand by me, then I swear that no matter what happens In the future, I will always stay beside you, and there one more thing that I want to say, you might get sad In the future about something or the other, you might even get scared about stuff, but I guarantee you one thing, there is one thing you will never be in your life, you will never be alone baby, never.' I said.

She stopped crying, there was silence for a long time.

'Hey, what happened?'

'Nothing Dev, I was just thinking that how some people come into your life and change it completely, a year ago, I didn't even like you, and look at us now, you have just said the sweetest words that I have ever heard from anyone, I can't believe this is happening in my life, I always thought that this day would never come, the day when someone would stand and fight for me to make me his own. I love you Dev, all I want to say right now is that I love you.' And then she slept, it was one of the most calm nights of all.

Now, we had to be aware at the school if we wanted to meet or even talk about something, it was like we were under surveillance all the freaking time.

'How is this going to work Dev?' we sneaked out into the basement during the lunch break, our school basement was always empty, It was the place where other couple came when they wanted to spend some "alone time" together.

'It's only a matter of time now baby, after that we will be out of here and nobody will bother us again, see, our second semesters are already approaching, after that only the board exams and then we are done with this school, we won't be coming here again, so these people can't do anything about It, they can only threaten us, so my baby, just chill.' I said, and then we made out in the basement. Yeah, that was the other plan; it had been a long time after all.

We were still having a lot of trouble communicating in the school premises, so Harshaali came up with a plan.

'Let's break up, Dev.' she said.

'WHAT? NO, not again, what is the matter with you girl? Have you completely lost you mind? You want a break up again?' my voice echoed in the basement, we had been sneaking into the basement whenever we had our chance, mostly It would be the lunch time or the activity class.

'Listen to me first dumb. I am not saying that we actually have to break up, we just have to pretend. Just for some time, so that the word spreads that we are not together anymore, sooner or later this news will reach the bitch and we won't be in trouble anymore. What say?' she said and winked.

'I just love it when you use the evil side of your brain and enjoy it. I love you so much, oh no, wait, I hate you, bitch.' I said.

'What?'

'Arre, I am just pretending that we just had a break up. I would surely call you a bitch if we are pretending now, ok?' I said and winked at her.

'Oh really, what do I call you then?' she asked. I was too busy kissing her face by then.

'I don't know, you come up with a fake abusive name for me, that's your job. Hey, want to make out again?' I said.

'We are going to be late for class; the other "bitch" is taking the extra class this week.' She said.

'OK, then we will just make out a little, and then we will go back to class. What say?' I suggested.

'I know you won't let me go without this, such a horny boy you become sometimes.' She said and then we did exactly what I wanted.

We planned out everything during our late night phone call, I had made a script, we had to breakup In front of our friends first and It had to sound convincing. If you can fool you best friend with some made up story, then you can fool anyone with the same story. So I had to ask Vinay to come with me and she called Abhilasha and Aditi with her.

'What do you think of yourself Deven, that I will be scared of you? Well, then you are hugely mistaken mister because I am clearly not afraid of you or what you show that you are, because I know that you can do nothing.' These were the opening lines of our "play".'

'Oh really, I will show you what I can do If I see you talking to that son of a bitch again.' I said.

'What is he talking about Harshaali? What is wrong with you guys and why are you fighting like this?' Abhilasha bought the opening lines and I guess Aditi did too.

'He is insane yaar, he wants me to stop talking to Ajay, just because he and his sick friends think that there is something going on between me and Ajay.' She said, she was playing her part pretty nicely. It was my turn to get into the character now.

'Listen Harshaali, I just don't like seeing you talk to that guy, I just hate it when you talk to other guys.' I said.

'Well, then you are a narrow minded guy and maybe I was wrong jumping into this relationship with you. I don't want it anymore, do you get that? She said, for a second I thought she was serious there.

'Fine by me yaar, even I am done running after you. It's over now.' I said, and started walking back to the class with Vinay.

'Dude, are you sure about this? I mean, I know you love her, I think you guys should think about this first.' He said, he bought the act, YESSS…!! This was the entire plan, I was supposed to sell my store to Vinay and she was supposed to do the same In front of her best friends. The plan was working.

'This Is bullshit yaar Vinay, I mean, she should see who she Is talking to na, that guy clearly likes her and all she Is doing by talking to him Is encouraging his behavior.' I said, I was really trying not to laugh.

'But Dev, remember last time this thing came up? You ended up apologizing In front of that shitake, you want to do that again?' he said.

'Bro, I didn't apologize last time either.' I said.

'What do you mean by that; you told everyone that you did.' He had so many questions today, this was the PLAN.

'Well, Harshaali asked me to apologize to him for threatening the crap out of that guy, so I called him up, and threatened him again that If he tells anything to Harshaali, I will kick his ass In front of the whole class. And he did exactly as I said.' I actually wanted to tell him about this. He had been making fun of me for apologizing to a guy because my girlfriend asked me to.

'Are you serious? Man, that was nice, but seriously, talk to Harshaali tonight, ok? Clearly you guys are not good at talking face to face.' He said.

Our little drama had created a commotion in the entire class. Apparently some girl overheard Harshaali's conversation with Abhilasha and told every other student in the class. Now, normally this would have created a problem for me and Harshaali as well, but this was exactly a plan. Actually, I would like to tell you the exact plan. I called It, THE FAKE BREAKUP.

THE FAKE BREAKUP

Step 1- *First have a fake fight In front of your best friends and make it look real.*

Step 2- *Then your best friends, being your best friends, will try to talk you into fixing things up between you two.*

Step 3- *Ignore them completely.*

Step 4- *Sooner or later the whole class will know about your breakup but each one of your classmates will pretend that they don't know anything.*

Step 5- *Wait till that bitch Class teacher get the wind of it.*

Step 6- *She might call out Harshaali to talk to her in private again.*

Step 7- *Keep pretending till the Board Exams.*

The whole plan was going really well, we had already reached step 4 and now all we had to do was wait until the bitch found out about it.

The same night I was talking to Harshaali when Dad knocked on my door.

'Harshaali, wait a minute, dad is outside.' I said and disconnected the call.

I opened the door and saw him standing outside.

'Yes Dad.' I said.

'Who were you talking to? It's almost 2 a.m. in the night.' Dad said, I was nervous now.

'Dad ahhhh, it was just a friend from school; we were discussing the English project that we are working on.' As I was saying this, a voice inside my head was screaming at me, 'DON'T SAY THAT... THIS IS NOT THE BEST LIE YOU CAN COME UP WITH YOU DUMBASS, THINK OF SOMETHING ELSE RIGHT NOW...!'

'You have the whole day and you choose this time to talk about the project? Hmmm.. Who's the girl?' he was my dad, and he had just asked me the most unexpected question of my life.

'Girl? What girl? There is no girl, dad.' I said, I didn't even realise that I was talking too fast.

'Son, I don't think that you realise that I am your father and I know everything about you, just sleep on time ok? You have school tomorrow.' He said and left me thinking.

'WHAT THE HELL JUST HAPPENED?!' I was talking to myself now.

My father had just caught me talking to my girlfriend and all he had to say was that he knew, man, this was really out of the blue. I had no Idea that my father was this Interested In my life.

I called her again.

'What happened? Did he say anything to you?' she asked.

'Nah, he was just checking up on me, I told him today that I had cold, he just came by to see if I was Ok.' I didn't want her to know that my father already knew that I had a girlfriend and he was really cool about it. I always thought that if my father found out about me and Harshaali he would flip out, but what I just witnessed was the signs of the coolest dad in the whole damn world.

'Oh, you take care Dev, you are really careless.' I had a smile on my face for the rest of the night.

The plan that we had made was going really well, she was getting calls from her friends just to check up on her, if she was alright and stuff like that, Vinay only had one thing to talk about now, my stupid fight with Harshaali. Things went pretty well with our acting and mostly lying skills, people now thought that me and Harshaali were broken up for good this time.

We used to laugh on this as we discussed it every night, what Abhilasha suggested, what Vinay wanted me to do, what these guys were planning, everything was actually funny to us. We knew we were wrong lying to these people as these were our best friends, but we also knew that if these guys didn't believe that we were broken up now, nobody else would buy it, so we continued our plan for a long time.

The second semesters were approaching and Harshaali made sure that I studied at least three hours a day. She came up with a schedule that helped me study and also allowed us to talk for some time in the night. She always copied her notes for me and as usual her notes were really helpful.

'Dev, are you studying according to schedule I prepared for you?' she asked on the phone.

'Baby, you shouldn't be asking this question. You make sure that I study every night and give each and every subject appropriate time, you check my notebooks for last night's work, you help me with my problems, you do everything that a good tuition teacher does, you should already know the answer to that question.' I said and she smiled. She knew she was doing a hell of a job making me study like that.

'I know, but still, it's really good to see you like this, you have got brains and I just want you to use them in the right place at the right time, and believe me Dev, this is the best time. If you clear the second semesters with good grades, you will not have to worry about the finals, boards are pretty easy as compared to these exams.' She explained all this to me just to make sure that I understood the importance of second semesters.

Baby don't worry about me, I will do everything as you say, Ok? I am sure I will score well this time, far better than the first semesters.' I said.

'That's really good, I believe in you baby. I love you, and that's the reason I do all this. You understand that right? Please don't mind if I ever get mad at you or yell at you when we are studying, I really want you to score well.' She loved me so much that she took out time from her schedule to check up on me, I got a text from her within every hour, and she would just ask one question, 'Are you studying?' and my reply as always the same, 'Yeah baby, you study too, stop worrying about me.'

Our relationship was all I cared about now, we were about to complete a year now and we had already been through so much together that we were really grateful to God that we were still together.

Our second terms went as we had figure, she topped again and I managed to secure the 4th position in the class. I score great in mathematics, science and social studies, English was my strongest point and I managed to score the second highest in the same. I was happy and my parents were happier than I was. They knew that I could score well and I did, they were proud. Harshaali's efforts had made it all possible, she was happy for me too. Finally, everything was going great in life. My parents were happy, my girlfriend was happy and so was I.

Our anniversary was also approaching now, but we could not celebrate as we wanted, it wasn't official that I had a girlfriend and making it official wasn't even the plan for a long time ahead. So we decided that we would just talk to each other all day and celebrate our anniversary that way. At this poInt in my life, I actually knew who mattered the most to me; I knew who my life partner was going to be. Most people spend their life searching for "the ONE", I was lucky enough to find that One at such a young age. Sometimes I felt like she meant the world to me, sometimes I felt like she meant even more than the whole world, the feeling of having that one special person in your life standing right beside you the whole time cannot be put down into words.

CHAPTER 9

THE BAD DECISIONS

A MONTH BEFORE THE FINAL EXAMS, my father called me into his room, sat down on the bed, and gave me a look that I had never seen before in my life.

'I want to know something from you.' I bet I missed a heartbeat there, I thought he was going to talk about Harshaali again.

'What do you want to do next? You will pass the final examinations, everyone knows that. But what are your plans for the future?' he asked these questions in a very serious tone, so I had to get into my serious mode too.

'Dad, honestly, I think I want to become a doctor, but I am considering going for Arts, as I want to join the Indian Police Force too. So right now I am torn between the two choices. Let's see, if I score better in science I will go for Medical, and if I score better In English, I will go for Arts.' I said.

I had not given this a lot of thought, but when dad brought up the topic; I couldn't resist thinking about it. I wanted to know what Harshaali's plans were, because it was clear that even after school, we were going to be together.

The next day as I was gettIng ready for school, Vinay called me up.

'Dude, don't bring your ass to the school today, It's an off. I don't know these people can't inform us the day before. I had to wake so early and walk so much to reach here and the watchman says it's an off, what the fuck dude. Anyway, I just wanted to save you from the suffering, stay home.' He said so much in just a few seconds, I only understood the part where he said that it was holiday today because of some unknown reason.

'If this is a joke, I will kill you, if it's not, then *Ha ha ha* dude, you had to go all the way.' It was funny actually, Vinay was the laziest person I knew, and he had to go through all that. Just thinking about it made me laugh.

'Shut up you bastard, I am already passed off, do not poke me, bye now.' he said and disconnected the call.

As soon as I got the information I called up Harshaali to tell her that the school was off today, she didn't pick up. She called me back an hour later.

'Please tell me you got the information and you didn't leave for school today.' I said.

'I didn't get the information and I am coming directly from the school right now, God these people just don't get that we get really pissed off when they do this. They should inform us a day before, why do they wait for us to reach there and then tell us? Bloody idiots, you know how much I love sleeping, and more than that I love seeing you every day, this is not fair. Now I can't do any of those things.' She almost cried, whenever she complained about something, she turned into a cute little baby that didn't get what she wanted; I loved that side of hers.

'Why are you not saying anything?!' she screamed at me because I wasn't replying to what she had just said.

'I love you sooooo much baba. You have no idea how much I love you, and you never will.' I said.

'Yeah, now where did that come from? I am crying like an idiot here and you say you love me, I don't get it.' she said.

'Baby, it's better if you don't get it, because if you do, the romance will die.' I said and gave her a kiss through the phone.

'You are getting weirder day by day Mr. Deven Dhaanak, but I still love you like crazy and you mean the world to me.' I could feel her love in her voice, she did love me like crazy and I knew it.

'Did you see what I did just now?' I asked.

'What?' she replied with a question? She never guessed any of my questions.

'I just made you smile when you were in the worst of your moods, and I did that on the phone, this shows how much I affect your life and also that you are really happy with me and this makes me happier.' I said.

'Obviously dumbo, all I ever want to do is talk to you for hours, trust me, if you were here right now, I would have just hugged you tightly and stayed like that till fall asleep.' The way she said it was so romantic. In that moment I knew I had the best girl possible.

We talked till we were both sleepy, then we decided that we will meet in the school basement the next morning.

I reached school before her and was waiting for her in the basement, when she showed up with her bag still on her back.

'You came straight down here? Nobody saw you coming?' I asked.

She didn't say anything; she threw her bag away and kissed me.

'What happened baby?' I said, before getting interrupted by another kiss.

'Shut up and keep kissing me.' she said.

I did as I was instructed. We made out for a long time that day, during our make out session; my hands played their role pretty well. By the time we decided to head back to the class, her hair was all messed up, her dress was all messed up, and I had entered and reached places that I shouldn't have during the school time at least.

As we were about to enter the class together, we recalled our little charade. We were not supposed to be seen together in the school.

'I think we shouldn't walk together like this.' She said, Harshaali didn't want to get into trouble again.

'I know and I was just about to say that, I am going that way, you go inside.' I said, as I went into the boy's washroom.

The worst person I could see in the boy's washroom, Vinay. He saw us walking together and talking.

'I thought you guys broke up. What's up with the long corridor walk?' he was such a pain in the ass sometimes. I didn't know how to answer that question.

'We were just chatting casually, I just wanted to talk to her, I know I made a stupid mistake bro, but still, I thought about what you said, and I think you were right when you said that we should sit and solve the matter.' I had to come up with something, I know this wasn't the best, but it worked.

'So are you guys getting back together?' he asked.

'No dude, not so soon. I want to give it some time, I have always said the first sorry every time, even if it wasn't my fault. I want her to apologize this time.' I said, I got inside the washroom just to avoid being seen with Harshaali, but there I was, answering stupid questions of my stupid best friend, and now I actually had to pee.

'Dude, you do love her, see, I only want you to be with her because you have got something that I never had. Sure, I have had girlfriends, but none of them even stood close to that girl in comparison. I have seen her with you and I have seen her without you, I can tell the difference. She loves you a lot Dev, think about it.' He said, but I didn't know if he was seriously saying all this stuff or he was just playing with my mind, but I needed to hear what he actually thought of Harshaali.

'Let's go, sit with me in the class, I need you to tell me something, ok?' I said.

During all that "Harshaali talk" I didn't even realise that we were getting late for the class, Harshaali was sitting comfortably in her seat because I had sent her directly to the class as I walked towards the boy's washroom.

'You are late, stay outside you two.' our class teacher, again, she didn't like me at all.

We had no other option except to stand quietly outside.

'What did you want to know, Dev?' Vinay said.

'Yeah, I think now we have a lot of free time on our hands. I want you to tell me what you feel about Harshaali, I mean, do you think she is good for me?' I tried to make my question as simple as possible.

'I think, even if you tried, you cannot get a better girl than Harshaali. She cares for you, she loves you dude, I have seen it in her eyes, I see her sometimes, and she stares at you for some time during class and then smiles. This only happens when a person is madly in love with the other.' He said, I didn't expect this from him, he was never in favor of love, he was always in favor of flings and casual affairs, but whenever anything even close to a relationship came up, he ran away. Getting this statement from a guy like him, it showed how much he cared for me and what I meant for him.

'But there are differences now, I never wanted this, but she.' he interrupted me before I could even finish my sentence.

'What differences man, the only thing that should matter now is that you love her and she loves you. You guys have been through so much together; promise me you will clear things out with her.' He said, now he was freaking me out with all this Idealistic talk.

'What is wrong with you dude? How come you are supporting a relationship?' I said and I laughed, but he didn't.

'My parents are getting a divorce Dev, and I can't stop them, they are going to do it and my life is going to be screwed. I can't see my parents like that.' The moment he said these words, he started crying. We were standing outside the class in the middle of the corridor; all I could do at that point was just hug him. He was my best friend and I had never seen him cry before. This was the first time he actually opened up with anyone and he chose me to do that, seeing him like that brought tears into my eyes too.

'Hey, Vinay, everything will be fine brother, please calm down.' I could hear my voice cracking too. The bell rang for the next class to start.

'See, now we have to enter the class ok? So cheer up man, everything is going to be fine, trust me.' I could only give him false comfort right now.

'Hmmm... let's go.' He walked ahead of me quietly.

That day I saw a very different Vinay, the one who gave a damn what was going around him. He was pretty vulnerable; I couldn't see him like that. He made me promise that I wouldn't talk to anyone about this, but I broke his promise, Harshaali was my girlfriend and I had to tell her. I couldn't keep such a thing to myself.

'What is he going to do now?' she sounded sad too.

'I don't know baby. I have not talked to him after that, I couldn't actually. I just cannot see him like that, I cannot see my best friend cry because his life is going downhill, and I can only see him happy like I have always seen him. Why do people do this? Why can't they just live their lives happily?' I was depressed as hell, if only I could do something about it.

'You think they do this on purpose? Dev, life is never easy, it throws difficulties at you, it has always been that way, you just have to work hard on things and things settle down themselves. Just like in a relationship, if you don't work on it, it won't work, you have to put in efforts, life doesn't get easy itself, you have to make it easy for yourself.' She said.

'Hmmm. Ok, I know things are hard for him now, but I believe in God, he gave me the blessing so that I could be with you, I know he will do something good for my friend too.' I said, and then we talked for a while and went to sleep. At least I thought I was going to sleep.

As soon as I disconnected the call, I started thinking about how Vinay had been acting a little weird these past few days. He was a little distracted all the time, he was too interested In me and Harshaali, he wanted us to patch things up between us but actually what he wanted was to get a little distraction from his own family life, he just wanted to keep himself busy so that he didn't have to think about his parents splitting up.

It is always difficult for anyone to help a friend when the friend doesn't want to be helped. But I knew Vinay needed help dealing with this. He was trying so hard to be normal that he stopped talking about his parents to anyone, even with me, he said that only I knew about this, so I guess he stopped talking about them with because now he felt weird talking about them In front of me.

'Hey, you know you can talk about anything with me right? You are like a brother to me and I cannot see you like this.' I said, we were standing in front of the canteen and we had a "Mountain Dew" bottle each.

'I know, that's why I told you, that's why we are still talking bro, although, If you ever tell any girl that I cried In front of you and then hugged you, I will kill you In cold blood, always remember that.' He said, he was still acting like he was OK.

'Well, about that, I guess Harshaali knows.' I said.

'You son of a bitch, well, It doesn't even matter, she is a friend only.' He said and gave me a smile.

'And by the way, I know you guys are together again, but don't worry, your secret's safe with Me.' he said.

'But how do you know about that? I didn't tell you, did Harshaali say anything about that?' I was surprised to know that the one person I have been lying to this whole time actually knows the truth.

'Look bro, I don't care about what you want or why you felt the need to hide the truth from me, I really don't, all I want is for you and Harshaali to be happy, but seriously, why did you lie to my face you son of a bitch?' this was my friend Vinay, just negated everything he had just said.

'Look, there Is something I didn't tell you, a few days back, Meena "the bitch" called Harshaali and asked her about us, Harshaali tried to get out of it but she couldn't, after that Principal called Harshaali in her office and said the same thing, to stay away from me, so we had to do all that drama just to stay safe In this school, because after that nobody Is going to bother us.' I said and that felt so good to take off my chest.

'You have been dealing with this the whole time and you didn't even think about telling me? Whatever your plan was is it working?' he asked, curiously.

'It seems so, almost everyone thinks that we are broken up, so nobody will tell that bitch otherwise, you get my point?' I said.

'OOOOKKKKK, so if nobody knows that you and Harshaali are in a relationship, how will they tell the Teachers about It, that was a nice plan bro.' he said, he was actually Impressed by my thinking.

'Well, who said that only you know how to be with a girl, though it doesn't mean that I see you as an inspiration or something, because if I did, I would be getting slapped by Harshaali.' I said and we both laughed so hard that his Dew came out of his nose and that was gross, by the way.

'Dude, that was a cheap shot ok. That was actually all your faults, you made me break up with all those girls in one bucking day. I mean, how you managed to do that, I still don't get it, but it was all worth it.' He said, we finished our drinks and walked back to the class in a nice and happy mood.

It makes you happy to see that people around you are happy, two of my favorite people in the world were happy right now and that was really boosting up my spirit, I was doing well at studies, I was doing well with my guitar lessons and I was great with the dance practices. Everything around me was going good for once. But there was still something that was bugging me, my career choice. I wasn't sure what I wanted to do.

'What do you plan after the board exams?' I was talking to Harshaali; it was one of our late night talks on the phone.

'I want to go for Arts, I want to become a Journalist, but my father wants me to go for medical studies. I don't think I want to become a Doctor. What about you?' this was not good, both of us were confused and here I thought that she had everything planned for her.

'I don't know either, I mean, I am really interested in going for Police services but even my Dad wants me to go for medical. I am not against the idea of becoming a Doctor at all, hell; I will be the first Doc in my whole family. But I want to do something where I can make a difference, you know, like being a loyal Police officer could do a lot for the city, I don't know, what do you suggest?' I said.

'Dev, I am really happy to hear that there is at least one person who thinks that the system can be changed, I am even more surprised that it's you, I never thought that you had such thinking. But if you are not sure, then I would suggest that you go for career counseling. That can really help you out in all this stuff; I have seen it that's how I know.' She was so wise at times that it made me think that maybe I don't even deserve this girl, only because in my mind I was never that confident about myself.

'I really want to do the Police thing, but only If Dad agrees.' I said.

'It's good that you respect your parent's decisions this much. You are getting wiser, maybe it's the effect of your company. See, I can really be a good Influence.' She said and laughed a little.

'You were always a great Influence baby.' I said and gave a kiss through the phone.

'But can I ask something?'

'You can ask anything baby doll, go ahead.'

'Why do you want to do a Police job when your whole family is into politics and all? I mean, if you really want to make a difference, go for the bigger stage, I am sure that can be more helpful.' Her question didn't sound like a question to me.

'Baby, I know my family background is more of a political one, but I think that if I become a politician, I won't be able to help the common people as I desire. My goals are simple, become a Police officer at a suitable rank and then become an example for all Police officers. I want people to look up to me if they are in a problem, even the smallest ones, I don't think I can do that as a minister or a politician. I can only do that when I am at a position where I can freely talk to people about their problems. I don't want to be the Police officer who scares people, I want people to be happy about the fact that I am around. That's what I want. I don't how it sounds, but this is true.' As I was speaking, there was complete silence; I thought that Harshaali fell asleep while listening to my speech or whatever that was.

'Hey, what happened?' I said.

'Nothing, just your ideas of making India a better place to live sees unreal, but somewhere I still believe In you, I believe In your talents and I sure as hell believe In your hard work. I know the type of person you show people you are. You want people to think that you don't really care, you want them to think that you are a bad person, but I see It,

I see the real you. I see a mask on your face that you put on every day when you step out of your house, you think that nobody knows about it, but I do Dev. You are a beautiful person and right now I feel like the luckiest girl on the planet that I have you around.' Her words were like Inspiration for me to change. She was right, everything she said was true.

'How do you know so much about me baby? You just pointed out the one thing that was only mine to know of, nobody has ever seen that side of me.' I said.

'Dev, you just don't know how much I love you baba, leave It. Just promise me one thing. Take off that mask and start being the person you really are.' She said.

'Hmmm… I promise baby, I won't stay like this now, I will change into a better person.' I said.

'I love you the way you are, I love the rough exterior and I love the Inner Dev the most. He is carIng, loving, hez fun to be around and most importantly he understands me the most.'

'Hmmm.. I love you too Harshaali. But we still have to fIgure out what we want to do In the future. Let's make a pact, we talk our parents tomorrow, whatever they say, we do. OK?' I said.

'AlrIght, we will talk to them, but I know what that's gonna be like.' She sounded depressed.

'What's wrong baba?'

'Nothing, we will talk about this tomorrow, its Sunday right? That's good, my parents will be home, I will talk to them tomorrow morning only. I will text you the detaIls, ok?' she said.

'Alright, just stay strong and put forward all that you want to do. Remember, I am with at all times ok?' I wanted to cheer her up.

'Yes baby I know and I really love you for that.' She said. I knew she smiled.

The next morning I got a text from Harshaali.

'Medical it is.' my reply to her must have made her sad too.

'Mine too, hope for the best (fingers crossed).'

CHAPTER 10

THE UNPREDICTABLE

WE WERE PREPARING FOR OUR board exams which were supposed to be held in two weeks. We had already studied the whole syllabus one, now we were revising the subjects.

'Baby I think we should talk to them again.' She said.

'Baby listen, I have no problem talking to them, but the thing is that they have made a decision and I know they are not going to change it, at least my parents won't, you can surely try another time with your parents.' I said.

'Devuuuu, please talk to your parents baby, for me, pleaseee.' She had me trapped in her delightful voice.

'Ok baba, but if they say the same thing again, it's final, ok?' I said.

I was supposed to talk to my parents now, all I had to do was tell them that I don't want to study medical and I wanted to go for arts, but what happened was something I did not have In mind at all.

'Dad, I need to talk to you about something, It's Important.' I said.

'I have something that I want to talk to you about. Come, sit here.' Harmandeep uncle, an old friend of my father's was visiting us today; he had a brochure in his hands that he was talking about.

'Yaar Manoj, this is an opportunity for your son, he can have a remarkable career as a Doctor, just think about it. First of all, Dentistry is not a bad option at all, secondly, you have no idea how much this University is going to do for him in his future. Just think about it and talk to him, make him understand.' He said these things and left the brochure on the table and then he left.

'Dad, what Is this about? What University?' I was confused with whatever I had just heard.

'I was just talking to your Uncle, he was telling me about this University in the U.S, he said that it is one of the best In the world, and it is for medical aspirants, so I think you should go there.' His words were like a 40,000 volt shock to me.

'Dad, I was here to talk to you about not choosing medical for a career option, now you want me to leave all of you here and stay in some unknown place for what, like five years of my life? Do you really think I can do that?' I said, I was furious at him at that moment, I was never like that in front of my father, I had misbehaved today, he just wanted the best for me and the way I reacted was not good at all. I could tell by his expressions that he was sad.

'I just want the best for you son, I have spent my whole life struggling with business just so you could have a better life and a wonderful education and if I have to send you away from me for some time, I am ready to do that. You will do as I say, you are my son and you have to obey me, this is for your own good. You will thank me later.'

All I could hear was a father talking to his son, well, not actually talking, ordering him to do exactly as he said, it was the first time in my life I thought my father was wrong. I couldn't say that to his face but I sure as hell felt It In my heart.

'Alright dad, I am ready to go. Make the arrangements as soon as possible.' I said and left the room.

My whole life I didn't have anyone special, the one that I could call my own, now that I had Harshaali, everyone around me was trying really very hard to take her away from me. for a moment there I wanted to scream in front of my father that even I have a life, I have people that I just cannot leave behind like that, I wish I had done that.

I called up Harshaali to tell her the worst news ever; I knew this was going to be depressing for her more than it was for me.

'Baby, what are you doing?' I asked.

'I just came back from Dad's room; they want me to go for medical only. What about you baba, did you talk to your parents?' she had no Idea what I was about to tell her.

'I have a really bad news for us.' I said.

'What happened? Is everything alright at home?' her first question concerned my family; it was amazing how she felt that closeness with my family just like that.

'No, your baby is going away from you, soon.' I said. I couldn't hold back my tears though I wanted to.

'What are you saying Dev? I don't understand. Please tell me, you are scaring me now.'

'My father wants me to go to a U.S. college for medical studies, he wants me to have the best in the world, he wants me to do something that no other child in my clan could ever do, I don't how it became my responsibility, but I really don't care what my family or my parents have achieved year, I want to make my own life Ions. I don't want to leave you here baby, I just can't, you are my life now. I can't live without you, please do something Harshaali.' I said as I cried with it.

'Baby, calm down, please stop crying, you will be fine baba. You once said that you believe in God, just do the same now also, he will help you somehow.' She said and her words always worked on me.

'I can't believe my Dad would want me to go away, I mean, am I that bad Harshaali?' I asked her just for reassurance.

'No my baby, you are not bad at all, you are the best trust me. I love you a lot Dev and I promise we will find a way out of this. But you know what we have to do first? We have clear our boards, please forget about this for a while and start focusing on the board exams, please.' She was right; I had not picked up a single book for such a long time

'I know Harshaali, I will study, I just need some time to process all this Information. I will TTYL baby, bye and take care. Love you more than myself.' I said and disconnected the call; I was so upset with whatever was happening around me at that time that I wasn't able to focus on a single damn thing.

'Dad, you cannot do this to me.' I said, we were having dinner in his room; everybody was eating quietly until I broke the silence.

'I can, I am your father, so shut up and eat your food.' He said.

'Dad please, I won't be able to adjust there, I will have problems. What will I do I do If I have a major problem there, who will help me?' I said, trying to convince him as much as I could.

'You just stay out of fights, everything else will be taken care of, worry not.' He said, he sounded so confident.

'But dad…..'

'Shut up Dev, this is the best thing for you, if you do this, you will be proud of yourself one day, and I will be proud of you too.'

'Hmm… so this is your final decision? I am really going to United States of America??' I asked him for the final time.

'Yes, I have arranged everything for you.' He said. 'You will be living in an apartment there with a roommate, oh yes, you don't have to give any entrance exams, they call it a medical school there, the grocery shops and everything that you might need on a daily basis is more or less on a walking distance from that place, the college is in the best parts of New York. What else do you need son? Just tell me.' I wanted to say that I wanted only one more thing, to have Harshaali as my roommate, but obviously I couldn't.

'No Dad, you have done enough. When will I be leaving?' now I had no Interest in talking to my father in this regard, I was done talking now.

'Soon after you board exams are over, you will become a doctor before any of your friends and that too from one of the most prestigious colleges in The United States, come on, that's got to make you happy.' He said, he was really excited about this, he wanted me to be excited too, but it just wasn't my day.

The same night me and Harshaali talked about this for a long time, she was really upset, she consoled me before when I cried on the phone, it was my turn now. I wanted to be there for her, I wanted to be the one who supported her In the long run, but thanks to my father's plans, I was not going to be the one for Harshaali, I knew that in my heart now.

'Baby, don't worry, we will work this out, we will work a long distance thing, ok?' she said, she didn't even know what she was saying.

'Harshaali, that's never easy baby, we are going to be in different countries, do you understand that?' I said. I wanted her to realise what was actually going on.

'Hmmm... I just cannot deal with this right now Dev, believe me I am trying, just yesterday I told you how much you mean to me and today I have to prepare myself to say good-bye soon, this is not fair Dev, this is not fair....!!' She didn't care who heard her talking on the phone now, she was emotional, hurt, she wanted everything to be normal for once; I know that because I had the same feeling. I wanted the same things that she did, I wanted her to be happy and her happiness lied in this relationship. This wasn't going to be easy, I knew I had to break up with her now; it was my turn to do the right thing.

I loved her, so I knew that it would destroy her when she saw me going away from her forever, she couldn't do that in her dreams, she loved me that much. She always sad that I had no Idea how much I loved her, but I did, I knew what I had to do.

'Vinay, meet me in the school library, NOW.' I needed to talk to him and tell him what had been decided and what was going to happen.

'What is the matter dude, I was just starting to hit it off with Aditi there. What was so urgent?' he asked.

'I need to tell you something, I might be leaving for U.S. soon after our exams, my dad has booked a seat for me in a college there, it's a medical college and I have to go.' I said.

'Congratulations dude, *party kab dega?*' he said.

'Fuck the party; this is just half of the thing I have called you here for.' We were sitting in a corner in the library and our librarian was looking at us like we had committed a crime by sitting there together.

'Oh sorry, there is more? Go on, bro.'

'I am going to break up with Harshaali now, I know this will break her Into pieces, trust me It's going to break me too, but it is for her own good, if she stays with me and we try long distance, we will fail, I know, and I don't want that. At least this way I can break up with her in a decent manner. But, I have a request, I know you guys are going to be in different schools and streams after this, but just keep her safe, stay in touch with her always and take care of her for me, please, can you do that?' I asked him for the biggest favor I could ever ask for from anybody.

'*Oye, bhabhi hai wo meri*, I will definitely take care of her for you man. I love you, and yeah, I am going to miss you a lot.' He said, we could have hugged each other if we were not sitting in a fucking lIbrary.

I was preparing myself for the speech I had to deliver in a few minutes in front of Harshaali. I had to breakup with the love of my life, just because I had an arrogant father, I never thought he would make me do this, it was his fault.

I talked to Abhilasha first about my situation, why I was doing it, what was the need, why we couldn't go for long distance. I had to answer all these questions too, but after twenty minutes of struggle, I got through to her, she understood that I had to do this.

'Where is she?' I asked Abhilasha.

'You don't really want to know Dev; she will be back in a few minutes.' She said.

'What? Where is she, tell me.' I got all squeaky in a matter of seconds.

'She is in the girl's washroom and she is crying. You cannot do anything about it right now Dev, just let her cry for some time, she needs to.' Those were some of the stupidest words I had ever heard in my life.

I ran towards the girl's washroom, she wasn't out yet, I could hear her crying even through the washroom door.

'Harshaali, please open the door baby.' I said. I really didn't care if it was the girl's washroom door I was just knocking on.

'What are you doing here Dev? Go from here please, someone will see you standing out there, people have a tendency to misunderstand you, please leave.' She yelled from the other side.

'I don't really give a fuck about the rest of the school, you know that right? Open this door, I want to say something.' I said.

'I know why you are here Dev, I know what you want to tell me, I know we have to break up now, I know there is nothing we can do about it, I know we can never be happy together, I know people don't like to see us happy, anything else you want to say, say it now.' she was crying and talking at the same time.

'I am never going to leave you alone, not even for a single second you dumb bitch, now come out and let me hug you or I will start crying too.' I didn't realise but I was yelling too now.

'Are you sure you want to see me like this? I really look like a mess now.' she said.

'Either you come out now, or I am coming in and you know I will.' I warned her to open the door for the last time.

She opened the door and I saw her coming out through that wooden door, her Kaajal was all messed up because of her crying, her hair in a rough look, she didn't have that coconut oil today, she smelled really great though. She came towards me, barely able to control herself from crying, she hugged me as tight as she could.

'Please don't leave me here Dev, I will die without you, I won't be able to handle all this alone. Take me with you, please.' Her tears wet my shirt and my chest. We were just a couple of teenagers, madly in love with each other and we had no other option but to say good-bye.

'You know I don't want this right? You know how much I love you, how much I am going to miss you there, I wish I could take you with me, but It's just not possible baby. I am so sorry for doing this to you again; I once said that I will never hurt you ever, when actually all I have been doing this whole time is hurt you again and again. I am really sorry for coming into your life like this and leaving so soon.' I said, now I had wet eyes too.

She didn't say anything after that, she just leaned on me and we hugged for sometime before we realised that we had to go to the class now.

We were almost at our breaking points, but we were somehow handling ourselves.

Living like this was hurting us both, but then she decided to stop thinking about all this and start concentrating on the upcoming exams. She made me promise to her that I would study as much as I could and score really well In the boards, as my whole future was dependent on them.

'Just do this and call me, ok? Then I will tell you what you the most Important questions in mathematics and science.' She said, it had been almost a week and we had not discussed that thing again, but the tension was always there.

'Ok *jaan*, I will complete this in around an hour, then mathematics.' I said and disconnected the call.

It was all about the exams now, only a week left for the theory exams and I was almost fully prepared. Not for the exams, but to leave the country as soon as I was done with the exams. I was still in disbelief that I was going to another country in less than a month, I was not prepared for this, I had never thought that my father would make me do such a thing, but I think he was right in his place.

'You can carry only twenty to twenty five kilograms of stuff with you, so make sure that you carry the most important things. Don't forget your books, I know you love reading, carry them with you, and son, please don't think of this as a punishment or something, all I want is a better future for you, that's all.' Sometimes it felt like he was totally right, but at other times I wished that he had asked me once if I actually wanted to go or not.

'Dad, I know you love me and I know this is all supposed to be for my own good, but I really think that should have asked me about this first.' Damn, I shouldn't have said that.

'Listen, I know it's hard to leave your friends and family behind, but until you learn how to set priorities, you will never succeed. All you should think about right now is how you are going to manage yourself there. Just keep in mind, I am sending you there for a reason.' He said and left the room.

I was still packing the small stuff that was required, a gun, a knife, some hand grenades and a brand new Baretta M12S; obviously I was packing all of this stuff in my mind. I couldn't possibly get all that stuff and take it with me to one of the most highly secured countries in the world.

A country I liked so much was now looking like hell to me, I should have been happy, my father had spent so much on me and my future, most people can't even get their visas and I was lucky enough to have a fully prepared father by my side. He was one of the most organized people I knew, he had connections almost everywhere, which was the reason I got my visa so soon. He was really excited, but I still wasn't thinking straight.

Soon our final board exams took place In Satluj Public School in Panchkula, it was our exam center. We both had prepared really hard, and were really excited about the exams. We knew we were going to score well. It was all because of Harshaali's efforts with me that I was so confident.

We had a really nice time during our exams, we would reach our exam center early so that we could spend some time together and revise a little bit, she helped me with the really important questions and made me revise all of them again and again, her methods always worked. The questions she thought were important were always in the question paper, so it made almost all my exams really easy and successful. Soon our exams were over too and we knew that it might be the last time we were seeing each other.

'When are you leaving?' she asked.

Most probably next week, I told you that all the preparations were made already.' I saw her face and I knew how sad she was to hear that.

'Can we meet outside once? I mean, just us.' She said.

'Obviously, why would I say no to that? You just text me the place where you want to meet, Ok?' I said.

We sat in the school ground for a few more minutes and then her dad came to pick her up; it was our last exam so we knew we didn't have a chance to meet in the school after that. I didn't know what she had in her mind. But later that night I had a pretty good Idea about that, when I got a series of texts from her.

'Come to my place tomorrow morning.'

'Nobody is going to be home.'

'You have to meet me tomorrow. I don't give a fuck how you do that but I want you here tomorrow, 10:30 sharp.'

I saw these texts in the morning when I woke up around 10:00 a.m.

'Oh, fuck, she is going to kill me if I don't get there by 10:30.' I was talking to myself, actually I was yelling at myself.

I jumped out of the bed in a jiffy and got ready in less than ten minutes. I called her up.

'Baby, are you serious? Do you really want me to come there?' I asked her on the phone and her reply scared the crap out of me.

'You have twenty minutes Dev, if you don't get here in twenty minutes, you will miss on a lot of stuff. Come ASAP...!' a lot of stuff? Oh my god, I was not going to miss any stuff now, I knew this was my last chance to be with my girl. She was waiting for me and now I just had eighteen minutes.

I took the keys and ran out, I told my parents that I was going to meet Vinay and I would be out with him for quite some time.

Normally it would take any driver more than twenty five minutes to cover that distance; she lived almost in the opposite end of the city. But I magically covered that distance in merely fifteen to sixteen minutes.

I rang the doorbell and had a chewing gum. She came up on the door looking as pretty as she could.

'You actually made it here and that too in less than twenty minutes.' She said.

'Are you going to open this door or are we going to stand here and talk like this?'

As soon as I said this she opened the door, I got in and bolted the Dorr behind me.

'So, nobody home?' I asked.

'Naaah, that's the reason I called you today.' She told me.

'Then what are we waiting for baby? Take me to your room.'

She guided me towards her room; I was already so horny just by lookIng at her, that I could not control myself any longer. She had decorated her room for me, all our pictures together, all our memories were on her wall, the song I played for her on our anniversary was playing on the audio system in my own voice, and everything was so romantic. That moment meant so much for both of us, we needed this, and we had been through so much in the past few months that we needed a break.

'Nice set up, I love it, and I love you so much.' I pulled her closer and kissed her forehead, the fact that this could be the last time we were together made her want me even more. She kissed me with such passion that all my emotions of losing her and not being able to see her or touch her anymore turned into passion themselves. I pushed her towards the wall and took off her shirt; in the process I noticed that she had something on her shoulder.

'What's this babe? OMFG, is that a tattoo?!' I had so many exclamation marks in my mind at that moment.

Her tattoo was nothing else but our initials, **D.H. (for Deven and Harshaali)**

'Why did you do that? It must have hurt you so much.' I looked at her tattoo but I was scared to touch it as it was still sore.

'All I want is you to stay with me forever. I know you think that long distance won't work, even I think so, but I would still like to try it because Dev, I seriously cannot imagine my life without you.'

Her words made that moment even more special for me, she wanted me so much, and she just didn't know that I wanted her just the same, maybe even more.

I kissed her again, with even more lust and tongue than before, her tongue just playing it's course in my mouth, I loved the closeness we had in that moment. She pushed me on to her bed, took off my shirt and asked me to lie down on my back.

'Hand me your shirt, I will be back in two minutes.' She said and left me there, all alone in her room.

'Now that's weird.' I said to myself.

Moments later she came back, she was wearing my shirt and nothing else, and seriously NOTHING else.

'Whoa, now that's what I call a surprise.' I said.

She walked closer and made herself comfortable in my lap, the she gave me the sweetest of the kisses ever, and I don't know if it was her lip balm or what, but that kiss actually tasted sweet.

The next thing I know is that we were all hot and heavy for the next hour or so, we made some of our most memorable memories in that one hour.

'I was clearly not expecting that today.' I said.

'Consider this as my parting gift to you.' She said and gave me kisses all over my face.

'You want to know what else I did for you?' she said.

'There is more?' today was clearly a special day according to my baby, and she had made It her mission to make It special for me too.

'Come with me.' she took my hand and took me in another room where I found a whole meal prepared just for me.

'This is the second surprise for you today. I made it all for you. Would you have lunch with me today?' she asked innocently.

'Baby, if it was up to me, I would have all my breakfasts, lunches and dinners with you only, every day of my life.' I said.

We sat down and she served me everything, it was the first time I was going to try her cooking. It was really awesome; I had never imagined me and Harshaali sitting in a place that peaceful, without any drama or any tension in our heads. We had the most amazing meal together. But then, the time came when I had to say good-bye.

'Please think about what I said about long distance, Ok?' she said, walking with me towards the door.

'You already know what my answer is going to be. I am always with you baby, no matter what,' I said.

'You just said something I really needed to hear from you Dev. I love you so much. Call me when you reach home, Ok?' she said. I kissed her good-bye and walked towards my car.

CHAPTER 11

A New Life

OUR FINAL RESULTS WERE ANNOUNCED on the internet, as expected she had scored a perfect grade. She was the only one who scored a perfect score, I scored a little less than her, but it was sufficient for me and my U.S. admission. My new life was waiting for me now, I wanted it to wait a little longer but it couldn't. I had to move away from my life here, all the good memories, all the amazing stuff that I had here, all my friends and family and my girlfriend, my Harshaali, I had to leave her behind too. The saddest part about this was that we were going to try the long distance thing, for some special couples, it might even work, but me and Harshaali, we were not special, we were the worst actually. We had been in so much trouble when we were in the same city, Imagine what our lives would become if we continued this mess through different bucking countries.

I knew this was a bad Idea, she knew too, but we were actually so desperate for this relationship to work. The simple reason that we were desperate was that this was the only good thing that was going in our lives, we were not quite fond of our families, I was, but after my dad decided to send me away, to an entirely different continent, It became hard for me to see them in the eye and tell them that they meant a lot to me, sometimes it felt like only Harshaali was feeling bad that I was leaving. Nobody else gave a crap about it, well, that was because I had not told many people about it. But still, the people who knew didn't even show any Interest In talking to me or spending time with me. Not even my best friend, Vinay. So I thought, 'Damn it, even I should spend time with the ones who actually care about me and will miss me after I am gone.'

I wanted to congratulate Harshaali on her perfect score but I couldn't, she said she was going to be really busy for some time as her relatives were visiting, so she won't be able to talk or text for like two three days. I was OK with it, but I started missing her so bad that I just had to talk to her that day.

'Hey baby, I know you are super busy but I am really missing you, please meet me tomorrow.' I texted her.

I waited for her reply but I don't think she even saw my message that night, I got a text from her the next morning though, it said

'Meet me in sector 17 today. Can't really talk right now, with relatives. Text me around 6:00 in the evening, I will tell you where we are meeting. Ok bye, love you so much.' Now that was weird, she hated sector 17, she always said that the place was really crowded and didn't even have a decent place to sit. Sector 17 was actually a shopping hub in Chandigarh where you could find the biggest brands and the small shops too, people started visiting that place so much that it became an actual tourist attraction In Chandigarh, now people come from place to shop there in some of the biggest outlets ever, but I don't think Harshaali wanted to buy something, I was confused, still I drove all the way to sector 17 without any questions.

'Hey, I am here, where are we meetIng exactly?' I called Harshaali.

'Start walkIng towards the front door of *Neelam Theatre*, I will meet you at It's front gate.' She said and I did exactly what I was asked to do.

There I saw her standing in front of the theatre, I walked up to her. She hugged me so tight I could barely breathe.

'Ok ok, now we have established that you called me here because you wanted to hug me in a public place, but baby what are we doing here?' I said.

'Just walk with me for a while.' She said. I was happy to see her again, we thought that we won't be able to see each other, but we made time for each other again, for one more night maybe.

'I really don't need a reason to be here you know, we could just walk here for the whole night, if you are with me, I don't mind it. I don't mind if we are meeting for the last time here, because I have such good memories of us being together, they will stay with me for life.' I said as she held my hand tight and looked into my eyes as we stood In front of a night club.

'This is where we have to go.' She said.

'I never knew you liked night clubs and stuff, you like them?' I asked her.

'Just come with me.' she pulled me inside the dark, smoky room in that club.

'SURPRISE…!' a bunch of my friends was gathered in the club holding signs that said "We Will Miss You Dev" and "HAPPY BIRTHDAY". This was actually the biggest surprise of my life.

Vinay was there with Rohan and Ankur and some of my other classmates, I went up to Vinay.

'I will surely miss you, dude. But still I can never forget that you made me breakup with three girls in one day, I still don't get how you convinced me to do that you son of a gun. I love you man.' And then he hugged me, I could tell he had been drinking.

'Did you plan all this? And what the hell, my birthday isn't for another month dude.' I asked him as I really had no idea this was going on.

'Yup, but I had a little help too, your girlfriend volunteered. She helped me out with all the decorations and stuff. And man, who knows what future has for us, I wanted this to be our last celebration together, your nineteenth birthday, with us.' He told me all about how long they had been planning all this and how Harshaali helped him, then he told me how Harshaali had been coming here for the last three days in the evening just to help around a little.

'So that's why you didn't talk to me for three days?' I asked Harshaali, I saw her smiling at me from a distance, standing with some of our friends, in that moment I saw the love she carried in her heart for me, and here I thought nobody cared.

'Yes, you like It?' she asked me if I liked it, dumb girl.

'I loved it, I love everything. I love you.' I said and hugged her

'I know Dev, I cannot say it much, but I love you too, baby.' She said.

We danced and drank for the rest of the evening, I had some beers and some vodka shots, I had no Idea how Vinay got a liquor licence for the party as we were all teenagers there. Vinay got into a fight with some club members, but it all got sorted out and then we all had dinner. Having my last meal with all those people brought back memories,

memories that I would cherish all my life. Sitting next to that girl, the girl that made my life so special, the girl that loved everything about me, the girl I loved the most In the world, It gave me a feeling that I was complete In that moment, I felt like this was all I wanted from my life. A life with Harshaali was all I wanted, but I was going to be away from her again, for a long time.

'I can't believe this is the last time I am holding your hand.' She whispered in my ear.

'I know baby, but maybe It's not, maybe It all works out as we want It to, maybe our lives have something special for us, just waiting for us, please think of It that way, and everything will seem alright.' I didn't want her to be sad when I left her; I wanted her to feel like it was a new beginning. She meant the world to me and I could not see her in tears.

'Promise me that you will try, promise me that you will stay connected all the time, we will talk and chat and stay like that till we figure out a way to make all this work, promise me, Dev.' She held my hand so tight when she said all that stuff. Everyone around us, our friends, our well-wishers, they were all looking at us, probably wishing the same thing for us.

'Guys, I would like to make a toast, for a friend who has been there for me when I needed him the most, for a friend who always stood by me even when I was wrong, well, sometimes he made me do stupid stuff, but that was still ok, because I always knew that if I was in need of a friend, he was the one I would turn to. To my best friend, now and forever. Love you bro.' after a few beers in him, Vinay became all sentimental and made a marvelous speech that brought tears to my eyes too.

I was going to miss all of this, all of these faces had been in my life for quite a long time now, but this day had to come, the time always takes its course and throws different challenges and opportunities in our faces. What I had now, was an opportunity as well as a challenge for me, I had to settle down in an entirely new environment, adjust with new people, live a whole new life, this was a big challenge for a guy who is set in his ways. On the other hand, the career opportunity was as bright as It gets, It was a hell of a chance that I was taking, but It was going to be worth It, at least my father thought so.

The evening came to an end, people left the place in a hurry as we were all late, but there was one person who didn't want to let go, that person was Harshaali.

'You should go home now Harshaali, it is getting late now. I don't think you should go alone at this time, I will ask Vinay to drop you home, ok?' I said and she kept staring at me with a blank face.

'Give me a hug, Dev. Make it a hug that stays with me for a long time, till the day you get back and hug me again.' She said and came closer. I held her as tight as I could, I could feel her heartbeat rising, I could feel her waist from the dress she was wearing.

'I love you Harshaali, I always have and I always will.' These were the only words that I could gather up as my good-bye to Harshaali.

She lifted her face to look at me and I saw tears, I hated when that happened, I wiped off her tears with my fingers.

'Promise me you will stay strong; promise me you will not cry, please.' I said and she nodded her head like a cute and innocent child. I kissed her forehead and I knew that now it was time to let go.

'Good-bye, Harshaali. I hope I will see you soon baby.' I said, she just smiled at me and said, 'You sure will Dev, I am not going to leave you so easily.' We both shared a memory and then started walking in opposite directions.

I had asked Vinay to drop her home after the party. He did me that last favor before I left the country.

The day finally arrived when I had to say good-bye to my old life and say hello to my new life. I was In Delhi, we were all leaving for Indira Gandhi International Airport, and I was scheduled to board my flight at 7:00 a.m. in the morning, I was already half an hour late because of all the traffic in Delhi, even at 6:00 a.m. in the morning, the Delhi traffic was at its peak.

We reached the airport at around 6:55 a.m. and I ran towards the terminal from which I was going to board my flight.

'Do you have all the things that you need on the flight? You got the address of your uncle staying there, right?' my dad was talking to me as we were headed towards Terminal 5.

'Yes dad, don't worry at all, I have got everything with me.' I replied. We reached Terminal 5 but there was still a long line for the security checks and all, so we were at least assured that we were no late or anything.

'Everything is fine now, this Delhi traffic irritates the hell out of me, I hate travelling by a car in Delhi.' Dad complained about Delhi's traffic, but he never did that before, there was something else on his mind.

'What are you thinking dad, you want to say something?' I said.

'I want to, but I don't know if I should, the thing is son, I know you didn't want this at all, but you have to understand, this is all for your future, I am thinking the best for you and the only thing I want from you is your dedication. It will be a long road to success, but if you do everything right, even God helps you, always keep that in mind and always know that I am right here, you need anything at any time, call me directly, ok?' I knew he was making me do this for all the good reasons, he wanted so much for me, he dreamed about my success only, not his. That was the moment I realised that the man standing in front of me was my actual hero.

My mom was already in her soap opera mode, she had tears filled up in her eyes, I had never been away from her before in my life, but this was something that we both had to deal with. I loved her so much, I had no clue as to how I was supposed to live without my mother I had never experienced it ever.

'Take care of your health, eat healthy and never smoke, if I ever have a doubt that you smoke I will stop talking to you.

Call every day after getting ready for college, having lunch, leaving college, reaching your apartment and before sleeping. I know it's going to be hard, but you have to do this, It Is an order.' My mother's instructions were repeated to me again.

As I was approaching the security check post, I remembered that Harshaali had asked me to call her before boarding the flight.

I dialed her number.

'Harshaali? It's me baby, get up, I am just about to board the flight now.' I said.

'Baby, I was up all night, I couldn't sleep at all. When is the flight?' she asked.

'I am standing in the queue for checking actually, I will leave in another ten minutes. I just wanted to call you because it's going to be a long flight and I won't be able to use my phone. I wanted to hear your voice.' I said, I was missing her already, I had been away from her just for a few days and now I was missing her.

'Baby, have a safe journey, I love you so much, now stop talking to me and board the flight. And please text me if you can later, I will be waiting to hear from you.' She said.

'Obviously, I will text you once I board the flight; I just wanted to wake you up so that we could talk.' I replied.

'*Chalo* now go, and text me ASAP. Bye, love you and miss you so much.' She said and we hung up.

I was next for the security check and my luggage was already scanned. I cleared the security post and went forward to the boarding area, but before that I turned back and touched my father's feet. It was a sentimental decision, I don't know, It just happened. After that I hugged him and told him that I would call him as soon as I reach New York. Then I went to touch my mother's feet and told her the same thing. It was time to say good-bye now; I had to board the flight.

I didn't see their faces after that as there was a huge crowd, these were all those people who had come to leave their loved ones and wanted to have a glance at them before they left. I wanted the same thing but I couldn't see them and had to get into the flight after that.

That was it; the good-bye period was over too, I had officially said good-bye to my old life in India and my relatives and my parents and my friends and last but not the least, my girlfriend. It was time to get on with the new life ahead. I had twenty two hours to prepare myself for the biggest city in the world, I was going to live in New York for I don't know how long now, and that was going to be my new life and my new address now. I got seated quickly and texted Harshaali.

'Hey baby, I am on the plane now, you there?' I didn't get her reply for some time after that.

I was waiting for her reply only when I got a text from her saying that she had to go for some urgent thing with her mother and would not be able to talk for some time. I said that I will talk to her anytime and she should continue whatever she was busy with.

I got a text from her later, saying that she and her mother had to go meet some relatives.

'Baby, I am so sorry I wasn't available at that time.' she said.

'Its ok baby, what happened?' I wanted to know.

'Arre baba some relatives from my mother's side called and wanted me and maa to visit there place, they had some kind of "*pooja*" or something, so I had to accompany maa. She gets bored in these events.' She explained everything to me. 'You tell me, how is your flight?'

'Well, my flight is great, it has got great food, great staff and I bet they have great wines too, but the sad thing is that I am not allowed to have any.' She sent a laughing emoji on my description of the flight.

'Baby, don't think that if you are living in another country you get to do all that stuff, and moreover, you are going for studying there. Do you know anything about your roommate?' she asked.

'My roommate? Yeah, I know some things about him, like he is a Punjabi boy, who has been living there for quite a while now; he is also a student and does part time jobs at places. I think I will also take up a job, just for some extra money and work experience. What do you suggest?' I was a little shaky on this guy's details.

'Are you serious? You don't anything about your soon to be roommate?' she exclaimed, although she was talking to me via text messages, I could Imagine her reaction pretty well.

'Ohhoo, calm down baby, I will know a lot about him once I see him, I will tell you everything too.' I said, just to calm her down a little.

I was a little tired by the journey, I needed some sleep, so I asked her to text me an hour later and then we would continue talking. She agreed and told me to sleep for a while. I called the flight attendant and ordered some food.

I woke up an hour later due to some turbulence in the plane, the air hostesses came to check if all the passengers had their belts on.

'Is something wrong?' I asked the air hostess who was checking up on me, she said that it was some minor turbulence and I need not worry about. Just after that I checked up my phone for any messages from Harshaali.

I had a bunch of texts from her asking me if I was ok and still sleeping and asking me to text her as soon as I woke up.

'Hey baby, I guess I overslept, what are you doing?' I texted her the moment I read all of her messages. I got a reply from her a few minutes later.

'I am fine baby, you tell me, Is everything alright?' she said in her reply.

'Yeah everything is OK here, don't worry.' I said.

'I am not worried baby, I will always ask this, you like It or not. By the way, I was just filling out forms for the medical Institutes in Chandigarh, there are plenty. Lucky you, you don't have to go through all the entrance exams and stuff that I have to deal with.' She said.

'I know, in a lot of ways this thing is good for me, I know I don't have to clear any exams, I will just go there and start my college life and soon I will be a dentIst.' I said.

'Yeah well that's not going to be that easy for me, I have to attend classes for two more years and stuff like that. But Dev, what if I get MBBS? That might be a problem you know.' She said.

'Baby I will tell you only one thing right now, I wanted to be with you, but I don't think that's going to happen soon, so I don't want any more pressure in my life, let's just see where the road leads us, and also, think about this, by the time you start going to college, whenever that may be, I will have completed half of my degree and by the time you complete your college, I will be a dentist and I will be practicing in the greatest city on the planet. I will be rich, that's what I mean. Your father will never say no to a guy like me, so worry not baby. I will work hard there.' I said I knew I was going to become a dentist, but I also knew that I was going to be a good one at that.

'I guess you are right, and baby, please don't think that I am pressuring you or something, I was just saying, I know that you will do wonders there. Make a lot of friends baby. I love you.' She said and I got a big smile on my face.

'Baby you know what, there Is a couple sitting next to me, they are New Yorkers only I guess, they must have had a tour of Chandigarh, they were just talking about it and I told them that I was from Chandigarh, they got so excited, they were really happy to see one clean city in India at least. They said that before Chandigarh, they were in Delhi for some time, well; you can make out the rest. They just loved there stay In Chandigarh.' I was so proud of my city, although I didn't actually live in Chandigarh, but it was the same thing, it was our tricity and we took pride in it if anyone praised it in front of us.

'Baby calm down, you are going to there city now, use some sense and ask about New York dumbo. You already know everything about Chandigarh, don't discuss that.' She said.

'Oops, good point babe. Ok listen; I will talk to them for a while now ok? TTYL?' I asked her.

'Yes of course, I am here only, take all the information you might need, you don't know anything and I know you, you didn't even research properly, so go get some info. Bye, love you a lot.' She said and we stopped chatting for a while.

I started talking to the couple sitting next to me about their city, and everything I had ever heard about The New York City was actually true, they told me all kinds of stuff, from dining to attractions to the best hotels to the best cinemas on the streets. The information was intriguing. Now I could not wait to get off that plane and see the city with my own eyes.

There were still ten whole hours left for the plane to land at the John F. Kennedy airport and I still had so many questions in mind. I kept asking questions and that couple kept answering me politely.

By the time I was in 10th standard, I had started watching Hollywood movies as well as T.V. series like Two and a half men, how I met your mother and F.R.I.E.N.D.S, and these were all the comedy shows based on either shot in New York or actually based on the city of Manhattan. I already wanted to see the places where these shows had been shot; I was a really big fan of Hollywood TV shows.

Being only a few hours away from my destination, I was quiet excited now, as the night went by In a drift, I realised that I had not talked to Harshaali In almost seven hours. I tried to contact her but it was way past hours, she would have been sleeping for hours now. I was a disappointment again. I told her that I would talk to her but I didn't, so there was nothing that I could do now but wait for her message.

It was a long journey but I liked it, I wasn't alone, the couple sitting with me was really sweet and was talking to me all the time, so I didn't get bored even for one moment. The flight was about to land now and we were asked to put on our seat belts again, so we did. I was pretty excited to see the new world I was about to step into, it was going to be my new world now.

The flight landed and we all left the airport. I made sure that I took the contact number of that couple, I was sure that I was going to see them again. So I talked to them for some time outside the airport till they waved a cab and the cabbie picked them up and they rode off in the crowd. I had the address of the apartment that I was supposed to stay in, I walked towards a bank that was just across the street and asked for some money conversion. My dad gave me a large sum of cash because he knew the currency difference was huge. I gave the bank accountant all the money my father gave me to convert it into U.S. dollars. A few minutes later the accountant came along with my cash and I stepped out of the bank to order a cab.

I took some time before calling out for a cab just to admire the beauty of the city I was going to live in now, I was feeling a little cold so I took out a jacket from one of my bags and wrapped myself in it. I looked up at the airport building and then I looked straight to my right, this city was so busy, it seemed like people didn't waste time here at all, they were always either on the phone or talking to someone or the other or just walking on the busy road. They didn't stop for anything. The clean roads and bridges showed how different U.S was from India, people actually cared about stuff here, stuff like the cleanliness of their own city, road management and other minor stuff too, all the building were so high that it would take you ages to count the number of floors In each building, the city seemed beautiful, the people seemed sweet, but now It was time to reach my new home.

I ordered a cab and gave the driver the slip that had the address on it.

'Sir, you new in town?' the cabbie started a conversation with me.

'Yes, my plane just landed here a few minutes earlier.' I replied to his question.

'How do you like the city, sir?' he asked a question again.

'Well, It has just been half an hour, I don't really know the city and the people here, so for me it is like a blank paper right now, let's see what stories are going to be written on the paper, good or bad.' I said.

'I wish they are all good stories sir, do you know the neighborhood where you are going?' the cabbie looked like a guy who knew every Inch of the city, so I thought that taking out some information from him wouldn't hurt.

'No, I am totally new to the city. Can you tell me how long it would take to reach that place?' I asked, I was anxious to see my new home.

Twenty minutes later the cab dropped me outside a brown colored building; it looked a little older In comparison to the other buildings. The neighborhood was again, really busy, people walked past me without even noticing me standing there.

'That's the address on the paper you gave me. It will be an even eight dollars, sir.'

'Thank you so much, here, eight dollars It Is.' I said, as he drove off.

I was standing In front of a building that was supposed to be my address for the next, I don't know how many years, the thrill of having the first look at my new room, the eagerness to meet my new roommate, and it was all so simultaneous. I entered the front door of the building and an old man, around sixty of age, crossed me, we shared a glance but I chose to ignore the man for the moment. The level of curiosity was so high. My apartment was on the second floor, there was no elevator so I was carrying my entire luggage at once to my apartment. I lifted the heavy suitcases and started climbing the stairs as fast as I could. I reached the second floor easily, all thanks to my busy schedule at my school; my body had been prepared for challenges like this any time. I walked through all the doors searching for the number. Moments later, I saw myself standing outside apartment number 231.

'This is going to be my new home now.' I thought to myself and knocked the door.

CHAPTER 12

THE CITY THAT NEVER SLEEPS

As I was waiting for my roommate to open the door for me, I thought that as soon as I set up my room and get all unpacked, I would go outside and get a new phone and a new sim card. I needed to talk to Harshaali and I was now missing her badly. I wanted to tell her everything that I had seen from the airport till that moment. I heard footsteps leading up to the door. The door knob turned and I saw my roommate for the first time.

'Hey, are you Deven?' he said as he looked at all my luggage.

'Yes, Hi, I guess I am going to be your roommate now.' I said and shook his hand.

'Hi, I am Ritwik Benipal. Come in, you need any help with unpacking?' he offered help like a good guy and a nice roomie, but I didn't actually need any help.

'No no, it's ok, I will do it myself, just tell me which room is mine and I will start unpacking ASAP.' I said as I entered the apartment.

It was a two bedroom kitchen set and had blue all over it. The walls were blue, the carpet was another shade of blue, the sceneries had the dominance of shades of blue and almost everything in the kitchen was also blue.

Before leaving for New York, my father gave me a bracelet; it was just like the one Salman Khan wore all the time, except the stone.

'Nice bracelet, silver?' he asked.

'Yeah, actually it was a gift from my father.' I said.

'Ohh good, which room would you like to have?' he asked. As he asked me this question, I noticed some of his stuff in one of the rooms already.

'How long have you been here? I mean in the apartment.' I asked.

'I came this morning, the landlord gave me a spare key for you, and he said that you should meet him before you unpack. His apartment is on the top floor.' He said.

'So I guess I will take that room, and don't worry, I will talk to him. My father has already told him about me, he will not say anything.' I said as I picked up my luggage and walked towards my room.

'OK dude, I will be in my room if you need Me.' he said.

I looked at my room, it was small but it was good, it could be managed easily. I already had an Image In my mind as to how my room would look. It already had a double bed in it with mattresses. I started unpacking, that was going to be hard, my room had a small admiral, so I had to manage that too, it was going to be tough as I had no managing skills and had servants at home for all that work.

Setting up my room, cleaning and dusting took all afternoon, I came out of my room and saw Ritwik sitting on the couch and watching F.R.I.E.N.D.S on the T.V set.

'You like this show?' I was actually surprised to know that the first thing I got to know about my roommate was similar to me.

'I love this show man, come watch It, It's really fun.' He said.

'Man I know that, I love this show, I have been a fan of this show for a really long time. I have seen all the episodes, till season 10.' I said.

'Let's watch it then.' He said.

'Before that, do we have something to eat?' I asked him as I had not eaten anything since I got off the plane.

'No dude, I told you I just got here this morning, but I know places where we could get good food, want to go out for lunch?' he asked.

'I am starving here, come let's go.' I said as I picked up my jacket. I took my wallet; I wasn't sure how much it would cost, so I took a few hundred bucks.

'There are some nice restaurants in our neighborhood, but I will take you to the best place I know. You order any variety of chicken, you taste it and I can bet you will love It.' He said.

Stepping out of the building, I saw an old man, very sharply dressed in a three piece suit and walking with a phone in his hand.

'How long have you been living In New York, Ritwik?' I asked him.

'My family moved here from Punjab when I was just three years old, that's the reason I have been living like a New Yorker my whole life. I don't know anything about India or the people living there, but I sure hope that I will get that Information from you, I would love to know about the country I actually come from.' He said, with a smile on his face.

'How long do you plan on living here?' he asked.

"Well, I don't know as such, but I really want to settle down here. I already like this city so much.' I said and we reached the restaurant Ritwik had told me about.

'Here is the place I was talking about before. You will love this place.' We entered a small hut; it had a sign saying *"Punjabi Style"*.

'*Punjabi style* haan? You have no idea what India is all about but still you know the best Punjabi restaurant in the city. That's great. Let's just order something fast, I cannot wait another minute.' I said as I read the menu card of the place. Names like *Murg Masallam*, *Tandoori Murgi* and *Kadhai Murgi* made my mouth watery.

A fair guy, who actually looked older than me, came to our table to take our order.

'Yeah, one *Murg Masallam*, one *ChIcken ChIlly*, one Lemon ChIcken and one *TandoorI MurgI*, as fast as possIble, what about you Ritwik?' I said.

'You mean all that was for you only?' he sounded shocked.

'Yeah, I have been on a plane for twenty three hours and I have been in a room cleaning it for half of the day, what else do you expect?' I said.

'Ok Ok, one Chicken salad for me.' his order with a chicken salad and stopped right there.

'What? You are not hungry?' I asked.

'I am, but that's my diet. I am a fItness freak; I cannot afford calories in my body.' He said, I called him stupid in my mind but looking at him anybody could tell that he was a Gym maniac.

The guy was in a really good shape, his biceps and triceps were all bulky and perfectly shaped. Anyone could tell that he was a regular at gym just by one look at him.

I was also planning to start some exercises soon. But right now I was starving. Food arrived in fifteen long minutes but the wait was actually worth it.

I finished all my dishes and a slice of apple pie in less than twenty minutes, the whole time, Ritwik kept looking at me with a stunned expression on his face. But I didn't stop chewing and biting the hell out of those chickens in my plate.

'Slow down bro, we have plenty of time.' he said.

'No we don't, we have to go shopping after this, and I have to get some stuff and a new phone. Eat fast; I have finished five times the food you have in your plate.' I said as I was full of energy once again, I wanted to explore some more shops and some more streets of the area.

'I am done, bill please.' He screamed looking at the counter and the bill arrived a minute after that.

'What? It's that cheap here? Only a hundred bucks for the amount of food I just inhaled?' I was shocked. Obviously I was new to the place and had no Idea how much a hundred dollar bill meant in this country.

'Dude, this is not cheap at all, you just think that because you are new and are here for your graduation. Start working here once, then you will know how much value money has here.' He said with a serious tone, but then he offered to share the bill with me.

'No it's alright, I will pay for what I ordered and you pay for what you had. I think it's only fair.' I said.

'Don't be stupid; let's just split the bill for half each. You give your half and I will give mine.' He said.

I agreed with the guy and paid my half for the first meal I had in New York.

'What do you want to shop for? Do you have a list or something?' he asked as we were leaving the restaurant.

'No list, just stuff like a sim card, mobile phone etc etc.' I said. 'You know a place for that too?' I asked.

'Dude, one thing you must know about me, I know a place for everything around here.' He said with a wicked smile on his face.

He took me to a store that was quiet close to the restaurant, people knew him there.

'Hey Jimmy, what's up bro?' he started talking to one of the salesmen in the store.

'Same old man, you tell me, what are you up to these days? Haven't seen you here for quite a long time now.' Jimmy said.

'Was a little busy past few days, hey, meet Deven, he is new in town, a friend from India, he is going to be my roommate from now on.' He said and signaled me to shake Jimmy's hand.

'Hi, I don't know much about this place, I just got off my flight so I was thinking if you could help me get a new cell phone.' I said.

'And set us up for a new landline number with a voicemail machine.' Ritwik added.

'You guys are just at the right place.' Jimmy said and went inside to get the stuff that we had asked for.

'How do you know this guy?' I asked Ritwik.

'Let's just say that he is a friend, he helps me, and I help him whenever he needs Me.' he said and winked at me. I really had no Idea why he winked. In the meantime, Jimmy came out of the storage room with a box and a landline phone.

'Here is all the stuff that you need, here is your new cell phone, and it comes with a camera, a 3.5 mm earphone jack and a memory card slot. It is a great purchase if you ask me, and here is your landline and voicemail machine, brand new. You can get your numbers and sim card from the next counter.' Jimmy explained almost everything that we needed to know about the landline and the new phone.

'Thanks man, see you around.' Ritwik shook his hand again and we moved to the next counter.

'OK, now I need to know what you do for a living and how do you know all these people.' I said.

'Come on Deven, I will tell you everything once we get back home alright?' he said and winked at me again. I really had no Idea why he was winking at me so much, it wasn't like we were best buddies and I understood everything he did.

'How can I help you, sir?' a really pretty girl on the next counter looked at me and asked me if she could be of any assistance.

'Yeah, I need a new sim card, can you tell me the procedure for that?' I asked the sweet lady for some guidance.

'Sir, I would love to help you, first you have to have a personal ID, then It Is almost compulsory to have a residential proof of some kind.' She said.

'See, that's the problem, I just moved here from India, I have no ID's or residential proofs, what should I do now?' I asked her again.

'That's not a problem sir, you could just ask any of your friends to provide an ID on your behalf.' She said.

'I just told you that I am new here, how am I supposed to have friends?' I was Irritated now.

'Why do you worry so much man? I am here with you.' Ritwik said as he pulled out his wallet from his pocket.

'Here, will that work?' he asked the lady if his ID and residential proof would be enough for me to have a new number.

'Yes sir, this is all that I need. Just wait for a moment.' Saying that, she started doing something on the computer on her desk. A few minutes later she gave me a sim card and asked me for two passport sized photographs of mine. I gave her what she asked for and after a few minutes she handed over the sim card that I needed badly now.

'Your card will be activated soon, sir.' She said.

'Thank you so much.' I said and she turned towards Ritwik again. 'Here is your ID and residential proof Mr. Ritwik BenIpal.' She said and gave him the documents that he gave her.

'Well, we also need a new landline number, can you do that for us too?' he said.

'Then maybe I should hold on to these documents for a little bit longer.' She said and dived back into her computer again.

'Here, this is going to be your landline number now, anything else, sir?' she asked, to which we both replied in unison, 'NO, that would be all.'

For buying so much stuff from the store, Jimmy hooked me up for a new Memory Card for free.

As we were walking out of the store, I opened up the box carrying my new phone.

'What are you doing?' he said.

'What does it look like? I am putting the sim card and the memory card in my phone.' I said.

'Do it when we reach home. Come, I have to get some stuff for the apartment too.' he said and started walking in the opposite direction.

'Where are we going now?' I asked.

'Nowhere, the place has no name, I am just going to get some beers for our place, and maybe some cigarettes too, do you smoke?' he asked me.

'No, and I don't even like the smell of it, it irritates the hell out of me.' I said.

'Don't worry man, I will smoke inside my room, you won't be bothered.' He said and went Into a Wine shop.

Moments later, he came out of the store with two six packs of beer and two packets of cigarettes.

'You are going to keep all that stuff in our apartment?' I asked.

'Yeah, where else do you want me to keep it?' he asked, making a joke I guess.

'No, It's just that, I don't drink or smoke or anything.' I told him.

'What? Not even beer?' he asked.

'Yup, not even beer.' I said.

'Dude, we have to work on you, we will start as soon as possible.' He said and we started walking towards our apartment building.

'We should have brought some food too; it's already 06:00 p.m, in the evening.' Ritwik said.

'We will manage; we can just buy some stuff that we can make at home.' I said.

'You know how to cook?' Ritwik asked.

'Yeah, I mean I know that much that we can eat at least tonight. Right now all I am thinking about is talking to my family. How long did she say it will take for my new sim card to be activated?' I asked him.

'At least two hours, bro, you can at least wait for two hours, right?' he said.

'Yeah, I can.' But I couldn't, I wanted to talk to all of them. I wanted to talk to my family, my friends and my girlfriend. God, I missed her so much.

'Let's go home, I need to set up this landline and the voicemail too, and also, we need to record a message for the voicemail machine.' He said.

We climbed the stairs to our apartment and Ritwik unlocked the door. I went straight into my room, inserted the sim card into my phone and placed it on the side table.

I came out and saw Ritwik placing the beer bottles in the refrigerator.

'You like this stuff, haan?' I asked him as he closed the refrigerator door.

'Yeah, a beer and a cigarette, the perfect mixture to calm you down and release you from all the stress from the day.' He said and took a long breath.

'Nice, I would like to do that someday, just not today. So, tell me something about you, I mean, all I know about you right now Is that you love beer and cigarettes, you like gymmIng and you know people around here. What else should I know?' I said.

'Hmmm, let's see, where should I start, yeah, got It, I come from a pretty rich family, I have a graduate degree In Software Engineering, I am looking for a job right now and I want to study further. I want to make a lot of money, although I know I don't need to, as my father is filthy rich. He is a businessman, well known, has connections and can set me up with any job or any business I want. My mother wants something different for me, she wants me to study and do a decent job and marry a nice girl and settle down as fast as possible. But I don't want that, I like my life the way It Is right now. I want to enjoy each and every second of It.' He said and sat beside me on the couch.

'Hmmm. Impressive, I didn't know you were an engineer, how old are you?' I asked.

'How does that even matter?' he answered my question with another question.

'It doesn't, I just want to know, I am just a teenager, seventeen to be precise, and I am here to study, become a good Dentist, earn as much as I can, even I want to earn craploads of money. But I just want to get better at every stage of my life, I don't say that I don't want to make mistakes, I just want to learn something from each mistake I make and move forward.' I said and took a long breath.

'Dude, the way you talk, you don't look seventeen to me, and by the way, I am twenty one.' He said.

'That's nice; I am living with a guy who is old enough to drink.' I said and we both laughed, this was the first time I had laughed since I got there.

'You tell me something more about you, like your family in India, your friends, your girlfriend.' He said.

'How can you be so sure that I have a girlfriend?' I said.

'Dude, nobody on this earth is this eager to talk to their parents ever; you are just waiting for your phone to work because you want to talk to her. Believe me, I know this stuff.' He said and winked again, this time I knew what the wink was about.

'Haha, ok ok, I cannot argue with you on this, I have a girlfriend back in India, I come from a place called Chandigarh, and you must visit that city if you ever have a trip to India, It Is just beautiful. My family is quiet rich itself, that is the reason I am here, my dad is also a businessman, owns several factories and earns quite well, my mom, she is a house-wife and a great cook, I just like to mention that a lot.' I said.

'That's good, to be frank, I didn't actually want a roommate, but my father said that I should have a roomIe, so here we are, roomIes now.' Ritwik was now openIng up too, even I was feeling comfortable around him now.

'It's almost seven; I guess your phone should be working by now. Go call your parents, they must be worried.' He said.

'Yeah, let me check my phone.' I said and got up to go into my room.

'Yes, it's working now.' I yelled from inside my room.

'That's great, call home.' Ritwik yelled back from the kitchen I assumed.

It was going to be my first call to my home. The first number I dialed was my father's.

'Hello?' I said.

'FInally you got time to call me, what took you so long?' My father yelled at me from the other sIde.

'Dad, calm down, I was just stuck with some work, plus my new sim card just got actIvated. So I called you late, I am so sorry.' I said, I was happy to hear his voIce after so long.

'Where is maa?' I asked dad.

'She is right here with me, talk to her.' He passed the phone to maa.

'Hey maa, how are you?' I said.

'Beta, you should have at least called us when you reached, you know how worried I was. You tell me, how you are and where are you?' she asked.

'Maa, I miss you so much, I am at the apartment, I have been waiting for so long to hear your voice, it is so weird that I have to live without you, I don't know what I am going to do without you by my side.' I said. My voice choked up a little.

'Beta, don't cry, you are a strong boy, you will manage, I know, besides, who says that you are alone, I am always with you, call me up whenever you want to talk ok?' she said.

'Obviously maa, I will, how's Tamanna, Saman, Naman, Maasi and Taau ji?' I asked.

'Everybody is fine here; we all miss you so much.' She said.

'I miss everyone too, save this number ok? This is the new number I bought from here, I and Ritwik also got a landline, and it will be activated by tomorrow.' I said.

'Ritwik is the name of your new roommate?' she asked.

'Oh yes, I forgot to tell you about him, he is an engineer, a little older than me, but he is great.' I said.

'Is he around?' she asked.

'I guess he is in the bathroom, I will send you pictures of the apartment on Whatsapp ok?' I said.

'Ok, I will talk to you soon, beta. Take care and stay healthy. Bye now.' she said and disconnected the call.

It felt so good talking to my parents after such a long time; it was the first time I had to wait this long to hear their voice.

Now it was time to call Harshaali, I just didn't know if she would pick up or not. So, I decided to Install Whatsapp in my phone first, so that I could text her first.

I Installed Whatsapp, it didn't take long as the internet speed In U.S. was way faster than in India. I added her number in my contact list and texted her.

'Hey baby, my new number, text me ASAP.' I said and put my phone on the side table again.

I went out to get some groceries for the apartment; after all I was cooking tonight. I bought some noodles, some veggies and some fruits, picked up some milk cartons and cookies too.

When I was walking back home I realized that I didn't but any oil for cooking, so then I went back to the store and bought some vegetable oil for cooking. I got back home after almost half an hour and saw Ritwik In front of the television screen again.

'Dude, stop watching T.V. and help me with this stuff.' I said and Ritwik took almost all the stuff from my hands.

'Where were you, man? You should have told me that you were going out, I would have come with you.' He said.

'Oh no, I just wanted to get this stuff, also I wanted to see the city on my own, the good thing Is that now I know the way back to the apartment, I didn't get lost or anything In the streets.' I smiled at him.

'Haha, that's good, it would have been hard for me to find you as you didn't even have your phone with you.' He said and we laughed again. I was almost starting to like this guy.

'So, you talk to your girl yet?' he said and I realised that I didn't.

'Oh fuck.' I ran towards my room and checked my phone. There were texts from Harshaali. I called her up instantly.

'Baby?' I said.

'I miss you so much Dev, I have been waiting for your call for so long, you didn't even talk to me on the plane. I got so worried.' She said. I was smiling as I had heard her voice after so long.

'Baby, I am so sorry I didn't talk to you sooner, but It wasn't my fault you know, I didn't have a phone until two hours ago, and then the sim card took time to get activated, I called as soon as I could, believe me.' I said.

'I know baby, I believe you, and how are you and how everything is going so far?' she asked.

'Everything Is just great here, I have been waiting to tell you everything for such a long time, you know, I am at my apartment, It Is In such a nice neighborhood, the people are so nice over here, I have a roommate he Is a Punjabi too, but get this, he has been living here since I don't know how long. I don't think he knows Hindi or Punjabi at all, but he is an Indian for sure.' I said, I was so excited that I was finally telling all this to the person I wanted to.

'Baby, I am really happy to hear that, at least you have a friendly face there now, how is he?' she asked.

'Well, he is older, twenty one, he is an engineer. And a great thing, he also likes watching F.R.I.E.N.D.S.' I said.

'Oh my god, Dev, how many times do I have to tell you that almost everyone loves that show?' she laughed on the other end.

'No, but still, at least me and my roommate have something In common.' I said.

'I know, it's great, you are enjoying yourself at least.' She said.

'Did you fill up the forms and all for the Institutes?' I asked her as this was the last thing that we talked about.

'Yeah, I am waiting for their call now, I don't know which Institute to choose, there are so many.' She said.

'It's quiet OK to be confused right now.' I said.

'Yeah, easy for you to say babe. Leave that, send me some pictures of the apartment and your roomie as soon as possible, OK?' she said.

'Yes baby, I will send you the pictures right now, you check them out, now I have to go, have to make dinner for both of us, Ok? Ttyl?' I said.

'Obviously talk to me later, go show off your cooking skills. Love you and miss you a lot, baby. And take care.' She said and disconnected the call.

I took a long breath and lied down on the bed with a big smile on my face, it felt so good talking to Harshaali, I was feeling depressed before, but now I knew she would be just a phone call away from me.

I got up and stepped out of my room, I could smell something good in the living room.

'Did you cook something, Ritwik?' I asked.

'Yeah, I made some soup for you and me from the veggies and fruits you brought, taste It and tell me how It Is.' He said.

'OK, will be happy to do that.' I said.

I tasted the soup and it was delicious.

'It's really nice man, thanks for doing this.' My pleasure, come sit, let's watch some television.

We took one bowl each of the delicious soup that Ritwik prepared for us, it seemed like it was going to be our dinner tonight as there was a lot of it.

We sat down on the couch to see some repeats of our favorite show, F.R.I.E.N.D.S, we saw the episodes and ate our soup with it, and it was all nice and happy at that time and life felt easier somehow.

'So, any news from the college?' he asked.

'Naah, I will go and meet the Dean tomorrow, I guess it's going to be easy, I just want to know when I can start attending classes, I just can't wait.' I said.

'That's good, do you have the address?' he asked.

'Yeah, obviously, It's in my bag, wait let me go get It.' I said and walked into my room to get the address of the college.

'Here, do you know where this college is?' I asked Ritwik who was still enjoying his first bowl of soup.

'Yeah, it's right where my college used to be, I mean my engineering college. This is really close; I can take you there if you want.' He said.

'You can come with me if that's not much trouble for you.' I said.

'No not at all, I will go with you; even I have some work in that neighborhood. We will share a cab tomorrow, OK?' he said.

'Yeah, It's Ok for me thanks.' I said and smiled at him.

'No need to say thanks, man. I am your friend now.' he said.

'Hmmm…' I kept on eating the soup, no, the delicious soup.

The next morning I woke to the smell of coffee, I came out in the living room and saw a new coffee maker on the shelf with freshly made black coffee In It. Ritwik was in the bathroom taking a shower.

'Did you get the coffee maker this morning?' I asked him through the bathroom door between us.

'No, I had this coffee maker with me; I bought the coffee and sugar though.' He yelled from the other side of the door.

'Nice, can I have some?' I asked.

'It's for you only bro, I had my morning cup of coffee already.' He said.

'Thanks dude.' I said.

'Stop saying that already.' He yelled again.

I poured some coffee for myself and turned on the television, Ritwik came out of the bathroom.

'Take a shower and get ready soon, OK? We have to leave for your college in an hour.' He said and walked straight into his room.

'OK bro, it will take me just twenty minutes to get ready.' I said and sipped my coffee.

An hour later, we were both ready to leave the apartment, Ritwik already knew the way to the college and also knew the city better than me, so he was going to be of big help around.

We hailed a cab and Ritwik gave the driver the exact address of my soon to be college, the cab driver started his car and we were headed towards the college in no time. On the way I saw a lot of tall buildings, some of them had signs on them. I thought to myself.

'Wouldn't it be great if I stayed in this city, called it my home and had an amazing career in the States?'

I looked at Ritwik, sitting next to me, he looked tensed, the work he had must be really important, I wondered. My hopes for the college I was going to study in were really high, I wanted it to be the best; I wanted my college experience to be extraordinary.

CHAPTER 13

NEW YORK UNIVERSITY, COLLEGE OF DENTISTRY

WE WERE ON OUR WAY to my new education center, Ritwik was sitting next to me in the cab, talking to someone on the phone, he had some work over there so he decided to come along. We reached our destination in no time. I got out of the cab and Ritwik took off.

I was standing In front of the college gate, admiring the building, the great infrastructure, the greenery its campus had, and I had the appointment letter and the recommendation letters in my hand. I walked through the gate into the beautiful building that it was. I saw some students rushing towards their class that said Chemistry on its door; I knew I was going to attend these classes too.

'Where is the Dean's office, can you please show me the way?' I asked a sweeper standing in the corridor.

'It's right in front of you boy, look.' He said and pointed towards a brown door.

'Thank you so much, sir.' I said and he smiled at me.

I knocked on the door before entering.

'Yes, come in, how I may help you?' the Dean said.

He was a bald, short man around the age of fifty, his voice was heavy and his office was huge. I walked in and started talking to him, telling him who I was and why I was standing there in his office.

'Sir, my name is Deven Dhaanak, I am here to join this college, sir.' I said and showed him the recommendation letters.

'Yes, I have heard about you, you are the Indian boy right?' he asked.

'Yes sir, I am from India, I guess my father had a conversation with you over the phone.' I said.

'Yes he did, take a seat.' He said and I did exactly as I was asked.

'So, you want to become a Dentist? Can I know the reason?' he asked.

'Sir, actually I just wanted to be a doctor, this was my entire father's Idea. He asked me to study here, so here I am.' I said, I was quite comfortable talking to him.

'You are an exception you know, we have an acceptance rate of just seven percent, you might be the first Indian student that will study in this college. Are you prepared?' he said.

'I am sir, I am here to become a doctor, a Dentist to be precise, and I am ready for the hard work.' I said.

'Then I am glad to tell you that you can join from tomorrow. The classes start at 9 a.m. in the morning, you can get all the information you need from the reception outside.' He said.

'Thank you sir, I will join from tomorrow only.' I said and took his leave.

I walked towards the reception just outside his office and got all the information that I needed. My classes were to start from tomorrow, now I had to call Ritwik to pick me up.

'Hey, where are you?' I dialed his number.

'I am standing outside your college. Are you free now?' he asked on the phone.

'Yeah I am, just leaving the building now. I see the cab.' I walked towards the cab and where Ritwik was eagerly waiting for me.

'Did you get the admission?' he asked.

'Yeah I did, let's go home, I need to go buy some books and notebooks and stationary.' I said and we took off.

We reached our neighborhood and Ritwik asked the cabbie to stop In front of a shop.

'Why are we stopping here? Our building is still really far away I guess.' I said.

'You only said you need to buy some stuff. That's the shop you can buy everything related to your stationary.' He said and I got off the cab again.

'I am waiting here only, come soon.' He said.

I bought some pens, books and notebooks for my first day of college. I took out my phone to tell Harshaali everything, but then I thought I would call her once I am in my room.

We went back to our apartment and ordered some food over the phone; we were too tired to go out again to eat.

'What was your work in that neighborhood?' I asked Ritwik.

'Nothing, it was some personal stuff.' He said as he took out a bottle of beer from the fridge.

'Ok, the Dean is a nice man, he looks scary, but he is nice.' I said, he wasn't listening to me, I knew that.

'Is something wrong, Ritwik?' I asked.

'It's just, there used to be a girl in my life, some time ago, when I was in college. We broke up, it wasn't good at all.' He said.

'Yeah, breakups are supposed to be bad, what was the thing today? Do you want to get back with her?' I asked. I knew I was asking a lot of questions.

'No, I don't want anything from that girl, she wants me back, but I just can't go back to her now. I made a mistake; I made a horrible mistake, man.' He said and with that he took a big sip from the bottle.

I got up and went straight to the fridge, took out a beer and opened it, and then I took a big sip myself.

'Want to share?' I asked him.

'I thought you didn't drink, what changed now?' he asked me.

'The situation changed, if we have to talk about this, we can't be sober, at least I can't, so, you were telling me what big mistake you made.' I said.

'It's not that simple, and by the way, you are younger than me, I am supposed to be better at situations like this.' He said.

'I am not trying to be better than you or anything, I just think that you need to talk about this, I am just here to listen, if you don't want to tell me about this, it's OK.' I said and got up from the couch. As I started walking towards my room, Ritwik called me back.

'Wait, sit.' He said and I did.

'It's not simple, going back to her, that's because I am now in a relationship with her cousin sister.' He said and the beer in my mouth came out of nose.

'What?! You are dating your ex-girlfriend's sister now?' I said with a huge exclamation mark hanging right above my head.

'Yeah, that's the reason I didn't want to tell you. See, it wasn't my fault actually.' He said.

'Wait wait, is that the reason she broke up with you?' I asked Ritwik.

'No, she has no idea that is the problem. I am not going to tell her that, and I don't think Shelly will take that risk either.' He said.

'Shelly is the cousin?' I prompted.

'Yeah, it was just a stupid mistake at first, I slept with her by mistake, we were really drunk and then it was just the alcohol talking between us.' He said and held his head between his hands.

'Hmmm, so you slept together, that always ruins things.' I said and he looked at me.

'You have got to be kidding me, you have slept with girls? You are just nineteen; you guys do this in India too?' I looked at him and there was only one thing that came in my mind.

'I am being questioned by the guy who got drunk and had sex with his girlfriend's sister, WOW. Isn't that incest or something?' I said.

'It's not at all funny; Jane was a really great girl. We were at this party, I had a lot of vodka and was about to leave for home, that's when Shelly caught hold of me and stopped me from leaving, she said that I was too drunk to drive at night and she carried me up to her room. I was so drunk that I actually thought that Shelly was Jane, but that was also not my fault, these sisters look so similar that anybody would get confused.' He said, our beer bottles were now empty.

'Want to have another one?' I asked him.

'I need a cigarette, whenever I think or talk about this I feel guilty, and a cigarette is all I need. I will get some from my room. Can you open up another beer for me, please?' he said.

He came back from the room holding a cigarette in his right hand, between two fingers. The smoke made me uncomfortable and Ritwik sensed it.

'Oh fuck, I am so sorry; I will just go into my room.' He said.

'No it's Ok, come on sit.' I said.

'You sure you want to have another beer?' he asked me.

'What's there to be sure about? I like the taste.' I said and we both sat down on the couch again.

'You still want to talk about this?' I asked him.

'No man, let's just drop this, thanks for listening though.' He said.

'Anytime bro, listen, do you think we need some furniture for the apartment?' I asked him.

'Like what?' he replied.

'Well, now as my college is going to start from tomorrow, I think I would need a study table, and I think we should probable get a proper center table and dining table.' I said.

'Alright, when do you want to do that?' he asked.

'I am thinking we should do that today only, because I will get busy from tomorrow and I will be coming back late, I am free now, what do you say?' I told him what I had in mind.

'That's actually a good idea. Come on, I know a guy.' As usual, he knew a guy.

We locked the door behind us and took all the cash we needed, I still had a lot of it as my dad made sure that money won't be a problem for me here. Ritwik took his wallet; I assumed he also had a good amount there. We came out of the building, it was almost dark, we didn't even realise how long we had been in the apartment. It was around 7:00 already.

'Is the place close from here or do we need to get a cab?' I asked him.

'No, we don't need a cab, its right around the corner.' He said.

It took us almost fifteen minutes to reach the place, it was quiet cold outside and I forgot my jacket in the apartment.

'What's wrong?' Ritwik turned towards me and asked.

'Nothing, I am just a little cold, that's all. Are we there yet?' I asked him.

'Yup, this is the place.' He said, looking at a huge building, it was a shopping mall.

'We are going to buy furniture from a shopping mall?' I asked him.

'Yeah, I know a guy here; he has a furniture shop inside the mall.' He replied.

We walked in through the huge glass doors; passing the security we entered a shop called "Benipal's Furniture".

'Let's go.' He nudged me from behind as I was staring at the sign, trying to remember where I had heard that name before.

'Hey Dad…!' he screamed as he walked inside the showroom, it struck me that second, Ritwik Benipal you dumbass, it's his own shop.

'Hello uncle.' I said as his dad looked at me.

'Ritwik, you made a new friend?' he said.

Ritwik looked just like his father, but he was shorter than him. His father was almost totally bald, had a golden glass frame and looked like a villain from the bad Bollywood movies; he was holding a cigarette in his hand too.

'No dad, I mean yes he is a friend, but he is also my new roommate, this is Devin Dhaanak from India. Hey Deven, where did you say you were from?' Ritwik asked.

'I am from Chandigarh, uncle.' I replied to Ritwik's question and my answer brought a big smile on his Father's face.

'Dad, do you know that place?' Ritwik asked his dad.

'Yeah, your mother used to study in Chandigarh, her college was really famous, and all the Punjabi boys were out there looking for girls all the time. I used to be one of them, until I met your mother outside her college.' His father told him exactly how he knew Chandigarh.

'So, you live in Chandigarh?' Uncle asked.

'Actually I live in Panchkula, uncle. But they almost the same so that's the same thing I guess.' I said.

'Yes it is. What do you do my boy?'

'Well, I am here to study Dentistry; I have been accepted in the NYU College of Dentistry. I join from tomorrow.' I said.

'That's impressive, so, I will try to be a salesman now, how may I help you?' he said with a smile on his face.

'Actually Dad, we want to buy some new furniture for our apartment, like a study table for junior here and some other stuff.' He referred to me as "Junior" that sounded so weird.

'Alright, come let me show you some designs, you choose from them.' He said and guided us towards a staircase. Their shop was actually a big showroom, the ground floor was just used as the staging area, it had only a few pieces of furniture, and the actual stock was kept on the first floor.

'Here, select whatever you like. I will give you both some time to make your choices.' Uncle said and went back downstairs.

'What do you think we should select first?' I asked Ritwik who was already doodling with some study tables.

'Obviously your study table, that's more important.' He said.

'I think this one is nice.' He said and pointed towards a big study table with a lot of drawers on it, I didn't like it.

'I don't think we should buy something this big, I mean, we have to manage the space we have, this will look so bulky in our living room.' I suggested.

'You are right; we should go for something smaller in size.' He said and the he pointed towards another table.

'Yeah, something like this would work, it's of the accurate size, limited number of drawers, this is nice, and I will buy this one.' I said, we had decided the first thing. Now we had to select a Dining table too.

'I think we should buy a small Dining table too, you were right, we don't have much space in the apartment.' He said.

'What about this one?' I liked a brown polished piece that was small, but it was really a beautiful table to have in the apartment, it was just perfect.

'I like it; I think we have just selected our first piece of furniture together, good job Junior.' He said.

We walked back downstairs to let uncle know about what we have decided.

'Did you boys get what you came looking for?' uncle asked.

'Yes uncle, we have decided to get the compact brown study table and the brown, polished dining table, they look nice.' I said.

'Good choices boys, come let's discuss the prices.' He said an we sat down on the wooden chairs that were at display for other customers.

'Here, this is your bill.' Uncle came with a register in his hand.

'Uncle, you have only mentioned the price of the dining table on this bill, we also want that study table.' I said and looked at Ritwik.

'I know, that is a gift from my side, you don't have to pay for that Ok? Just study hard and become a really good Dentist, I will need your help after sometime.' He said and pointed towards the cigarette packet in his pocket.

'But uncle, how can I accept such an expensive gift? No no, you have to take the money, please.' I insisted on paying him, I didn't know if it was right to accept a gift from my roommate's Father.

'Just take it, if Dad says he won't take money for it, he won't.' Ritwik said.

'But Ritwik, how can I...' I was interrupted by uncle before I could finish that sentence.

'No buts and ifs now just fill out this address box and both the tables will arrive at your place in no time.' he said.

I did as Uncle asked me to do, I took the register from his hand and started filling up the address box on it.

I walked out of the store as Ritwik was talking to his father, I saw him smiling and his dad was saying something, he hugged his father and came outside.

'You are really close to your father, aren't you?' I asked Ritwik as we walked outside the mall.

'Yeah, I love him, I love my mother too, but I am really open with my father, you know, before I told you about all this Jane and Shelly stuff, he was the only one who knew.' He said.

'You told your father about that mess? What did he say?' I asked him.

'Well, he made me sit down and then he told me about his youth and what mistakes he made at that time, he made me realise that I had to tell Jane the truth about what happened that night. But I still don't have the courage to tell her that I slept with her sister.' He said.

'Whenever you talk about Jane, you become sad, is that the guilt or you miss being with her?' I have no idea why I wanted to know about my roommate's love life.

'It's a little of both you know. I know I made a huge mistake, but that mistake led my life in another direction, Jane was really special, but what I have with Shelly, it's just something else. I can't even eplain that in word.' Listening to Ritwik talk about his girlfriend, I started missing Harshaali. We agreed that whenever she would be free, she would text me and then I would call her and then we would talk. But today I received no text from her; she must have been busy with the institute admissions and stuff.

'Whatever it is, I just hope you do the right thing, Senior.' I said and looked at him with a smile, he smiled back.

We reached our apartment and I saw an old man standing outside, in the middle of the corridor, with a cigarette in his hand, wearing a long robe and big black glasses.

'Are you the Indian guy?' he asked looking at me.

'Yes sir and you are?' I had no idea how he knew who I was.

'I am your landlord, I asked you to come and meet me at my apartment, didn't you give him the message?' he asked Ritwik.

'He did, didn't my father already talk to you?' i got offended by his tone.

'Your father did, but he is not going to live here, is he? I needed to talk to you, tell you the rules of this building.' He said.

'I am standing right here, tell me the rules.' I said.

'You are cocky, it's just because you are new here, but I will let that pass, there are only two rules. One, you don't disturb your neighbours with loud noises or anything. Two, you don't get any animals in the building. No pets allowed.' He said, I didn't like this man, he was the first rude guy I had seen in New York, he thought he was going to scare me or something, but he was wrong.

'I will keep that in mind, are we done here?' I said.

'For now we are, just don't give me any reasons to throw you out in the middle of the night.' He said and threw his cigarette in the alley.

'Good night.' He said as he walked away towards the staircase.

'What's his deal?' I asked Ritwik who tried to unlock the door.

'I have no fucking idea, dude, I just think his age is catching up to him.' He said and we both entered our apartment laughing.

We ordered dinner from the same restaurant that we had our lunch the first day, we turned on the T.V. and Ritwik lit up a cigarette again.

'Don't you get tired of the smoke?' I asked him.

'Sometimes, but right now I needed one.' He said.

'That thing you said, about cigarettes helping you calm down, does that really work?' I asked him.

'It does, I have experienced it so many times, it's just like meditation, the only difference is, meditation doesn't kill you.' He looked at me when he said the last words of his sentence.

'You know this is harmful, still you do it. Is it that satisfying?' I said, I was excited now.

'You wouldn't know that unless you try it yourself.' Ritwik said and offered me one from his pack.

'No no, I don't think I should, I am a medical student, and that too Dentistry, I know the effects, I don't want to become an addict.' I said.

'You worry too much, Deven. It's your wish though, if some day you change your mind, let me know.' He said as he put the packet back in his pocket.

We had been waiting for our furniture and our food for a long time now, I asked Ritwik to call up his father and ask him if the delivery was scheduled for today only, meanwhile I called up the restaurant to get the status of our food.

'Sir, the delivery boy will be knocking on your doorstep any second now. I am really sorry for the delay.' The man on the phone said.

'Food will be arriving soon, what about the furniture?' I asked Ritwik.

'On its way, do you know where you are going to put the study table? In your room or in the living room?' he asked.

'I think I will keep it in my room only, if I keep it in the living room I will be distracted by the T.V. all the time.' I said.

'Good point, it's better you keep it in your room only, the dining table can go near the kitchen slab, it will be easier to grab stuff from the kitchen then, less efforts you know.' He said.

'Yeah, you are right.' I said.

The food that we had ordered arrived moments later, we took out plates and sat in front of the television again to have our dinner. But before we could have a single bite, our furniture arrived too.

'Now that's called bad timing, you eat; I will sign the delivery papers.' He said and got up to take the delivery of our stuff.

'Where do you want these tables to be placed, sir?' one of the three guys carrying the tables asked Ritwik.

'Deven, you sure you want the study table in your room?' he asked me, I was still sitting on the couch having Murg Masallam.

'Yes, let me see where I want the table, man, this tastes so good.' I said as I got up from the couch and went inside my room.

'Bring the table in.' I yelled from inside my room.

'Keep it here, next to the almirah.' I instructed the two really huge delivery boys.

'It's all set up now, sir. Anything else you would like us to do?' the third guy asked me.

'No, that's all I needed help with, thanks a lot.' I said.

The three guys walked out the door as Ritwik handed over the papers to them.

'Well, now we have our dining table, wanna shift the food to the table now?' Ritwik asked.

'Sure.' I said.

After having dinner, we both sat down on the couch again, the food was so good, even Ritwik decided to cheat on his diet for the night and have the taste for once. We were literally tired of eating now.

'Wanna go out for a walk?' I asked Ritwik.

'What's the time?' he asked.

'Around 10, why? Is it unsafe?' I asked.

'Nope, was just thinking, there's a really nice café just around the corner, want to grab a mocha?' he asked.

'Always ready for a good tasting coffee, let's go.' I said and we grabbed our jackets.

Ritwik picked up his cigarette pack as we headed outside the apartment. He just couldn't live without them.

'So, you know some guy there too?' I asked as we passed the "Punjabi Style" restaurant.

'Yeah, the guy who owns the café is a friend of mine. I will introduce you to the guy as a friend, you will never have to pay for your coffee ever.' he said and we both laughed.

We walked for almost fifteen minutes before we reached an old looking building, the windows were covered with curtains so nothing was visible from the outside. The sign on the top said, "Café Mocha".

'And how do you know the guy who owns this place?' I asked.

'He is a high school buddy of mine; we practically grew up together.' Ritwik said.

As we entered the Café, Ritwik started a conversation with one of the workers there.

'Hey, where's your boss?' he said.

'Sir, he is upstairs doing some work.' The guy in the white apron said.

'Work haan? Let's see.' Ritwik had that mischievous smile on his face, I knew something was wrong.

I followed Ritwik to the staircase, he climbed the stairs in no time, and he seemed really excited. The first floor of that building was really messed up. It was almost like it had been abandoned many years ago, it didn't have a new paint work, there was dust all over the place, but there was one room that looked quiet maintained. Ritwik started knocking on the door hard.

'Come out you bastard, I know what important work you are doing inside. Come out or I will break this door.' He yelled from the outside.

'Don't you think that's a little inappropriate?' I said.

'Just wait and watch.' Ritwik's reply confirmed that there was something wrong with this scenario.

Moments later the door got unlocked from the inside and a girl rushed downstairs.

'You son of a bitch, you have the worst timing ever. I was just about to score with that chick, you ruined it all.' He said as he wore his shirt.

'I knew your urgent piece of work, how are you?' Ritwik asked him and then they hugged each other.

'Man, I haven't seen you since that party, where have you been?' Ritwik's friend said.

'Just around places, hey, meet Deven, he is my new roommate.' Ritwik introduced me to his friend, who by the way was still a stranger to me. I shook his hand, 'Kevin Rogers, I am the owner of this haunted house you stand in.' he said.

'Deven, nice to meet you.' I said.

'Where are you from Deven?' he asked, we were now climbing down the stairs to actually order a coffee.

'I am from India, this place is quite nice, you don't like it?' I asked Kevin.

'No I don't like it here, actually the thing is, my father gave me this place to manage because he thinks I am good for nothing, so he thought that a place that is good for nothing will suit me just perfect.' Kevin said, 'Three mochas over here.' He yelled at one of his waiters.

'How have you been? I mean, I can see you are still whoring around, but still.' Ritwik asked Kevin.

'Dude, it's not whoring around, OK? I love that girl. She just ran away because she just wasn't ready to be seen with me, I can't even imagine how she must be feeling right now.' Kevin said.

'What a load of crap, tell me her name within three seconds and I will believe everything you just said.' Ritwik replied to Kevin's hurtful love story.

'Ahhhhh, Damn it, I wish I had asked her name before getting her naked. Leave it. You tell me something about you Deven. You here for some work?' Kevin asked, our coffees had arrived by that time.

'Well, I am a Dental student at NYU College of Dentistry, tomorrow would be my first day.' I said.

'Well that's great, you will be getting a lot of girls in that college, seriously, that place is full of nerdy girls, but they are hot as hell, man. You are going to be really happy tomorrow.' Kevin said.

'I don't actually care about these "nerdy hot girls"; I already have a girlfriend in India.' I said as I sipped my coffee.

'What did you just say?' Kevin exclaimed.

'Hey Kevin, leave it, he is just a kid.' Ritwik said to Kevin.

'You are telling me that you are in a long distance relationship with a girl? Dude, you live in different countries. Even if you do something stupid here, like say, you slept with a really hot chick, it doesn't matter, nobody has to know, OK? Live your life and have some fun, that's all I want to say.' Kevin said and then rested his back on the couch he was sitting in.

'Whatever it is, if I see myself in a different place in some time, if my relationship doesn't work, maybe I will break up with her and start doing what you just said.' I told Kevin.

'Hey Junior, you don't have to listen to this idiot, he has always been like this, against relationships and commitments and stuff, you shut the fuck up Kevin.' He told Kevin to keep his wisdom to himself and leave me out of it.

'It's OK Ritwik, I don't mind at all. He is your friend and everyone has their own opinions. Let it be. I think we should leave now, it's late.' I said and got up from the couch.

'Hey listen, I am really sorry if I offended you in some manner, I didn't mean to.' Kevin apologized to me.

'There's no need to apologize, Kevin. I will be here a lot now, so I think you can call me your friend from now on.' I said as I extended a hand towards Kevin.

'Sure man, why not.' He said and shook my hand with a smile on his face.

We left the café and started walking for our apartment, it was the first time I was walking in the New York streets in the middle of the night.

'I am sorry about Kevin; he is just like that sometimes.' Ritwik said.

'I liked the guy; he just said what he thinks about life, that's really nice. Infact, I liked his idea about the "nerdy hot girls".' I said.

'Sometimes I just don't get who you actually are, and I don't like that.' He said in a funny way.

'Well, you just need to know me better then, that is not going to be a problem, we are going to be roomies for a long time I guess.' I said as we approached our building.

We entered the apartment and I started packing for the next day, kept my subject books and notebooks in the bag. As I was packing I checked my phone again, there was an empty screen, no messages or missed calls from Harshaali. I called maa and talked to her for some time and then I went to my bed as I was a bit tired as well as a little too excited for my first day of college.

Ritwik woke me up the next day, I had an alarm set for 07:00 a.m. but it didn't wake me up.

'Get up, it's your first day, you don't want t be late on your first day. Wake up.' Ritwik said in a sleepy voice himself.

'What? What's the time?' I asked.

'Its 7:45 now get up and get ready. I will make some coffee.' He said and I sprung out of my bed instantly as I realised that I was lagging behind on my schedule.

I got ready in like fifteen minutes, got dressed in five and had breakfast and coffee in ten.

'Text me when you reach, OK?' Ritwik said.

'OK sir, sure sir, bye sir.' I said and closed the door behind me.

I signaled a cabbie in my street and he came to pick me up.

'Where to, sir?' he asked.

'NYU College of Dentistry, go go.' I told him I was in a hurry and he said he understood.

'Are you new in the neighborhood?' the cabbie asked.

'Yeah, I just came two days ago, I am here to study, and I am really late right now.' I said.

'Don't you worry, sir? I will drop you there in no time.' he said.

He did as he promised, he dropped me off at my college gate before time, I saw the building again and started walking towards the main entrance. The last time I was here, I couldn't see many student faces, but at that particular moment, the whole college crowd was in the front lawn. There were all kinds of students, I could just tell by looking that it was a great atmosphere for everyone and I would make a lot of new friends here.

I was walking towards the classes when I heard a voice behind me.

'Hey you, new boy.' A guy standing with some of his friends called me.

'Are you talking to me?' I asked him.

'Yeah, I am. Are you the new boy from India?' he asked. His question brought a smile on my face, the smallest mention of my country made me happy in that place.

'Yes I am the new guy, from India, but how do you know that?' I asked.

'That doesn't matter, see there is a rule in our college, the new student has to perform a dare of our choice. So go to your class, place your bag in one of the seats and come back outside in less than a minute. Go now.' he ordered me, like I was going to listen, huh.

'OK, so you want me come out in less than a minute? And who did you say you were exactly?' I asked him.

'I am your senior, and you mind your tone you son of a bitch.' Ok, that was it.

'What did you just call me?' before he could say anything, I was choking him with my right hand and punching him with my left, his friends were trying to pull him away from me but I didn't let go. Calling me with that name, he made a huge mistake, I was going to be a decent student, but that wasn't going to happen now that a fellow student had abused me in the middle of the corridor.

'What is happening here?!' a man in a navy blue suit, around mid forty of age came running towards the commotion the "new boy" had created.

'Sir this new boy was trying to choke me, he punched me several times sir, and I didn't even say anything.' The senior guy said.

'You! What are you doing? Where are you from and why did you hit him like this?!' the man was yelling at me for no reason, that guy had convinced him that it was all my fault.

'Sir, if this is the kind of crowd you have here, then I am very sorry to say but this is going to be a huge problem. This guy who is now trying to show himself as a victim of assault here, he abused me, called me a son of a bitch, tried to bully me around and wanted me to do some kind of dare for him, said that it was a tradition. I am not here to follow any of your meaningless traditions, I am here to study, you bother me again, I will hit you even harder.' I almost scared the crap out of that guy, he was trying to be a bully in front of me, which I already didn't like, over that, he abused me, he just had it all coming.

'You are going to the Dean's office, Chris, and you, control yourself, control your anger. Now go to your class, I will be there in a minute.

Oh fuck, this man was my professor, I thought he just came there to stop me from hitting that guy, I guess he was about to enter the class when that happened and came back to stop whatever was going on.

As he instructed, I went to my class and sat on a single chair. The classroom was quiet large, but the strength of students in the class was a little less, I was told that it was going to be a batch of fifty students, but there were not more than twenty students in the class. The professor in the navy blue suit came in and kept his leather bag on the table.

'Silence class.' He said and all the students turned to see the professor.

'I am Stuart Whitman, I will be your Chemistry professor for this semester. We will be having 5 assignments in the session, 4 lectures per week in which two lectures will dedicated only to class revision, we have our semesters in early December, right after your winter vacations. I want proper discipline in my class. Now, there is something that just happened outside the class. I am very disappointed about what that boy did, mister?' Professor Whitman pointed at me, now I was suddenly the center of attraction in the class, all the students were looking at me and wondering what had happened.

'Deven sir, Deven Dhaanak, I am from India.' I told him.

'Deven, I apologize on behalf of Chris, whatever he did, he will be appropriately punished for it. But I just want to tell you one thing. I saw you outside in that moment, all I could see was rage in your eyes, if I wasn't there to stop you, god only know what you coul have done to him. I just want you to understand that there are going to be times when you feel suffocated, because of jerks like Chris, but in that moment, just think about the best thing in your life. Beating a guy won't be as satisfying as ignoring the bastard, Ok?' he told me something that I already knew, but looking at this man, I knew he was a friendly, I knew he wasn't upset with me that I kicked some punk ass in the middle of the corridor, he just wanted to see the best in me and that's what made me say what I said next.

'I am really sorry for the way I reacted, sir, I promise you it will never happen again.' I said and the Professor gave me the permission to sit down.

'Ok, so today we will not study as such, today I just want to know the people I am going to spend the next seven months of my life with. Let's have an introductory class, shall we?' he asked the class and we all said, 'Yes professor' in unison.

'So let's start with you, on the first seat. Tell me your name the place you come from.' As he instructed, the students got up and introduced themselves to the class.

'Good morning sir, my name is Emma Greg and I am from Chicago.' The girl in front of me stood up and introduced herself. It was my turn now.

'We all know you Mr. Daanak.' He said in his American accent. 'You can keep sitting.' He said.

The students sitting behind me continued the practice, but I was more interested in the girl sitting in front of me. Not because she was really hot or anything, but because her voice reminded me of Harshaali.

The introduction went on for a while, but I was still trying to catch a glance of Emma the whole time, she had long brown hair that she had tied in a bun, she was wearing a blue crop top and black denim jeans with matching blue heals. I was a little shy to talk to her directly, so I decided to let it go. The lecture ended after some time and Professor Whitman left. We were supposed to sit there and wait for the next teacher to show up, we had Biology next. I was sitting in my seat taking pictures to show Harshaali, when suddenly Emma turned around and called my name, in her accent.

'Ammm, excuse me, Deven, is it?' she said.

I looked up at her, finally I saw her face. Well, she was pretty, really pretty, big eyes, rectangular spectacles and three piercings in each ear.

'Yeah, Hi. Emma, is it?' I said, I don't know why I smiled.

'If you don't mind me asking, what happened outside? What was the Professor talking about?' she asked.

'Amm, is this your first day here?' I asked her.

'No, why?'

'On your first day here, did a group of guys call you and make you do a task or dare or something?'

'Yes, why? Did they call you too?' she asked, as soon as she asked this question, Chris "the bully" came into our classroom.

'Was that the guy?' I pointed a finger towards him.

'Yes, but he didn't have those bandages on his... wait, did you do that to him?' soon her expression of shock changed into laughter.

'Man, that was amazing, he is such a jerk, look he is staring at you.' She told me.

'Let him stare, he won't even dare talk to me now, atleast in the college, outside the college, even I am free to hit him as much as I can. Here Professor Whitman saved him, but outside the college, there are no Professors.' I said.

'Haha, so we have a badass in our class, hey, it's great meeting you by the way.' She said and extended a hand forward.

'The pleasure is all mine, but I am no badass, he abused me, that's why I hit him, if he would have talked to me normally, I am not a lunatic who will hit anybody without any reason.' I had this urge to explain my side of the story even though she didn't ask me.

'So, if he ever talks to you in a civil way, you will talk to him normally?' she asked me.

'Yes ofcourse, give respect and take respect, that's the rule, this guy, I don't think he deserves it, and he knows that too, that's why I said he won't even talk to me again.' As we were talking, chris got up and left the class, maybe because people kept asking him about the injuries he had on his face, the ones that I gave him. He was embarrassed I guess.

'See, he can't even tell people now, the reason he got beat up by his junior. Idiot.' I said.

'You are a safe guy, Deven.' She said.

'Safe?' this was confusing.

'Yeah, now if a girl is walking with you in this college, nobody will look at her and comment. See, even though this is a Dental college, cheap people come here in every batch, by cheap I mean, the guys who don't have any respect for girls or women and guys who just want one thing. You understand, right? She asked if I got what she was saying, haha. Clearly this girl had never been on a tour to India. A girl this hot, if walks alone on the streets of cities like Delhi or Chandigarh, she is destined to become a victim of eve-teasing. But, I have to love it, it's my country.

'I do get what you mean, but I still don't get what you mean by me being a "SAFE" guy.' I said.

'By safe I mean, with you any girl can walk freely outside.' She said.

'OK, so you think that if a girl is out with me and a guy says something cheap about her, I will start beating him up?' I needed to know this; I didn't want a "HITMAN" image in the college.

'Yeah, wouldn't you?' she asked.

'That depends on the girl. If the girl is my girlfriend, definitely, if she is my sister, I will literally kill the bastard, if she is just an acquaintance of mine; I will just defend her in some other manner.' I eplained all the scnarios to Emma as she listened to me carefully.

'So you mean, Mr. Dhaanak (in her accent), if I want to see you kick ass outside again, I should either become your girlfriend or your sister?' she said and started laughing, I also laughed, not out loud though.

'No that's not what I mean exactly, but whatever.' I said and smile again.

The next lecture started minutes later, it was Biology and it was a female Professor named Jenny McCarthy. She started the lecture with another introduction, another lecture was wasted I knowing names and places. At the end she told us that we had to get some lab equipmets for the next class. She gave us a list and told us where we could get those instruments easily.

The whole day passed easily, mostly because it was only comprised of introductions and classmates coming up to me asking why I hit "the senior". I gave everyone the same story, and by the end of the day, all I wanted to do was go home and sleep for a while.

I was about to leave the college when Emma came running towards me.

'Hey Deven, wait up.' She yelled from a distance. I was carrying the backpack that my mom bought me, it was black and had all the unused books and notebooks from the day.

'Hi Emma, what happened?' I asked from the first friend of mine in the class, I guess.

'Nothing, I just wanted to talk to someone, apparently I talk a lot and people get bored, so this is me experimenting on you. Why are you in such a hurry to get home? It's only p.m. in the afternoon.' She said.

'I am not in a hurry, I just didn't have anything else to do, apparently now I do, I am acting as a labrat for my classmate.' I said and she giggled a bit.

'So, can I ask some questions about you? Because basically, I don't know you at all, but you seem like a really nice guy to have a conversation with.' She said, she spoke at such a pace and with an accent that it was sometimes hard to understand what she had just said.

'Ok, you can ask me anything. I don't mind.' I said.

'Ok, then tell me, where are you from?' her first question was a stupid one, I had been repeating the same thing the whole day and she didn't know where I was from.

'I think the whole class knows this by now, but if you don't, it's Ok, I am from India, and I know you are from Chicago, see, I pay attention in the class.' I said.

'Oh crap, I knew that, I have been hearing that all day, how I could forget. OK, ammm, you live with your family or are you here on your own?' her next question made sense atleast.

'No my family is in India, I am here for the degree only, my dad sent me here for studying. I live on the lower east side of Manhattan, frankly speaking, I never want to go back to India, I love this country and I love this city.' I said, I don't know why I told her the last two things.

'Well, that's nice, even I love New York, all my life I wanted to live here, and by the way, I guess we are neighbours. I live in the lower east side too, where are you living?' she asked.

'Well, I don't really know the names right now, but there is a restaurant called "Punjabi Style" close to my buiding.' I said.

'Oh my God, I eat there almost everyday, the chicken there, it's amazing, it's right in front of my building. I have never seen you there though.' She said.

'I know the chicken there is amazing, I have only been there once, we mostly order food from the apartment.' I said.

'We?' her question comprised of only a word ths time.

'Yeah, me and my roommate, Ritwik. He is an engineer. He is also an Indian, but his family came here a long time ago, and now he lives here as a New Yorker only.' I told Emma.

'That's actually great that you found a fellow Indian as a roommate. How are you planning to go home?' she asked.

'I was about to call out for a cab when you called me, what about you?' I asked her.

'I am waiting for you to call for a cab now, you don't mind sharing a cab with a stranger, do you?' another question from her side.

'No I don't mind, besides, you are the second person I have had a decent conversation with in this country, so yeah, we can share a cab.' I said and called a cab standing behind us at a short distance.

We decided that we will split the bill and then we got inside the cab.

CHAPTER 14

LIVING THE DREAM

EMMA SHARED A CAB WITH me, we talked about all kinds of stuff during the ride, she told me all about her family and friends back in Chicago, I told her about my life back in India, it was nice to have a conversation with her. Also I learned that we had a few similar interests, like music, movies, t.v. shows etc. We had a pleasant cab ride and she became a friend instantly, she told me about her roommate who was also a a student, she told me how much she loved Chandler Bing in the t.v. show F.R.I.E.N.D.S, I told her that he was my favourite too.

We reached her place first and I finally recognised her building. I had seen it before while I was walking with Ritwik on my first night here.

'I have been here before; I bought my cell phone from that shop, right there.' I told Emma.

'Haha, can you tell me which building is yours? Just for future reference?' she asked.

'You see that tall brown building, looks kinda old and rusty? That's my building.' I told her.

'Alright then, see you around Deven, it was really nice meeting you. Bbye.' She said and paid the cabbie her half.

'Bbye.' I said and waved at her. Then the cabbie dropped me in front of my building and I paid him the rest.

I got in the building and started climbing the stairs, took my phone out of my pocket and checked it for any new notifications. There I saw a message from Harshaali. I literally stopped in my tracks just to read that text.

'Hi baby, I am so sorry I have been unavailable since past two days. I am at my naani's place actually, I don't get any signals here and I am nt able to use my phone much. I will be here for a couple of days. Please don't be upset with me, I know you will understand my situation. I love you and miss you so much, Dev, I just can't put it together into words. Just know this, I love you and I am always with you. But I have to go now, I will talk to you as soon as possible, baby. Miss me, bbye.' After reading that text I knew I won't be talking to her for a long time now, I knew this situation, this had happened before too, she would go to her naani's place, which was I don't know, how backwards that it didn't even catch proper mobile signals, and then she would just disappear for like a week or so. I hated her naani's place so much. I just never told her so, but God I wanted to tell her now.

I walked towards my apartment and knocked on the door.

'Ritwik, I am back, open the door.' I yelled from outside.

'Coming.' He said.

He opened the door and I walked in, I saw him talking on the phone with somebody, they were having a tense conversation. I tried to ignore but he was screaming now and it was even harder to ignore now.

'I know that, but I cannot go through all that again, please try and understand.' He screamed and disconnected the call.

'Jane?' I asked.

'Who else? Why the fuck can't she leave me alone? Oh hey, leave that, tell me about your first day.' Suddenly his gloomy face turned into a bright smiling face.

'Well, it was good, no, it was actually terrific. But the starting of the day was quiet vicious.' I said.

'Vicious? What do you mean?' he prompted.

'I got into a fight with a senior college mate, he was trying to bully me actually, when I tried to defend myself, he called me a son of a bitch and moments later I broke his nose.' I told Ritwik everything that happened in just two sentences.

'Oh fuck dude, you actually broke a guy's nose on the first day of college? That's got to be a record. Did anyone intervene?' he asked.

'Yeah, my Chemistry teacher stopped me from bashing his face any further, he didn't punish me or anything, I told him the truth and he punished that other guy for misbehaving with me, took him to the Dean and all, so basically, I created a ruckus on the first day and got quiet famous in the college for beating up a senior.' I said.

'Hahaha, obviously, you had to get famous after doing that. So, any new friends?' he asked.

'Yeah, this girl sitting in front of me, a really sweet and pretty girl actually, started talking to me about this incident, and we got along well. Actually we got along really well, after that I discovered that she lives in the building just across the street, behind that restaurant. So we shared a cab home.' I told him.

His expression changed again, the smile turned into a grin with his eyebrows upwards.

'What? Why that expression?' I asked.

'Nothing, how's Harshaali?' he asked with that same grin on his face.

'Oh come on, there is nothing like that going on, Ok? Emma is just a friend.' I explained it to him but I wasn't sure if he understood.

'Yayaya, have you eaten anything since this morning?' he asked.

'No actually, I guess the excitement of the first day and that fight killed my appetite. But now that you have mentioned it, I need to eat something.' I said.

'Yeah, I was hoping you'd say that, I had lunch at the restaurant, got some for you, it's in the fridge. Have some and get some energy, we need to go shopping again.' He told me.

'Shopping? For what exactly?' I asked as I pulled out a bowl full of chicken from the fridge.

'We have to get some electrical appliances. Now do everything quickly, we have to leave soon.' He said and went into his room, for a cigarette most probably.

I had my lunch and got ready for another shopping tour with my roommate. It was already five in the evening, when we left the apartment.

'Where are we going? Please tell me you know a guy for this too.' I hoped he would say yes.

'Yeah I do, we are going to the same store from where we got your cell phone, which reminds me, we still don't have a voicemail message.' He said.

'Hmmm, we will do that when we get back, Ok?' I said and he nodded in agreement.

We walked in the same store again and met Jimmy.

'Hey guys, how can I help you today?' Jimmy asked.

'We need a microwave, a toast maker, a juicer and some lamps for the apartment.' Ritwik handed him a piece of paper which had the list of all the stuff we needed.

'You have a list? I think you were home all day.' I said.

'Yeah, had nothing else to do, so I thought of some stuff we would need frequently.' He replied.

'That's good use of time.' I giggled.

'Come this way, I will show you all the varieties we have and then you can make a choice.' Jimmy guided us to the appliances section of the store. I saw the lady who gave me my sim card, I smiled and bobbed my head a little to greet her.

'Select everything Ok? That's your job now, I prepared the list, and you make the choice.' Ritwik said.

'Alright, let's see now, we don't need a big microwave, so I guess this one will do, lemme check out the rest of the stuff.' I said and moved towards the toasters and juicers. I selected one of each and told Jimmy to pack them up.

'What about lamps?' Ritwik asked.

'Oh yes, I forgot, let's get three lamps, one for my room, one for your room and one for the living room. What say?' I suggested.

'I think that's perfect.' He said and I selected three different lamps for each sight.

'Are we done now?' I asked Ritwik.

'Yup, let's pay them and leave, they will deliver the stuff at our apartment.' He replied.

We walked towards the bill counter and paid half each, for the overall bill. After that we walked out of the store and started walking back to our building. On our way back home, we stopped to get some take out for dinner. I was really tired now and all I wanted to do now was got home and sleep. What I didnt notice was that I was now crossing the street where Emma's building was located.

'Deven?' a voice called out my name but I was a little pre-occupied and didn't hear it.

'I think some girl is calling out your namee.' Ritwik said, I thought he was still making the same joke about Emma and me.

'Ha ha ha, very funny, I know there is no girl calling out my name, definitely not Emma.' I said and gave him a fake smile

He looked back and then looked back at me.

'Does Emma have brown hair?' he asked.

'Yeah, how do you know?' I asked him.

'Does she wear black spectacless?' he asked again.

'Yes, but how do you know that? I am pretty sure I didn't give you a desciption about how Emma looked.' I said.

'Is that her?' he pointed in the opposite direction. I turned around and saw Emma walking towards me in a haste.

'Slow down Emma, are you OK?' I asked, she was trying to catch her breath back.

'I have been shouting out your name since you left the store.' She said and I looked at Ritwik.

'Don't look at me, I told you.' He said.

'I am so sorry Emma, I thought he was just kidding. But tell me, was there something you wanted to talk about?' I asked her.

'No, I just saw you so I thought we could just talk about college and stuff. Where were you headed?' she asked, and then I realised I didn't actually introduce Ritwik and Emma to each other.

'Oh I am so sorry, this is Ritwik, my roommate, Ritwik, this is Emma, my friend from college.' I said and they shook hands after that, too formal, I know.

'I was just going to my apartment actually. So, tell me, what you wanna talk about.' I said.

'Well, I guess I will just go to the apartment and see if the store guys made that delivery. You guys can carry on. Bbye. Bbye Emma, nice meeting you.' Ritwik said and started walking back towards the building.

'So, that's you building, nice. Wanna join me for a walk?' Emma asked me.

'There's no harm in walking actually, you wanna have something to eat or something?' I asked Emma.

'What? You just know me for like, ten hours and you want to go out on a date with me?' she asked and I thought that maybe I had offended her in some manner.

'No, not like that Emma, I was just asking, I didn't mean to offend you in any manner, I'm really sorry if I did.' I said and then suddenly she started laughing.

'THAT was not funny.' I said.

'Oh yes it was, you should seen your face, why are you always so tensed up, Dev?' she asked.

'I am not tensed up, I just don't have any friends here, so basically, I just don't want to lose the ones I have made. The number is quiet small you know.' I said.

'Listen, I am a really nice girl, OK? Even if something happens, I don't ever leave my friends alone. I am like that only.' She said.

This thing with Emma was quiet decent, I made a friend in the college on my first day only, this was nice. Although, I did also make, sort of an enemy, but I didn't care about that at all.

'Do you think it's going to be a trouble, that senior thing? I mean, I am not bothered or scared or anything, but still, he was a senior in college, do you think he will carry a grudge?' I asked Emma.

'Obviously Deven, the guy was a senior, that's like the last thing you want to do in a college, make a senior you enemy, but in your case, it's more like, beating a senior on the first day. But I know he deserved it. The guy was a jerk.' She said.

'Well, if you say he was a jerk, I believe it. Do you know any other students in the class?' I asked.

'Yeah, don't you?' she replied.

'Actually, no I don't, they just don't seem like interested in talking.' I said.

'It's not them idiot, it's you. I saw the way you sit in the class, I saw the way you walk, plus that thing with beating up the senior, these guys are probably scared of you, or rather scared of beong seen with you.' She said.

'What is that supposed to mean?'

'Well, you know, "the guy who beat up the senior" has got to have trouble coming to his way. They probably just want to stay away from that trouble, not you.' She explained.

'Man, I have done that scaring thing again, you know, this has always been my problem, even in India, I have a lot of friends, but there are also people who think that I am a bad company. I don't know why.' I said, I was a little depressed learning that I might be the only person that my batchmates didn't wanna talk to.

'Awww, don't be sad, I am your friend now, first thing we do tomorrow morning, introduce you to the other guys in class, and girls too.' she said and punched me in my arm.

'Yeah right, the nerdy girls.' I said and we both laughed.

'Wanna have something to drink?' she asked me.

'What? Now you wanna date me?' I said and laughed.

'No, we have been out, just walking, it seems rude not to offer right?' she said.

'Yeah, that's exactly why I asked before. Tell me, what would you like to have?' I said and we walked towards a coffee shop.

In the midst of talking and walking with Emma, I just didn't realise that we had walked far away from our neighbourhood.

'Wait, where are we? I don't know the places around here. Do you know the way back?' I panicked.

'Yeah I do Deven, relax, it's not like we don't know anything.' She said.

'I am sorry, I just don't want to call my roommate to pick me up from somewhere, he might look really decent but I wouldn't hear the end of it after that.' I said.

We ordered two mochas to go, we took our glasses and walked out of the shop.

'You know Deven, I think we should go back now, it's getting dark.' She said.

'Yeah, I know. Let's go.' I said.

We walked back and I was relieved that she did actually know the way back. I walked her to her building and then I walked back to mine. Getting into the apartment, I knew I was going to be asked a lot of questions by Ritwik. But something totally different happened when I walked in.

I walked in and called out for Ritwik, he didn't reply, so I thought that he must have gone out for something. i went to the fridge looking for the food that we had brought for dinner. All I found was an empty bag from the "Punjabi Style".

'When did Ritwik start cheating on his diet regularly?' I wondered.

'Ritwik? Where are you man?' I called out his name again, I walked up to his room.

'Ritwik, are you inside?' I knocked on his door just to find that the door wasn't locked.

'Hey, dude, I have been…. OH MY GOD, I AM SO SORRY…!!' I ran out of his room. There was a girl with him and they were doing, well, "stuff".

'Fuck, I am so sorry; I didn't think you were going to be home this early.' He said, managing his towel. He didn't have the towel when I walked in on him and his, whoever she was.

'What did you think, dude? That I was going to stay at Emma's apartment for the night? Who is that?' I asked Ritwik.

'Well, she is, ammm, Shelly.' He said.

'Oh, then I am really sorry that I walked in like that on you and your girlfriend. But you know what, that's your fault.' I said.

'I know man, I should have called you or something, I should have told you that I had company.' He said.

'No, I mean, you should have locked the door atleast.' I said and we both laughed our guts out.

'I am so sorry, I shouldn't have come unannounced.' Shelly came out of the room and apologized.

'You don't have to apologise, really, it was my fault.' I said.

'No it wasn't, it was really inconsiderate of me to just come over. I am really sorry.' She said.

'Hey, you are his girlfriend, you can come anytime you want. I have no problem with that, I don't know about him though.' I said and looked at Ritwik who was just standing there holding his towel.

'Dude, I will tell you two things, one, you are still standing naked in front of your roommate, and two, you are ordering some food for your roommate after you get dressed, because your roommate is hungry as hell. And please for god's sake wear something.' I said as Shelly gave him the look.

'Oh, sorry.' He said and ran towards his room to get dressed.

I walked to the fridge to have some beer for myself.

'You want one?' I showed her the bottle.

'Yeah, I think I need one.' She said and I opened one for her too.

'I am really sorry, but I asked him to inform you, it's his fault he didn't tell you.' As she was telling me that, Ritwik came out of his room, fully dressed this time.

'That's because he was out on a date himself.' He said.

'Oh, really, three days in New York and you already have a girlfriend?' Shelly inquired, suddenly in her girly tone.

'She is not a girlfriend, she is just a friend of mine from college.' I told Shelly. 'And you better order some food for me now. I am really hungry and I just had a really long walk.' I told Ritwik.

'Yeah I was just going to ask you, what do you wanna have?' he said.

'Just order some *Kadhaai* chicken, or anything on the menu. I just want to eat something.' I said, as we were talking, Shelly kept staring at me.

'What?' I asked looking at her.

'Nothing, I was just trying to figure out your age, you certainly don't look seventeen to me.' Shelly said.

'That's just because of the beard I guess, I haven't had time to shave yet.' I said.

'Hmmm, so, tell me more about you, Deven, right?' she asked.

'Yeah, Deven Dhaanak. Well, there's not much to tell, I am from India, I am here to study Dentistry at the NYU college of Dentistry. My whole family is living in India only.' I told her.

'Oh, that's really nice. I am actually doing a management course in NYU. Though this is my last year in college.' She said.

'I have ordered some food for you, and dude, thanks for being so cool about this, and remember, you can also bring any girl up here.' He said and got smacked in his head by his girlfriend.

'Don't put ideas in his mind, he is just a kid. Please, don't listen to him Deven.' Shelly said.

'No no, I prefer not listen to his ideas most of the times, but right now his ideas seem really great, I get to have sex at least, it's been a long time, bro.' I said and we both bumped fists together.

'Well, you certainly have the looks, and believe me, if you can get a girl like Emma run after you twice; you can make her do anything, if you know what I mean.' He said, again got smacked in his head.

'Yeah, he knows what you mean; you have found just the perfect roommate for you, just like you. Don't you have a girlfriend in India?' she asked me.

'Yeah, I am not saying that I WILL do something right now, I will wait for the right moment, and stop talking about Emma like that you son of a bitch, how many times do I have to tell you. She is JUST A FRIEND.' I screamed at Ritwik and he laughed as loud as he could.

'HAHAHA, OK OK, I get it, you don't have any intention to screw your only friend at college, but whatever man, she is hot and in some time you will notice it yourself. Ok, I and my girlfriend are going to sleep now; you eat something and go to sleep, OK? You have college tomorrow.' Ritwik said and they both left the living room all to me.

'Hey, did the store guys make the delivery of the stuff we just bought?' I yelled from the living room.

'No, they called, they don't have any delivery boys tonight, and they will send the stuff tomorrow morning.' He yelled from inside his room.

'Ok.' My reply.

I sat there watching television as I waited for the food to arrive. After twenty minutes of all the channel switching fun I was having, the doorbell rang. I opened the door and received the order, paid the guy and sat on the dining table to eat. But as I was about to take my first bite, my phone started making noises.

'Hello.' I said.

'Hi baby, how are you?' it was Harshaali,

I looked at the time; it was 09:30 p.m here, which meant it was still morning in India.

'Did you reach home? How are you calling so early in the morning?' I inquired.

'Well, I am back home.' She said and stopped for a while, 'But the good news is, only I got back home last night, I came home because I had some scholorship tests for the Institutes and all. But now I am alone at home, which means that we can talk all the time.' she sand through the phone, she was really happy, and so was I.

'Really? That's the best thing that has happened in quiet a long time you know, I have so many stories to tell you babe, there is so much that happened in the past two days that we didn't talk.' I spoke at a really fats pace.

'Slow down mera *baccha*, we will be talking for a long time now, start with the college, tell me, how was you first day?'

And so we started talking that night. It felt great talking to her after such a long time, but it was actually worth it. I told her everything about my college, the first meeting with the Dean, getting accepted in the College, getting all the stuff and furniture from Ritwik's dad, my first day at college, my first fight within my first moments in college, my first friend Emma, everything.

'So, you managed to pick up a fight on the first day?' she asked.

'That wasn't my faut, he abused me, and you know I don't take crap from anyone, so I did what I had to do. I broke his nose.' I said and that made her laugh I don't know why.

'Yeah, that was so easy to do right? Dev, try to stay as calm as possible my baby, you are not there to get into fights or anything, you are there to become a doctor. OK?' she said.

'Yeah my baby, I know. I won't do that again. I promise.' I said.

'So, you made a new friend, what is she like?' she asked.

'Ammm, she is really, what is the word for her, ammm, she is really bubbly and one of those mischievous kids that you see running around in the class. She wears big glasses, just like me, talks a lot, walks a lot, and the best part is, she made friends in class, so I can improve my impression now, because I am a friend of the girl who is friends with everyone.' I told Harshaali.

'Haha, bubbly, that's nice. Don't you have college tomorrow?' she asked.

'Yeah I do, why?' I said.

'What is the time there? Check.' She said and I looked at the mobile screen.

'Fuck, I am so late, I am not gonna wake up on time now.' I cried.

'When do you have to wake up?' she asked.

'Around 7:30, why?' I said.

'I will call you, I have entered New York time in my phone in the World Clock, you sleep now, I will call you in the morning. Ok?' she said.

'OK baby, I will sleep now, I hope yours is the first voice I get to hear in the morning.' I said and we disconnected the call.

It was the best sleep I had in so many days; I had a chat with the person I wanted to be with. I knew being with her was nearly impossible for me now, but atleast I had the satisfaction of talking to her over the phone. I slept peacefully that night.

The next morning I woke up with the voice of my roommate's girlfriend instead of mine.

'Ritwik, I am getting late, where are my shoes?' she was shouting outside, in the living room.

'Here they are baby.' Ritwik said, these guys really didn't know how to keep it low. I mean, the whole night I heard noises from Ritwik's room, we shared a wall, the voices were really tormenting. It was really difficult for me to concentrate on anything else, so I picked up my phone and looked for my earphones and had to sleep while listening to the loudest song on my playlist. I got up and checked my phone. There were more than ten missed calls and a few messages from Harshaali.

'I tried to wake you up baby.'

'I think it's my fault I kept you up for that long.'

'I just hope you get up on time, if you do, just text me, Ok?' these were the texts that flashed on the screen of my phone. So, I texted her the moment I read all those messages.

'I am so sorry baby, I couldn't get up, but I am up now, and I am leaving for college now, so I will talk to you when I get back. Bbye *jaan*.' I texted.

I got up from the bed and went out in the living room, Ritwik was making coffee.

'Good, atlast you woke up, want some coffee?' he asked.

'Yeah, why was she in such a rush?' I asked.

'Well, she was also late for college, as are you. Go and get ready, have some coffee and leave ASAP, you are already late.' He said.

I knew I had to get ready quickly, so I skipped shower that day and sprayed a lot of perfumeon my self, had some coffee and rushed downstairs to order a cab for college. I was lucky enough that a cab was standing just outside the main door of my bilding.

'NYU?' I asked the cabbie.

'I am not free sir, I have to pick up someone, where exactly do you have to go?' he asked me. I was just about to leave just as he said that he would not go, but I still stopped to answer his question.

'College of Dentistry, why?' I asked.

'My other customer is also going to the same college, would you like to share a cab with her?' he asked, I was running really late now, so in an impulse, I said, 'Yeah, Ok, who is your other customer and why is she so late?'

'She will just be here in a moment, you can sit in the cab, I will talk to her, she won't have a problem, and she is a really sweet girl.' He said as I opened the cab door and sath behind the driver's seat.

'There she is.' He pointed towards a girl in pink.

'That's Emma, I know her.' I said.

'Well, I guess there is not going to be any problem the, right?' he asked.

'No there's not going to be any problem, she is a friend.' I said, Emma opened the cab door and sat inside without noticing me.

'I guess I have company... Deven? Hey..! What a coincidence. How are you? Wait, are we sharing a cab again?' she asked.

'Yeah, I am really sorry, but I was getting really late so I insisted on sharing the cab, you don't mind, do you?' I asked her.

'You crazy or what? Why would I mind? Let's go.' She said and the driver started his car.

'So, you got late today, eh?' she said.

'I guess we are both late Emma, aren't you worried at all?' I asked her.

'Worried about what? We are in a college Deven, we are not kids anymore, just relax, we will be there in no time.' she said and reclined in her seat a little.

'You worry a lot Deven, loosen up a bit, and enjoy the scenery outside.' She said and looked outside the car window.

There was nothing but skyscrapers in the whole scenery, there were cars going in a straight lane, people walking on the side rails, school buses picking up children, and elderly people walking outside. On our way we crossed the Central Park, one of the most visited places in New York, it looked so beautiful from the outside, the greenery and the smell f fresh flowers was to die for. Emma was right; all I had done in America till now was worry about one thing or the other. I needed some time out.

'Emma, are you free after college today?' I asked her, she opened her eyes and looked at me.

'Yeah, why?' she said.

'I just want to go out, like some nice place; I haven't really had a chance to know the city properly, what say? Can we do that?' I asked her.

'Of course, don't be so formal, we will go for a tour tonight, OK?' she said.

'Ok, thanks.' I said and smiled.

Moments later the cabbie dropped us in front of the college gate. I was thinking about Harshaali the whole time, I missed her and wanted to see her, but I knew that wasn't possible, that feeling of helplessness made me sad.

'What are you thinking? I have been watching you since I got inside the cab, is there something bothering you?' Emma asked.

'I don't know, maybe yes, I just miss my family, that's all.' I said.

'Hmmm, that happens to me too sometimes, but you know what, give it time, when you see that great stuff is happening for you here, you will be happy, and I am pretty sure your family will b proud of you.' She said and gave me a smile.

'Thank you so much, I feel like you are the only person that I can talk to here.' I said.

'Don't worry; we are going to change that today. Come; let's go to the canteen first.' She said and pulled me towards the canteen.

I saw a bunch of my classmates sitting in a circular manner and they had two chairs empty.

'Hi guys, this is Deven, he is…' she got interrupted before she could complete that sentence.

'The guy who beat up the senior yesterday, yeah, we all know about that. Hi, I'm Damien.' He got up and shook hands with me.

'Dude, you actually made the guy bleed, weren't you afraid of him, he was a senior after all.' Another guy said.

'No, actually, I would like to clear this out with you all, I am not the guy who just hits people without any reason, I punched him because he was abusing me and my family. He deserved it according to me, and after that, he didn't even have the courage to come up to me and fight again. Because he knows, I made him bleed once and I can do that again. But with you guys, I was really pissed by the fact that my classmates are not talking to me because I got into a fight.' had been preparing that speech for such a long time.

'It's not right guys, he is a nice guy, he is a friend of mine, just like you guys are. I think you should all give him a chance.' Emma said.

'And hot too, Hi Deven, I'm Tracy, this is my friend Laurel.' That was not what I was expecting. Tracy and Laurel kept looking at me and then at each other and laughing.

'Dude, we are your classmates, and now we are friends. Don't worry about us hating you or anything; we just thought that you were a bad news. Now that we know the whole thing, we respect you bro.' Damien said and raised his fist in the air, and I bumped it.

'So, we all OK now?' I asked.

'Yeah, and I guess we should head for the class now, we are late. Professor Whitman must have arrived in the class by now.' Laurel said and we all got up and walked towards the class.

'Hottie eh, didn't expect that.' Emma punched me in my back.

'What are you punching me for? It's not like I told these girls to like, but hey, thanks for doing that, now atleast I have some people I can talk to.' I said as we entered the class.

Professor Whitman started with Inorganic Chemistry and we all listened to him intently, I was also tryin to listen to what he was saying but my mind was wandering elsewhere. All I could think about was Harshaali and what she would be doing, although I knew she would have been sleeping at that moment, but still I wanted to be with her.

'Hey, do you wanna go out and have something? I am famished, didn't even have breakfast.' Emma passed me a note under her seat; she sat right in front of me.

'Ahemmm, ya.' I said in a really low pitched voice so that nobody would notice.

The lecture ended soon and Emma asked me to wait for her outside the classroom. I did as I was aksed, I stood outside the class and checked my phone for any new messages from Harshaali, but I wasn't that lucky. Suddenly, I saw Chris "the bully" walking towards me.

'You got some balls getting into a fight on your first day in college, and that too with me, do you have any idea who I am?' he said, I tried to ignore him and another fight in the college on my secondd day only. So I tried to move away from him.

'Listen to me you son of a bitch, last time you had the upper hand, next time, I will show you exactly who I am and what I can do, but not in college. Watch your back, kid.' He said and pushed me towards the wall. I lost my balance and almost took a bad fall, but Emma caught my hand.

'Hey, what happened? Are you alright?' she asked.

'What took you so long?' I asked her back.

'Nothing I was just talking to Damien about our fresher's party, he is the one planning it.' She told me. 'Is something wrong?' she asked again.

'No, everything's fine.' We walked towards the canteen.

'Two chicken sandwiches and cold drinks please.' I gave the order to the canteen waiter.

'Would you just tell me what happened, Deven?' she kept asking me the same question again and again.

'Why are you sure that I am upset over something?' I asked her.

'Because normally you are not like this, usually you talk about stuff, whatever is on your mind you say that, today you just sitting quietly.' She said.

'Ok, listen, in the morning it was just about missing my family, but now, just after I stepped out of class, that guy, Chirs came up to me and threatened me, I wanted to hit him again, god knows I did, but I just didn't want to create a scene agan in the college on my second day too, so I just kept quiet, you caught me from falling down back there right, that was because that son of a bitch pushed me, and yeah, he called me a son of a bitch again, I just remembered.' I told her the whole story, while she sipped in her cola.

'So what's the problem now?' she asked.

'What do you mean? Didn't you hear what I just said, it clearly means that he wants a fight again, and that too outside the college.' I told her.

'So? You kick his ass again and we have a good laugh over it, what's the big deal?' she said.

I looked at her with a smile on my face and said,

'You just want me to fight again, don't you?' I looked at her.

'Yeah, so? You are not gonna take bullshit from some lame guy, are you?' she asked me, more like, she suggested.

'Apparently, I'm not.' I said and then we ate our food. Then we went back in the third lecture and attended all the classes after that.

The day ended quiet smoothly, except that threat from that idiot. Emma and I were walking outside to call out for a cab, when he showed up again.

'I told you I was going to show you what a big mistake you made yesterday. Here I am.' He said, there were four other guys standing behind him, now I knew I was going to be beaten up. No matter how huge a Salman Khan fan I was, I couldn't take five guys at once.

'You mind if we steal your boyfriend for some time?' he looked at Emma, up and down, and asked her that.

'Yes, I do.' She said.

'Ahhhm excuse me?' he said, and so did I.

'Emma, go take a cab and reach home, I will see you later.' I said.

'No, you think you are really tough taking on a guy who already beat you in front of the whole school? Well, think again, because the moment you lay a hand on my friend, you are going to be facing a big Assault charge, now you decide, do you still wanna "kick his ass", or you wanna spend a week in jail.' She said, my mouth was open the whole time she was talking to him.

'You think you are really smart haan? Well, I am not scared of any charges or jail or anything, all I want to do is show this punk who I am, so just get out of my way.' He said, I could see that he was really pissed off now.

'Oh really, so you might even talk to the guys I called when you were threatening my friend.' She said and held her phone in front of his face. She had called 911, the emergency number in the States. Looking at her phone he must have realised that this wasn't just the right time to do what he had planned to do.

'You bitch, I will get my hands on him one day or other. Let's go guys.' He said and his minions followed him.

'Are you crazy? Why did you do that?' I screamed at Emma.

'I just didn't want to spoil my day out with you, also, I don't want to be seen with guy whose face has been bashed up badly. So, just chill, and call a cab, we have plans, remember?' she said, groaning heavily, I called a cab and we took off for the apartment.

'Do you want to change first or are you Ok going in the same clothes?' she asked me.

'I am Ok, why? You have to change first?' I asked.

'Yeah, obviously, I can't go out looking like this, this is just my college dress.' She said.

'Ok, we can stop by your place first.' I said.

The cab dropped us outside her building and I paid the guy. She started walking towards the door and I stood there.

'Want to stand out here in the cold? Why don't you com upstairs?' she invited me in.

'Ok, but make it quick, we don't have much time.' I said.

'Oh god Deven, relax, we are not late and we don't have any appointments or anything, we have plenty of time.' she said and pushed me inside the wooden door.

She opened the door to her apartment.

'See, that's my room.' She pointed towards one of the bedrooms.

'My roommate isn't home today, but I am really sorry for the way my place looks, I have a really messy roommate.' She said as I entered. I looked at her place, it was really messy.

'Yeah, that's ohk, my room used to look like this once, when I was in India.' I told Emma.

'You make yourself comfortable, I'll just be back in a moment.' She said and walked towardsher room.

'Ok, but make it quick.' I said.

'Yeah, sure.' She said.

CHAPTER 15

NY WITH A FRIEND

I WAS SITTING ON THE COUCH in Emma's apartment, I saw the the messy room from a different point. I was trying to compare it to my apartment; my apartment was a little bigger than this one, but this building had better facilities, like an elevator. I took out my phone to call Ritwik and tell him that I was going to be late today.

'Hello.' I said.

'Yeah buddy, where you are?' he asked.

'Amm, actually, I am at Emma's place and I ...' I was interrupted.

'Oh really? So what about your morals now buddy? Don't you have a girlfriend now that you want to be with your whole life?' he said.

'Shut up you pervert, I am just going to check out the city with her, she is just getting ready that's why I called, I will be late today, don't order any food for me either.' I told him.

'Yeah OK, and Shelly will be here, SO KNOCK.' He said.

'And you LOCK, Ok, bye now.' I said and hung up.

'Let's go, I am ready.' I turned to look at Emma, she wore a black short dress a little higher than her knees, cut from the shoulders, and she didn't put the glasses on, had her hair open and had some make up on too.

'Ahhh, you look… hot…' I said.

'Oh really, that's sweet, thank you.' She said.

'No glasses?' I asked.

'No, I got lenses too, you wanna get up now or are you going to look at me like the whole night?' she asked and I made a run for the door. I didn't even realise that I had been staring at her.

'So, where do you want to first?' she asked.

'Amm, let's go to the most famous places first.' I said.

'Like the Statue of Liberty, Central Park and Empire State Building?' she gave me a list of places to choose from.

'Let's go to the Central Park, have you been there before?' I asked.

'Yeah, and I am telling you, you will fall in love with that place. Trust me. It's one of the most beautiful and greenest places on this planet.' She said.

We came out of her apartment and she locked the door.

'You know anything else about that park? I mean, I have heard a lot about it from a lot of people, but I have no idea why it is so famous.' I said.

'Dude, you just came here, it will take time and a lot of roaming around for you to know about why New York is the best city in the world.' At this statement I realised something.

'Didn't you tell me that even you just moved to this city?' at this she turned to me, gave me a stare and started walking again.

'Sorry, I didn't mean to mock you.' I said.

'Just shut up and call a cab, genius.' She said and I smiled at her.

I tried calling a cab, but it took me more than five minutes to get even one of the cabs to stop.

'Central Park?' I asked the cabbie who was certainly cheecking out the hot girl I was standing with.

'Central Park?!' I screamed at him just to get his attention.

'Yeah, get in.' he said.

'That guy was totally checking you out.' I told Emma.

'Yeah, I know, I look pretty right?' she looked at me and giggled.

'Yeah you do, excuse me sir, do you know why Central Park is so famous around here?' I asked the pervert cab driver. It's a fact, if you want to know something about a city; the cabbies are the best people to talk to. They know the city inside and out.

'Man, you must be a tourist.' He said.

'No, actually I just shifted here, I am a Dentistry student. But that's not the answer to my question I guess.' I said.

'Well, the reason why Central Park is so famouswould be that it has all the right things in it, it has got lawns, playgrounds, fountains, castles and everything that makes it one of the biggest attractions of the world. You will just know more about it when you see it.' He said.

'See, I told you it was a big deal around here.' Emma said.

'Yeah I knew it was a big deal, but you didn't give me any significant points right? Now I am excited. Can you please drive faster, sir?' I asked the cabbie.

'Man, nobody ever calls me SIR around here, where are you from?' he asked.

'I am from India, why?' I asked.

'Must be a hell of a country, guys of your age here, they don't respect anything, and you, you my friend gave me respect. That's special.' He said, I felt a sense of pride in my country and I, we Indians are born to respect people, all our lives we are taught how to behave in front of our elders, then we grow up and we teach the same stuff to our children. This is something that is really remarkable about India. We respect everyone.

'Here's your destination, pal. Hope to see you soon, here, this is my number, call me up whenever you need a ride.' He said and gave me his card.

'That was simply impressive, making a friend just like that, I am speechless.' Emma said.

'Oh come on Emma, you and speechless, it's nearly impossible.' I said and laughed, she punched me again.

'So, this is Central Park.' I said as I stood on the Fifth Avenue, I wondered, why this park was so huge. Then I realised, this is the fucking reason this park is famous worldwide, I entered the park with Emma and a lot of expectations.

'This is huge, why didn't you tell me it was so big?' I asked Emma.

'I thought you already knew that this was the biggest park in the world, see, it's written here, this is a discovery kit, I just got one for you. This says that the park covers about 840 acres of land, imagine, this much land devoted only to greenery, that's so creative.' She said as she looked at the park, amazed, just as I was.

'Yeah, this is what makes it so special I guess.' I said and we started walking.

I saw Alice in Wonderland statues in the mid park, the Belvedere castle, the Bethesda fountain, Bethesda terrace and so on, and it was just the mid park are. There was a zoo situated in the South End of the park, a Discovery center in the North End, a separate place for people who came to the park only to play chess, there was a bridge named as Gapstow Bridge in the South End, Harlem Meer in the North End, a boathouse and so much more. This park was the coolest place I had ever been in my entire life. An ice skating rink in the South End, a ground or court for almost every sport like, baseball, basketball etc, this place was amazing. But however amazing it was, it was really huge and it was hard to walk through the whole park at once, so Emma and I decided to visit the place again sometime and we decided to get home, as we were getting late now.

'So, did you like it?' she asked as we were sitting in the cab.

'Like? I loved it, this is the best place I have been to my whole life, and you know what, this park has made me realise how much I want to stay in this country.' I said.

'Wow, that's really nice Deven, so you planning to stay?' she asked.

'I don't know Emma, I want to, but I will have to ask for my parent's permission if I want to stay and lead a life in the best city of the world.' I said.

'What permission? It's your life; you should get to choose how and where you want to spend it. Don't you think so?' she asked.

'No I don't, I know it's my life, but also, they are my parents, they have been there for me their whole lives, when they get old, when they need me, I want to be there for them, that's a bigger and more meaningful dream you know. Yeah, if I get to live here it would be nice, but if that makes my parents unhappy, I will gladly sacrifice one of my dreams for them, because I know, at some point in their life, they must have given up on one of their dreams just for my sake too.' I said.

'You really miss them, don't you?' she asked me.

'Yeah, I really do, I will talk to them as soon as I get to my apartment.' I told her.

Soon we were standing in front of Emma's apartment again, we paid the cabbie and I decided that I wanted to talk from there.

'Are you sure you don't want to come upstairs?' she asked me for the third time.

'No, I'm good, I just want to go to my room and talk to my parents now, and then I will sleep.' I told Emma.

'Ok, good night then Deven.' She said and went inside her building.

I started walking back to my apartment; I took out my phone again to check it for any new messages or missed calls. But there were none.

I reached my apartment and saw Ritwik and Shelly sitting on the couch, having beer.

'Thank god you guys are dressed.' I said and Ritwik laughed.

'What took you so long? Did you forget that you also had your own apartment?' he mocked me; he always did that when I told him that I was with Emma.

'You are not going to stop that, are you?' I asked him, taking out a beer for myself. I didn't have a habit of beer, but after living in the States for about a week, I had developed one, maybe there was something in the beer, they tasted different here, great, but different.

'So, where did you go?' Shelly asked.

'Central Park, I love that place.' I said and took a large sip from my pint. 'But I think I have a problem, I think your crap headed boyfriend was right when he said that Emma liked me.' I told Shelly.

'Really? How can you say that?' she asked.

'Well, after getting back from the park, I decided that I wanted to walk the rest of the way back home, so I got off with her in front of her building, she kept asking if I wanted to go upstairs to her apartment or not, she asked me three times, and the thing that made this suspicion was that earlier she had told me that her roommate wasn't even home tonight.' I told them.

'Duuuuuuuude, she so wanted you to stay there tonight.' Ritwik said.

'But why? For what?' I asked.

'To play tennis you dumb whore, why didn't you go?' he said.

'Because I don't know how to play tennis and moreover, because I have a girlfriend. Thankyou.' I said and took my dinner and another pint of beer to my room.

I called my mother that night, she was really happy to hear from me as I had not called for around two days. I told her all about college and Emma, I didn't tell her about the fights that I had been having with that bastard in the college, there was no use of telling her. I knew she would just panic and just catch the next flight to America, that's just how she was my whole childhood, severely over-protective. I talked to her and dad for some time and then hung up. I thought about calling Harshaali but I didn't have any idea about where she was and what she had been up to the whole day. So, I didn't. Instead, I had my dinner and beer and I slept.

The next morning I woke up and checked my phone, there were a lot of missed calls, all from my parents and my cousins in India. I instantly called back.

'Dad? What happened? You called me so many times last night, I am sorry but I was sleeping.' I said.

'I know you were. I need you to pack some stuff and get the first flight back home. It's urgent.' He said in a very serious tone.

'What's going on dad? Is everything Ok there? Is mom Ok?' I asked as I got scared by the impromptu call back home.

'Everything is fine, just get back home as soon as possible, get your tickets and text me when you land.' He said.

'Alright dad, I will tell my roommate that I will be coming home today.' I said and hung up the phone.

My father was never this serious, I mean, he was sometimes, but those times were really unhappy and distressing. I just prayed that everything was fine back home.

I got up and went in the living room and saw Ritwik and Shelly sleeping on the couch, they must have dozed off watching a movie or something.

'Ritwik, wake up.' I said.

'Huh, what?' he said in a sleepy voice, Shelly woke up too.

'I am just waking you up to tell you that I have to go home today; there is some kind of emergency.' I told him.

'What emergency? Is everyone Ok?' he asked.

'Yeah, that was my first question from dad when he told me to get the tickets. But he didn't tell me anything, he just told me to pack up some of my stuff and head back home ASAP.' I said.

'Ok, you go pack your bags, I will make you some coffee and help you out with the tickets, I will book them online and get the printouts. Worry not, everything will be fine.' He said.

'I know, but I am still worried, something is wrong man, otherwise my father would have told me the reason that he is calling me back.' I said.

Don't worry Deven, we are with you.' Shelly said, and looked at Ritwik.

'Do you want me to come with you? I will gladly accompany you if you want.' Ritwik suggested.

'No, if dad has called me in such a hurry, then probably it's just a family matter, must be something related to some property or whatever, I guess.' I said.

'Ok, I will get your tickets, you get dressed and pack your bags, and I will get you tickets for the first flight out.' He said.

'Thanks man, I will get ready. I will call Emma and tell her that I won't be attending classes for some time.' I said and went into my room to call Emma.

'Hello?' I said.

'Hi Deven, what's up?' Emma replied in her sleepy voice.

'I am just calling you so early to tell you that I won't be coming to the college for some time, I have to fly back to India for some important work.' I said.

'Hey, that's good, you were missing home, have fun and tell them about me and click a lot of pictures and send them to me, OK?' she said.

'Yeah, I will.' I said and hung up.

I started getting ready, took a shower and shaved, I needed to look decent if I was going home, and my dad didn't like my beard at all.

'Here, have some coffee.' Shelly made coffee and poured some for me.

'Thanks, hey did Ritwik leave to get the printouts?' I asked Shelly.

'Yeah, and he is going to drop you at the JFK, he just texted me your flight details, your flight leaves in two hours. Ritwik would be back any minute now.' she told me.

'Nice, I am all packed and ready to go now.' I said.

'Hey, are you ready?' Ritwik asked as he came through the door.

'Yeah, should we leave now?' I asked him.

'Yeah man, if you want to board that flight on time we have to leave now.' he said.

'Ok, let me get my stuff.' I said and got up to get my bag from my room.

We left the building and I called the cab driver who dropped me and Emma at the Central Park. He picked us up and we were on our way to the airport.

We reached the airport in an hour, all because of the traffic at that hour; it was the busiest hour on the NY roads as everyone was in a haste to get to their work places. Ritwik dropped me outside the airport.

'You take care now, and you call me as soon as you know what the problem was, Ok junior?' he said.

'Yeah man, thanks for everything you did today.' I said.

'Don't worry, that's the least I could do. Come back soon, Ok?' he said.

'I will try.' I said and we bid goodbyes to each other.

I was supposed to catch my flight in thirty minutes but I was still stuck in a very long security line, the checking at the JFK was really intense and it took almost half an hour. When I made into the flight, I called home again, to see if it was just a misunderstanding or did they actually wanted me there.

'Dad? I am on the flight, are you sure I have to come?' I asked.

'Yes, you have to. Call me when you land now, Ok?' he said.

'Yeah, I will, bye' I said and switched off my phone. I was not in the mood of talking to anybody after that, I just laid my head down and kept thinking about the worst case scenarios.

'What if something really bad has happened? What if someone has been in an accident of some kind? What if one of my relatives died?' all these creepy thoughts ran through my mind.

'Sir, any drinks you'd like to have?' a really beautiful air hostess asked, I needed a drink very badly.

'Yeah, can you get me a beer, please?' I asked the lady.

'Sure sir.' She said and went back to get me a beer. She came back with a tray that had glasses with brand names on it.

'Which one would you like, sir?' she said and I picked up the largest glass the tray had.

'Thank you.' I said and the air hostess moved on to serve the other passengers.

I felt like I was helpless in this situation, my mind kept on coming up with different scenarios, all of the bad ones, but I had to stay calm, it was still a long flight sit through and then I had to take a taxi or a cab or anything to reach Chandigarh from Delhi. I thought to myself that if I didn't distract myself, I would go crazy thinking about what the emergency was back at home. I didn't want to think of the bad stuff, so I decided that I would sleep through most of the flight or read a book or something, just to keep my mind wandering.

The announcement for the seatbelts was made and we took off, I was quite certain that whatever the thing was, it was quiet huge, otherwise my father would have handled it himself. I drank the big glass of beer that I had ordered and drifted off for a while.

I woke up three hours later and saw the same air hostess again, the one who brought my beer for me. I rubbed my eyes like a kid and realized that I had been sleeping since the plane took off.

'Excuse me, can you please tell me how long it's going to be till we land in India?' I asked her.

'Sir, it is going to be nineteen long hours, would you like to have something?' she told me.

'Yeah, another huge glass of that same beer, I would like to sleep a little longer this time.' I said and the lady smiled at me.

'I will get you the largest glass that we have, full of that beer, sir.' She said and went back again to bring the magic liquid.

She came back with a glass bigger than the last one.

'Sir, will this suffice?' she asked.

'Yeah, thanks again.' I said and picked up the glass from the tray.

An old man sitting next to me kept staring at me, he was an Indian, a tourist maybe, I thought to myself, what would the old man think of me, but then I realized that I didn't know him, and there was no way that he knew me, so I started drinking my second huge glass of beer.

'You look a little too young to be drinking alcohol, son? Are you Ok?' the old man finally said what he had in mind.

'Yeah, that's the thing uncle, normally I don't drink at all, but the situation I am in right now, it demands alcohol in my system, or else I would go crazy.' I told him.

'Whatever it is, it will be fine.' He said and touched my arm.

'Thank you, uncle.' I said.

I drank the whole glass till its last drop and felt a little dizzy in my head. I closed my eyes to catch some sleep, but the bad things started popping into my mind again. I knew I had to sleep, but it was just not possible anymore, no matter how much alcohol I had. I just wanted to know something about what had happened, but my father was adamant at his decision of not telling me anything, so I had to bear the pain of not knowing. I was unable to take my mind off from this situation, so I started thinking about New York; I started recollecting all the good stuff and bad stuff that had happened to me there. I tried thinking about Chris, and how I would go back and kick his ass once again, he was pretty annoying and I knew I would fight with him again, the way he stopped me and Emma that day that was his last move that he made against me.

Then I started thinking about Emma, how I made such a good friend in a matter of a few days, and how I started trusting her instantly, how she stood up for me when Chris wanted to beat me up with his friends. She was a really sweet girl, but a little idiotic too, she liked talking a lot; I thought that I would bring something for her from India when I got back.

Out of all the good things that happened in America till now, Ritwik turning out to be my roommate was the best. That guy was resourceful, he had contacts almost everywhere and he knew how to handle situations. I made a mental note that the first thing I would do when I got back from India, was get Ritwik to come clear with Shelly's sister, I mean, how long could they actually go on without telling her everything. Atleast by doing that Ritwik will give that girl a chance to get over him. Thinking about all these things calmed me down and my eyes became heavy, beer did most of the work in that, but now I could sleep.

It took me almost one and half hour to just sleep in peace, all that time I was planning how I would be welcomed back at home. Finally, after two hours of sleep seeking, I closed my eyes and drifted off.

After six long hours of sleep, I woke up, this time I was hungry as I had not even had breakfast. I called the same air hostess again and ordered some food, this was starting to become the longest trip of my life, all I could do was sit in my seat and think. But I was tired of that too, I had my dinner and then again called the air hostess.

'Do you have any books or magazines on the plane?' I asked her.

'Yes sir, we have a wide range of magazines, what would you prefer reading?' she asked.

'Just give me something that would put me back to sleep as fast as possible.' I told her.

'Hmmm, ok sir; let me see what we have.' She said and again went back to whatever magic place they had behind those curtains

'Here, I think this will help you sleep again.' She came back with a business magazine called Fortune; it had knowledge about business ventures, huge companies going bankrupt, corruption money and all that economy related stuff. It was just perfect to put me down to another nice, long nap.

'Wake up son, we are almost there.' The old man sitting next to me woke me up.

'Huh? Ohh, are we landing?' I asked the man and checked for my seatbelt.

'No, but we are about to, the pilot has made the announcement.' He told me.

I turned on my phone because I was supposed to call my father the second I landed.

'We are landing, wow; I have missed this place so much.' I said to myself.

As we were landing, the reality struck me hard, in a few more hours I was going to know what big emergency had shown itself at home, because of which I had to come back.

I got off the plane moments later, collected my bag from the checking area and walked outside the airport.

'Dad, I have reached Delhi, should I take the bus now?' I asked him.

'No, see, there must be a short, dark guy standing right outside your terminal gate, holding out a plank with your name on it. Go to him and tell him who you are, he will bring you home.' He said.

'Ok dad, I will call you again when I find that man.' I said and hung up.

I started looking for a sign that had my name on it, soon I saw the guy who was there to pick me up.

'Sir, are you Mr. Deven Dhaanak?' he asked.

'Yeah, I am, you are here to take me home right?' I asked him.

'Yes, sir. Please come this way.' He said.

He brought my father's car to pick me up, I texted my father that I was safely in the car and was headed home now.

'What is your name?' I asked the driver.

'Sir, Suresh, Sir.' He said.

'You don't have to call me sir, you are older than me, doesn't look nice.' I said.

'So, what should I call you, sir?' he asked.

'Call me bhaiya, or bhai, that sounds good.' I told him. 'Listen Suresh, do you have any idea what has emergency caused this sudden trip of mine back to India?' I asked him.

'I don't know sir, I was appointed by your father just today, his regular driver didn't show up.' He said.

'Oh, Ok, drive a little faster please, I really want to reach home as soon as possible.' I said and rested my head on the rear headrest. I was exhausted from the flight. Although, all I did in the flight was eat, drink, sleep and pee. I fall asleep in the car too, Suresh woke me up, and God knows I wish I had not woken up that day. I wish I never came to know.

Suresh pulled up in front of my house and woke me up.

'Bhaiya, wake up.' I woke up instantly and saw a huge crowd of people in front of my house, mostly my neighbors and my relatives. I saw a familiar face.

'Hey, Vijayent uncle, what happened?' I asked, he held his head down and didn't say anything.

'Will anyone please tell me what happened?' I screamed at the people standing outside my house, I could hear loud screaming and crying noises from inside, my heart started pounding.

'Deven?' Naman's voice fell onto my ears.

'Bhai, what's going on? Nobody is telling me anything. Please tell me what happened.' I said,

He looked at me with tears in his eyes, I kept yelling at him to tell me what was going on, when he hugged me and started crying.

'Deven, Saman is no more, we lost our brother, Deven.' His words made me a still picture, I didn't move, I couldn't cry, I couldn't speak. I just hugged him there and did nothing else. The moment I saw my father, it all became so clear to me, they didn't tell me anything because of this particular reason. If they had told me what had happened, I would have never showed up. I took Naman with me inside; I didn't have the strength to face my family in this moment. I couldn't face them if I wanted to.

We went inside the front door and I saw everyone sitting on the floor, my mother sitting in a corner crying and sobbing heavily, but my massi, she just sat there with a numb expression on her face. I went closer and sat in front of her. She looked up at me, teary eyed.

'Deven? Your brother is gone Dev, he's gone forever. Where were you Dev? Why were you not with him?' she screamed at me, she cried in front of me and all I could do was close my eyes and think that it was all a bad dream.

'Massi, I was gone for less than a week, if I had known this would happen, I would never have left him alone, never.' I had no idea what had happened.

Naman picked me and took me into Saman's room.

'He had an accident, his car ran off the Morin hills, stop crying, I have something to tell you.' I tried not to cry at all, but this was something that was never expected.

'Tell me, what happened exactly?' I said.

'He didn't come home last night, you know he never does that, I just thought that he might have been attending some party or something so I didn't say anything to anyone, mom and dad were not here, so for a moment I thought that he was at some friend's place and was having a night out or something, but here's the thing, his girlfriend called me this morning, she was with him last night, she told me that he was no more, and I have a strong suspicion that this was all planned. Do you know who his girlfriend was?' he asked.

'Yeah, that girl Neha, I have seen pictures of them together, but I have never met her or talked to her on the phone.' Saman was really secretive about his relationship with Neha, he never told us about her or talked about her in front of us.

'I think our brother was murdered.' He said.

'What?! How can you say that?' I was shocked at his judgment. 'Who would want to kill Saman?' I asked.

'Neha.' He said.

'Naman, this is a really huge thing to articulate brother; you have to have solid proof of this. We can talk about this later, we need to be with them, and they need us. Where is his body?' I asked.

'Postmortem is still going on, we need to know if he was drunk or it was actually a planned killing, if he was drunk, we cannot do anything, if he wasn't..' I interrupted him.

'Then I will go to that whore's place and kill her with my bare hands.' I said.

'Hmmm, let's go, we should be out there.' He said and we left the room.

Everything that I had thought of, everything that I was afraid of just became real and came rushing into my life, it was the most horrifying moment of my life, and I heard the ambulance siren.

'Saman is here.' Maasi screamed and ran towards the door, she fall a couple of times, the shock had made her weak.

'Maasi wait.' I ran after her just to catch her and stop her from going outside, I knew the only she was going to see out there was Saman's dead body, but she didn't stop.

Every once in a while there is a moment when all the people in your life and your surroundings come together for one cause. They had their cause, each and every person in our neighborhood and our family was standing in front of that ambulance just to see Saman's dead body. Naman and I stood there, trying to comfort our mothers and fathers, but that was our family's day of grief.

They opened the door of that ambulance and took out the body, it was wrapped in a white cloth, still tied so that the body wouldn't fall in the back of the ambulance, and his head was still bleeding so the doctors had put a lot of cotton around his neck and under his head.

'Saman, please wake up Saman.' Taauji stood there, helpless.

We had to see it all, we had to stand there and see our family shatter in front of our eyes. The hardest part was that we were not able to do anything. All we could do was stand by them and support them as much as we could.

'I have lost one of my hands today, my family is broken, I don't want to live anymore.' Taauji cried.

I had never seen that man cry in my entire life, but his fate had made him bow down to the reality, his son was gone and he was never coming back, Naman didn't cry in front of them at all. He wanted them to see that he was right there, he was standing there hugging his father, hoping that Saman would somehow wake up and join them, but he didn't.

My father sat there with his head hung low.

'They used to live with me.' he said.

'It's not your fault, Manoj. You cannot blame yourself, we all have to be strong, and we have to be there for them.' My mother said and pointed towards maasi and taauji.

What we could do, what could we possibly do in a situation where God had betrayed us in such a manner that we couldn't even stand together, our strength was gone.

For Naman and me, Saman was a pillar of strength, he was like a parent who used to take care of us, but now we had lost him and there was no way that we were getting him back.

'Tomorrow we will pay him his last respects, it is our humble request that all of you be there.' My taauji told everyone and we took his body inside. It was late, we were still sitting around his body that was covered in white, I sat there reliving all the moments that Saman and I had spent together, but not even a single drop of tear dropped from my eyes, atleast in front of our parents.

I got up and went into Saman's room where I saw Sakshi and Naman looking at the laptop screen and Sakshi was crying.

'What are you guys looking at?' I asked them.

'Don't come here, you won't be able to see this.' Naman said.

I ignored him and saw what they were looking at; these were the photographs of the accident scene. The police had taken some of these pictures and some of them were taken by Naman.

I saw the pictures and things became so clear, why Naman was suspicious.

'How can this happen? This doesn't make any sense, Naman.' I said.

'That's the reason we are going to file a case against that bitch, she will not live a happy life if she had anything to do with this, and I am pretty sure that she had.' Naman said.

'We need to tell taauji about this, he is a lawyer Naman, he has connections.' I said.

'Right now, if I show these pictures to him, he will take his revolver and shoot that Neha in her house, with her parents, do you want that?' he said.

'I actually do, but no, that would be wrong.' I said.

'That's why we have to show these pictures to the police first and ask some questions.' Naman said, he had a list of anomalies that he thought didn't add up in the scenario. When they found Saman and his car, his body was half fallen out of the backseat, the first thing that was suspicious was that how the hell did the body get there, how can a 6 feet man jump from the driving seat and end up in the backseat of the car?. The second thing that didn't add up in this equation was that, if he died in the car, how is it possible that there were not even a single drop of blood on the seats? The third thing was that, the left side i.e. the passenger side of the car was completely destroyed but the driving side was not harmed at all, then how did he get that wound on his head?

These were few of the things that we thought made this look like a pre-planned murder, but we were not sure.

Whatever it was, we were bothered, but we were so preoccupied with other stuff that we didn't have time to think about this. The next morning, after all the last rituals for Saman, we took his body for cremation purposes. That was the time when we had to do the hardest thing in our lives, according to Indian values, we had to pick up his body and take it to the cemetery, where the holy rituals of cremation of his body were to be performed.

'This is the last time we can see his face, I want to see it, it doesn't matter how spoiled it is because of the accident, I don't care, I want to see him, the last time.' I told Naman and he took me there, he told everyone to leave the room for some time.

My hands trembled, I was about uncover my dead brother's face for the first and last time, it was the hardest thing I had ever experienced in my life. The moment I picked up the white sheet from his face, which became the first moment I cried with an open heart.

The best looking out of all of us, he lied there with his eyes closed. All the memories that I had of him came running back in a second, all the times we were singing together, all the times we played cricket in the front lawn, and everything became a last memory. I remembered the time when I had just started driving, he was the one who took me for my first drive, he was the one who taught me the rules, he had such a huge part in my life, but now all I had was his memories.

Naman picked me up and hugged me, he cried with me in that moment, we were exhausted but we had not cried, we tried to maintain our strength, we wanted become our parent's strength. In all this, we forgot that we were still humans; we also had emotions that had to come out. I stopped crying and wiped off Naman's tears too.

'Let's call everyone and take him, I cannot see him like this anymore.' I said.

'Hmmm… Ok.'

We called everyone inside and picked him up, a priest started his departing hymns and we started walking, the ladies in this ritual are not allowed to be in the cemetery, so we left all of them behind and they all cried as we were leaving and taking Saman with us.

We reached the cemetery after a long, hard walk with Saman on our shoulders, and we prepared his body for the last rights. The priest carried the out and it was Naman's turn to pay his last respects by giving fire to his brother's body. He did the most unbelievable task and cried all along.

'Brother, we will miss you.' He said and burned his body.

That as the end, the end to our brother's life with us, with his family, the people who needed him the most, he had just abandoned them forever. We came back from the cemetery and took a bath as we were supposed to. There was so much that we had endured, so much that we had seen in the last few days that we had become habitual to consoling people and see them cry in front of us. People came to us and told a lot of stories about Saman, we knew some of them, but some of them were new for us. That was it, now all we had of him were his memories.

Naman and I went out for a walk that evening.

'What have you planned now? When are you going to show those pictures to taauji?' I asked.

'Tomorrow, you should leave Dev, you should not be here now, trust me, I can handle everything here.' He said.

'Hmm, I know what you think about me brother, but you have to promise me one thing, you will get to the bottom of this and promise me, the moment you find those bastards who did this to Saman and all of us, you will give me a call, promise me.' I said.

'I will, I promise, I need you to be with me at that time, I need a hand in killing those bastards.' He said, the rage in his voice was so clear.

'I will leave tomorrow, is that Ok?' I asked.

'Yeah, I will drop you to the station, you should go and pack.' He said.

'Hmmm, I will.' I said and we came back.

I told everyone that I was leaving the next day, some of my relatives asked me to stay longer, and some suggested that I should go.

'You both are my pride, you both have to do something that everyone will be proud of in our family, not just me, all of our clan all of our friends, do you both get it?' taauji said as I touched his feet before leaving for Delhi.

'You just take care of yourself taauji, we will handle everything.' I said and left with Naman.

He dropped me to the train station and hugged me; he was just about to cry when I stopped him.

'I am leaving because you said that you could handle things, if you cry now, I will just stay, I won't go.' I said wiping off his tears and controlling my tears in front of my only brother now.

'I won't cry at all, I promise. I will take care of everything here, don't worry and study hard there, remember everything dad said.' he told me and I touched his feet before leaving. I had never done that in my life before, but it seemed like the right moment to start.

'Bye brother, I will see you soon.' I said.

'Bye, take care.' He kissed me on my forehead.

I didn't look back at him for even once, I didn't have the courage, and I knew that if I turned back and looked at him, I would just relapse and stay. So I decided not to look at my brother.

My train reached Delhi railway station in about five hours and I took a cab for the airport, I was exhausted but I still kept going. I reached the airport just in time for my flight, no matter how much I tried; I couldn't stop thinking about my family. I couldn't take my mind off it. I boarded the flight and ordered a large glass of neat vodka, on the rocks. After having that big glass of pure vodka, I cried for hours, I can't even remember when I dozed off while crying.

I woke up to the announcement of landing when the air hostess came to my seat to check if I had my seatbelt on.

'What? Are we landing?' I said.

'Yes sir, I tried to wake you up earlier for dinner and for breakfast, but you didn't wake up.' She told me.

'Screw dinner and breakfast, get me another glass of vodka, neat.' I said.

'Sir, we are not allowed to serve alcohol before landing.' She told me.

'My brother just died, I just came back after cremating him yesterday I need that drink, please get me one.' I told her, she gave me a saddened expression and brought my drink to me. I drank the whole glass in less than a minute. A few minutes later, we landed at the JFK airport.

CHAPTER 16

LIFE AFTER DEATH

I GOT OFF THE PLANE AND switched off my U.S number; I saw numerous messages and missed calls from Harshaali and so many other people. In the midst of all that had happened at home, I forgot to meet or even call Harshaali, she didn't even know that I was in India. I thought of calling her but I was not in that place, I couldn't tell her what had happened just now, I wanted to go home first, to my apartment.

'Hello, Ritwik?' I called him as soon as I got a cab.

'Hey brother, how are you? Are you back?' he asked.

'Yes I am back, where are you?' I asked him.

'I am home, come on home, I am waiting.' He said.

'Hmmm, Ok, I am coming.' I said and hung up.

I was in the neighbourhood soon; I pretty much had the idea of roads close to my apartment by now. I saw a wine shop and aksed the cab driver to stop and wait for a while.

'I will be right back, just give me five minutes.' I said and got off the cab quickly.

I went up to the wine shop and asked for two bottles of whisky, two six packs of beer and a few bottles of vodka, the same brand that I had in the flight. I paid the man and took all the bottles to the cab and started placing them in my bag.

I reached my building soon and got off the cab. Entering my building I saw a guy from the restaurant, "Punjabi Style", I stopped and asked him if he would take a home delivery order right there. He recognized me and took my order.

I entered the apartment and saw Ritwik and Shelly sitting in the couch and watching television. I walked in and kept the six packs on the kitchen shelf, they heard me.

'Hey man, how are you?' Ritwik came and hugged me.

'I am Ok, how are you two?' I asked.

'Wow, you brought beer.' He said with a big smileon his face.

'Yeah, and I brought these too.' I said and threw two cigarette packets at him.

'Woah man, what's wrong? Are you Ok? And what was the emergency back in India?' He asked.

'Hmmm, let's sit and talk, I am tired.' I told him, I picked up three bottles of beer and took out the rest of the alcohol from my bag.

'Keep it in the shelf, will you?' I asked Ritwik.

'Dude, will you tell me what happened?' he said as he took the bottles from my hands and placed them gently on the sofa.

'Hmmm, give me one of the packets, I need a smoke.' I said.

'The way you are talking now, even I need one, would you just tell me?' he yelled.

'My older brother died in a car accident. Can I get one now?' they both looked at each other and then looked at me with sympathy in their eyes.

'I am so sorry to hear that Deven, how did it happen?' Shelly asked as I lit a cigarette for the first time but as soon as i dragged the first puff out of it, it made me cough at.

'You like this shit?' I asked Ritwik.

'Hmm, I know you must have gone through a lot brother, but now you are here, try to forget it and move on with your life. I guess your brother would have wanted that for you.' He said as I kept on sipping in beer and dragging small puffs of that cigarette, my first cigarette.

'It does reduce the tension, you were right.' I said, tears started rolling down my eyes, I started thinking about Saman and his face kept blocking all the other images in my mind. All I could think about was Saman and what our family had to go through.

'Hey, come here.' Ritwik said and hugged me.

'I don't have anything left, my brothers were my power and my strength my whole life, everybody used to be jealous of us, we were that united, we never fought amongst ourselves, my family is broken in half and I have to stay here, alone and away from each and every person that I love, this is killing me.' I said and cried on Ritwik's shoulder. Shelly held my hand and took away the beer and cigarette.

'Listen to me Deven, I know it hurts right now, but in some time you will understand that the people who leave us behind to cry, they are actually our enemies, you will get stronger because of this, trust me, I have been through this myself, but all I did after getting over that incident was get my graduation degree and study, I have had my share of fun too, you know that right? I am always here with you man, whenever you need me and whatever you need me for. I am just a wall away, always remember that.' He said and tapped my shoulder.

'Can we all go out tonight? I don't want to stay in.' I asked looking at Shelly who now had tears in her eyes as well.

'Hey, what happened to you now?' I asked her.

'Yes, we will go out tonight.' She said wiping off her tears.

We all got up and Ritwik thought of a night club that was close by, we decided that we would go there and have some drinks and then get back home. All three of us got dressed and we took a cab for the place, we reached there in just about ten minutes. We got off the cab and I took a look around, the place was a little weird and the owner did not put a lot of thinking into the name of the place, the was was called "What's Up", like really dude, you open a night club and you name it what's up, that's just stupid. But whatever the name was, we went inside and I went straight to the bar.

'One large whisky, neat.' I screamed at the bartender, the place was so loud that I could barely hear my own voice.

'Sure sir.' He said and brought a glass half full of the golden colored fluid.

'Thanks.' I screamed again.

'Hey, you shouldn't drink this much, man.' Ritwik came up to me and said.

'Yeah, he is right, come with us, I think we know what could lighten up your mood.' Shelly said and pulled me into a corner where I saw a familiar face.

'Emma?' I said.

'Hi Deven, when did you get back?' she said, her voice sounded like she had been drinking for a while.

'I just got back today.' I said.

'Everything Ok back home?' she asked, i looked at her and she looked really happy and it seemed like she was enjoying herself, so I didn't tell her.

'Yeah everything's fine, you tell me, how's college?' I asked her, changing the topic instantly.

'Oh college is good, you know our Physics professor changed, there is some weird guy now, keeps on staring, I don't even know his name, so I call him stares-a-lot professor, isn't that a cool name?' she asked, laughing. Shelly was actually right, talking to a friend did help my mood a little.

'Come let's have a drink.' I told Emma and she followed me to the bar.

'What would you like to have?' I asked her at the counter.

'Ammmmm, I will have what you are having.' She said after thinking for a while.

'Are you sure?' I asked.

'Yeah, what is the order?' she asked me.

'Whisky, neat, two, large.' I signalled the waiter and he made our drinks for us.

'What was the emergency?' she asked again.

'I really don't want to talk about it.' I said and took a big, burning gulp of that liquid.

'Finish your drink; I want to talk to you outside.' She said and we finished our drinks to get out of that place.

'What did you want to talk about?' we were walking outside the club.

'Nothing, I just wanted to tell you something, I am pretty drunk right now, and I guess it is just the alcohol that's messing up my mind. But I am just going to say it out loud now that you are in front of me, see, when you were gone, whatever work it was that you were busy with, I was still here, I went to college, I went out with friends, I did everything that I do usually, but there one unusual thing that kept on happening again and again, I missed you, I thought about you all the time, I cursed myself for not having your contact number, I just couldn't get you out of my hean for a single second. I know this is too early, it's been less than two weeks that we have known each other, but I think I like you Deven, I really do.' She said and we both stopped, I looked at her in that moonlight and she looked beautiful, her hair was a mess, probably because of the dancing, she kept moving from right to left and then again from left to right just because she had had a lot of alcohol, but she looked beautiful, she didn't have he spectacles on, her hair was not tied like she usually tied them, but they looked great too. In that moment I had nothing else on my mind, maybe which was also because of the alcohol I'd had. I cleared my throat to speak.

'Emma.' I said her name and then looked up at her, she just stood there waiting to hear what I was about to say, 'You look beautiful tonight.' I said and she smiled like a baby.

'Thank you Deven, see I just told you that I like you and you just told me that I look beautiful, that has to mean something, because if it doesn't….' I kissed her and interrupted whatever she was saying, I didn't listen to a word she said because I was just busy looking at her face.

'You talk too much.' I said as I released her face from my hands.

'Yeah? I just dont remember what I was about to say.' She said and kissed me again, this time the kiss was more passionate, from both our sides, she leaned in and I held her waist, her skin was so soft, she was wearing a blue colored top and it slid up a little when she raised her hands to fold them around my neck.

'I guess this was exactly what I wanted to talk about.' She said.

'Is you roommate back?' I asked her.

'Yeah, what about Ritwik? Is he still living with you?' she asked and we both laughed at her silly question.

'Obviously he is, but you know what, he doesn't mind if I have company.' I said.

'I guess I am staying at your place tonight.' She said and we hailed a cab for my apartment.

We reached my building and I got a call from Ritwik.

'Hey, did you guys leave already?' he asked.

'Yeah, I am at the apartment, and I am not going to be alone, so KNOCK.' I said and he laughed.

'Oh really, yes I will knock I am pretty sure, here Shelly wants to talk to you.' He said and gave the phone to Shelly.

'What the hell are you doing mister? I didn't take you to Emma for this.' she said.

'Well, it's your fault now, I am leaving, and don't call, I will leave the door open for you guys, bbye.' I said and disconnected the call.

I took Emma upstairs, she looked Ok now, earlier she looked wasted but now she was fine. Although I was a little tipsy on my steps, I guess the neat whisky that I had didn't suit my system that well. I opened the door for her and she entered the apartment.

'You guys have maintained this place pretty well, it's like boys never lived here, you guys must be really organized.' She said as I took out some cigarettes from my bag.

'You smoke?' she asked me.

'Just started, do you?' I asked.

'No, you know this is a really bad habit right?' she said.

'I know, but the way I see it, it calms me down, there was a time I used to hate it, but now I don't.' I said.

'Hmmm, how many in one day?' she asked.

'2-3 maximum, no more than that.' I told Emma.

'Hmm, then it's Ok, just don't start smoking a lot.' She said.

She sat on the couch, close to me and held my hand.

'I know you are sad, I can just feel that, I don't know how, but I do. If you ever want to tell me, just know that I am always there for you.' She said.

'Emma, can I ask you something?' I said.

'Yeah, ofcourse.' She replied.

'Why do you like me so much? I have not done anything that special, and I am definitely not the best looking guy in the world, can I know the reason?' I asked her.

'You don't really need a reson to like anyone Deven. The moment I turned and saw you and then talked to you, I instantly had this liking for you that never stopped increasing, I tried to tell you before, but there was never a good time, I guess there never really is.' She said.

'Hmmm, to be frank, I knew this before you told me, I saw the hints, I just didn't want to say it myself.' I told her.

'Signs? OH MY GOD, do you all know? You, Ritwik and his girlfriend too?' she asked.

'Yeah, actually they are the ones who made me realise that, they knew it before I did.' I told Emma.

'Hmm, so why didn't you ever ask?' she said.

In that moment, I wanted to tell her about Harshaali, but I couldn't, I was so selfish in that particular moment that I preferred lying instead.

'I don't know actually, I just didn't know if I even should tell you that, I thought it would be best if you told me yourself.' I said, I genuinely felt guilty for not telling her the truth, but there I was, sitting with a smoking hot girl, who by the way, just told me that she liked me, who was talking

266

to me, who was giving me her time, man, I wasn't gonna screw that up. I told you, SELFISH.

'If you would have told me before, I would have just denied it and would have felt all embarrassed. It's actually good you didn't tell me before.' She said.

She was an adorable girl, she was like those kindergarten children who have no idea what's the world like and all they ever want to do is play around and have a great time, she was such a sweetheart and I had been through so much lately that I found it pleasing to be with her and just talk, although I didn't want to talk about Saman in front of her. I wasn't sure if she would understand, also, I didn't want to cry in front of a girl.

'Can I ask you something?' she said.

'Hmmm…'

'What happened there, I mean back in India, is everyone Ok there?' I looked at her and saw the honesty and care in her question, I knew she wanted to be a part of my life and that was the question that she had been wanting to ask the whole night, she just didn't want to ruin our moment together before. Looking at her, I realised how stupid it was to call her a friend, girls this pretty can never be friends, they are always your crush first, and when you know that you are never gonna get the girl, you decide to make her your friend so that you can just stick aroud her for some time, but that wasn't the case with me.

Her question made me a little emotional as it brought back a lot of bad memories, a tear rolled down my cheek as I was still looking at her.

'Hey, Deven what happened? Now you are scaring me, please tell me.' she said coming closer and holding my hand.

I wiped off my tears and controlled my emotions, and then I looked at her again, this time I knew I was going to kiss her, and I did. I just leaned in and she didn't stop me either, instead she shifted a little in her seat just to kiss me back, one of her hands on my right shoulder and the other one was on my left cheek, the kiss became more and more passionate as the seconds ran by, we both shifted on the couch and I pushed her, forcing her to lie down on her back. My hand shifting from her waist to her back, just caressing her soft skin as her top was lifted a little, giving me access to her back, I felt the hook of her bra in my hand and at my first impulse I opened it. She stopped kissing to speak.

'Deven, that was impressive.' She said and I just looked at her and gave her a wicked grin.

'Well, call it practice.' I said and kissed her again.

'We should move this to the bed I guess, your roomie must be on his way.' She said and I followed her to my room.

She sat on the edge of my bed waiting for me as I closed the door, I turned around and there she was, the first girl in America, and in my life to be exact who had a crush on me before I had a crush on her. I never in my wildest dreams had imagined that a girl like Emma would like a guy like me, but apparently she did, and she liked me a lot. I came close to her and held her face in my hands gave her a little peck on her lips and moved away.

'What happened?' she asked.

'Nothing, just forgot something. I will be back in ten minutes.' I said and ran out of my room and out of the apartment. The second I looked at her sitting on my bed, I knew it was going to be an amazing night, and I didn't want anything to screw it up. So I ran as fast as I could and reached a medical store just around the corner.

'Amm, can I get a pack of condoms, sir?' I asked the old man sitting on the counter and he ordered one of his workers to hand me one. I grabbed it and paid the old fellow and ran back towards my building.

'Hey buddy, what are you doing out here?' a male voice stopped me in my tracks, it was Ritwik.

'Ammm, I was just going to the apartment, where's Shelly?' I asked.

'She is at her parent's, had some work, she will be here after some time, but what are you doing out here? And where's Emma?' he asked.

'Ahhh, she is in my room, waiting for me to get these.' I said and showed him the thing that I had bought just now.

'Hahaha, that's great, so do you want me to come home or should I give you guys the apartment tonight?' he asked me.

'Dude, I am going to do it in my room, not the entire apartment, you can come.' I said and he laughed.

'Listen, she is waiting for me, do you mind if I leave now?' I asked.

'No man, not at all, goes have fun.' He said and I ran off again.

I reached the apartment in less than two minutes and opened my room; I kept the packet in my denim pocket to maintain a little modesty.

'Where were you, I was just about to call.' She said, she was standing in the living room waiting for me.

'Nothing, I just ran out to get something and then ran into Ritwik so I stopped to ask him a favour.' I said.

'What favour?' she asked.

'Let's just say that we have the entire apartment to ourselves tonight.' I said and she laughed.

'You are such an idiot Deven.' She said and came closer and kissed me on my cheek.

'You look exhausted, come let's lie down in you room.' She said.

'Ok, but tell me, do you want something to eat? We can order now, I am quite hungry.' I said.

'Yeah Ok, order some chicken. That would work.' She said.

'Ok, let me see if we have enough beer.' I said and opened the fridge, there were three rows in the fridge that we could use to keep our food and supplies, but all they carried were beer bottles.

'I guess you guys have nothing but beer, you drink that much?' she asked.

'Nah, we never actually realised that we had so much beer in the apartment, oh yes, now I remember, I bought two six packs on my way back from the airport today. That's why we are stashed up on beer.' I told Emma.

'You and your roommate are just so alike, I don't know what it is about you two, but somehow you guys are really similar.' She said.

'Well, it's good to have a roommate like Ritwik, he is a really nice guy, plus he takes care of me all the time and you must know, I need a lot of care sometimes.' I said and winked at her, yes, I had also learnt the art of winking, living with Ritwik.

'Hahahaha, Ok Mr. Deven Dhaanak, let me take care of you now.' she said and kissed me again, on the lips this time. I kissed her back and took her to my room again where I pushed her right back where she was when I ran out to get "medical supplies".

'Hmmm, I have been waiting for this, and I had no idea this would be so good.' She said while kissing me.

'You talk too much, really.' I said.

We kissed for a long time, I took off my shirt on a reflex and she took off her top seeing that I was getting ready, I had unhooked her bra before but it was still lingering by her shoulders, so I helped her take it off completely. Her soft, milky white skin was perfect, and the little black mole just between her breasts made her body look even more desirable. Her breasts looked so luscious, I caressed them softly first and she moaned, and then I pressed them more passionately. Her nipples became hard and perky and I nibbled on them softly, kissing them and rubbing them between my fingers. The interval beetween her moans decreased, I knew she was enjoying it. I kissed her neck again, giving her a soft and gentle bite on her shoulder, I reached for her lips once again, and the kisses became more intimate, her hands running up and down my back and my hands still playing with her breasts. Slowly and gently I kissed my way down to her belly, reaching for her belly button.

'Something in mind, just stay like this.' I said and went out into the living room to bring the vodka bottle that I had bought from the wine shop that day.

'What are you gonna do with that?' she asked.

'Hahaha, something I have always wanted to do, belly button shots.' I said.

'You are incredible with this Deven.' She said as I poured some vodka into her belly button.

'What are you waiting for, go ahead, fulfill your fantasy.' She said.

'Just wait, let it settle down completely.' I said and slowly went down to her belly button and covered it with my lips, I took that shot and it helped me turn her on even more.

'My turn.' She said pulled me onto the bed.

I looked at her, but there was no eye contact, she just started kissing my body all over, starting from my chest and then slipping down slowly to my stomach until she reached my denims.

'Mind if I take them off?' she winked.

'Not at all.' I said and she unbuttoned it quickly.

The stuff that she did with her tongue was just inexplicable, she was like a magician down there, half of the stuff she did down there, I didn't even know could be done by a girl. I already had a hard on when she unbuttoned my denims, but when she started the 'Licking and Sucking' action. She knew each and every trick in the book, she was an expert. Soon she reached into my pocket and took out the condoms I had bought earlier.

'Good work, this is why you ran like crazy, didn't you?' she said.

'Yeah, I didn't wanna take a chance.' I told her.

She carefully wrapped it in a condom and gave it a quick suck, and then she slowly sat on it and held my hands tightly. Her moans were irregular now and she leaned on my body, understanding her pain mixed with her pleasure I pulled her in, and she moaned a little more, now her voice turned into hushed screams, like she wanted to shout out at the top of her voice, but she couldn't because of some unknown reason. I held her breasts, each in one hand and kept on pressing them. She kept her body in a very regular to and fro motion, feeling each one of my inches inside her, she wasn't new at this, which was for sure. I started a little bit of movement of my own, penetrating even deeper, giving her all that she desired that night. Soon we switched positions, now I was on top of her, she lied there, her eyes indicating that she wanted

272

more, I was already deep inside her, but there was something missing, the passion, the excruciating desire of pleasure, everything that made it what it was till now, it was all there, but still there was something missing, then it struck me. I leaned in and started kissing her with all the passion inside me, she was still moaning as I continued the slow movement in and out, then I ineased my pace, the slow and measured movements suddenly changed and it took her at surprise, she took off her hands from my back and grabbed the bedsheets, now she didn't control herself, she let go of all the emotions that were running inside her body, all her desires were fulfilled, she was getting towards her climax and so was I, increasing the pace made her scream on top of her voice and finally, each of us had our climax, I did take it out before that, my sex-ed teacher taught me well, just figuratively, not literally. We both took a long breath and I lied beside her on the bed, looking at the ceiling and the fan rotating on top of us, we lied there in complete silence. For several minutes we were in the spot and in the same position, she didn't move an inch after what happened, I guess she was tired, I hope. I was about to say something when the doorbell rang.

'That must be the food you ordered.' She said.

'Yeah, I'll go get it, there's my wallet in my pant, can you pass it?' I said, as soon as she turned to me with my pants I kissed her, a long passionate smooch just as a thank you for being there for me.

'Go, get the food, Romeo.' She said and kissed me on my cheek.

With a towel and my wallet in my hand I walked out of the door, where another surprise was waiting for me.

'Here, that's the whole order right?' I saw Ritwik paying for the food and talking to the delivery guy, I didn't see Shelly around though.

'Hey, where's Shelly? Didn't she come back yet?' I asked Ritwik as he placed the bags on the dining table.

'I am right behind you and your towel is slipping away tiger.' A female voice, oh fuck, Shelly was standing right behind me, I ran back inside the room.

'Who is out there?' Emma asked.

'My roomie and his girlfriend.' I told her.

'But didn't you say that they were not going to be here.' She was really calm and composed about all this, whereas I was getting nervous.

I walked out of the room again, fully covered, and saw them both sitting on the couch, staring at me.

'Ahhh, hi.' I said.

'Hey, how are you?' Ritwik with his sick, wicked smile.

'I am fine; I am good actually, why?' I asked.

'What about Emma? Is she alive in there or did you kill her?' Shelly said and Ritwik laughed his lungs out.

'HA HA HA, when did you guys come home anyway?' I asked them, just to make sure how much they had heard.

'Well, let's just say that the movie was already playing when we entered the hall, but the climax and ending scenes, we definitely didn't miss those.' He said and I hung my head total disbelief, they didn't even tell me that they were going to be home, and then they heard everything.

'You sick bastard, you should have called atleast.' I said.

'Check your phone, Mr. Love Machine.' He said and I took out my phone from my pocket.

There were more than ten missed calls and several messages from Ritwik and Shelly, asking if they should get back home or not.

'Ooops, sorry you guys.' I said.

'It's Ok, call her out, she must be famished after all that you have done to her, and seriously, what were you doing man?' Ritwik with all his excitement asked.

'It just happened, I wasn't doing anything special.' I said.

'Yeah, Shelly will tell me that.' He said.

'Why? What does she know?' I asked him.

'Nothing right now, but she will soon.' He said.

'What? How is she going to know anything?' I asked him.

'Look behind you, you will understand.' He said and I turned around and saw Shelly and Emma going into Ritwik's room, Shelly looking a little too excited.

'What? They are just going into your room, what's with that?' I asked him.

'Bro, they are going to discuss what happened between you and your girl in there, and trust me, they do this the entire time, and girls discuss everything.' He said.

'They do? Really? Why?' I asked.

'They just do, they like discussing how hot it was, the details like girth, length, stamina and technique. Wanna have a beer?' he asked, after exploding my mind with that information. But I couldn't do anything about it, and I did want a beer.

'Yeah, get some cigarettes too.' I said.

'Hmmm, so tell me, you like her yet?' he asked.

'What do you mean? I obviously do, that's the reason all this happened.' I told him.

'No it's not; you just say that so you don't feel guilty about cheating on your girlfriend. Trust me, I have been there, with Shelly, it was just a big mistake first, but then I got to spending time with her and everything, I realised that I had a lot more stuff common with her than I had with her sister. That's why we are still together.' He told me.

'I am the worst person I know, I had sex with a girl I don't even have feelings for, and the girl I actually love is sitting miles away in India and she has no idea what I am going through, I don't know what I would tell her, I seriously don't know that, I think I am just going to tell her about Saman and then tell her about Emma, that's the only fair thing I can do now.' I said.

'I was just about to say that myself, you must tell her about Emma, but it's not necessary you tell her now, spend the night with Emma, you need that.' He said and we saw Emma and Shelly walking out of the room, Emma's face was all pinkish red and Shelly had a big smile on her face. I looked at Ritwik.

'What?' he asked the girls.

'Nothing, shall we have dinner? And can you two please stop smoking in the apartment?' Shelly said and took the cigarettes from our hands and put them in the ashtray.

'You guys ordered too?' I asked them, I had only ordered food for two people.

'Yeah, when you were humping her brains out, that's when we called the restaurant and ordered food for ourselves.' Shelly said.

'Shelly?!!' Emma screamed.

'Humping her brains out? Did you say that to her?' I laughed and asked Emma.

'No I didn't, Shelly, shush.' Emma signaled Shelly and she laughed.

'Yeah you didn't, come let's have dinner.' I said and we all sat down to have dinner like a good nice family.

For that night I almost forgot that my family had been through a tragedy and I was here to study, I just didn't want anything to screw up my mind again, but I knew I was going to be questioned and I was going to be hated soon.

CHAPTER 17

THE TRUST THAT WAS BROKEN

WE HAD AN AMAZING NIGHT and after that we went inside our respective rooms with our respected company. Ritwik told me that they had heard almost everything that happened in my room, now it was our turn. We couldn't close our eyes until Ritwik stopped "humping Her brains out" in the other room. Emma lied next to me holding my hand while her other hand caressed my hair.

'You know you are an amazing guy, Deven.' She said.

'Why did you say that?' I asked her.

'Because you are, and you know what, even though I was drunk tonight, I will remember each and every second of this night forever.' She said and kissed me.

'You are an amazing girl too, Emma, and I am not saying this because we slept together or anything, it's because you were there. When I needed a friend, you were there, and that's what makes you so special for me.' I said.

She closed her eyes and started humming a song.

'Piano man?' I said.

'You have heard that song?' she said.

'Oh yes, I love that song. You know what, I want to do something, but it's not possible for me to do that thing. Do we have college tomorrow?' I said.

'No, I don't think we have any classes on Sundays.' She said and smacked me.

'Oh, I completely forgot its Sunday tomorrow. I will go and buy something special.' I said.

'What could be that special?' she asked.

'Just something, you will love it.' I said. 'Now close your eyes and let me kiss you.' I said and she closed her eyes and then I kissed her. We slept through the night.

The next morning I woke up and went out for a walk, Emma was still sleeping and had no idea what I was going to buy. I took my wallet with me and started searching for a music store; I was going to buy a new guitar for myself. I found a store opened and it said **"Melody Rocks".** I went inside and found a really big showroom filled with music instruments, they had them all, even Indian instruments like *Dholak*, *Flute*, and *Sitar* and stuff like that.

'Sir, I would like to see the range of guitars you have.' I said to a salesman sitting on a wooden chair.

'Sure sir, please follow me upstairs.' He said and I did as I was asked.

I went upstairs and saw two rows of guitars hanging by the wall. One row had all the acoustic guitars from various companies and the other one had electric guitars. I picked out a black guitar with an inbuilt tuner and equalizer.

'How much for this?' I asked the man.

'A Hundred and fifty five dollars, sir.' He said.

'Ok, get me some plectrums too, pack them fast.' I said and rushed back towards the counter.

I paid the man and started walking back towards my building. I saw our landlord walking out of the door.

'So you have planned to disturb the whole buliding now?' he said.

'No, I just want to keep it in my room; I don't even know how to play it.' I said and gave him a quick good bye.

I ran upstairs and opened the door to my apartment and saw Emma sitting on the couch with both Ritwik and Shelly.

'Hey, where were you?' Emma asked before she saw the guitar on my shoulder.

'Is that a guitar? You know how to play?' Shelly asked.

'No, I just like to hang heavy stuff on my shoulders, just for fun dumbass.' I said and all of them laughed.

'Play something for us, Deven.' Emma said.

'What do you think I wanted to do last night? When I said that I couldn't do that?' I said.

'Ammm, we were listening to the Piano Man, wait, do you know how to play it on guitar?' she asked another dumb question.

I winked at her and poured myself a small glass of neat vodka, just to warm up my throat.

'Now was that necessary?' she asked.

'Yeah, I needed that.' I said and pulled a dining chair to sit and play my first song for Emma.

'Guys, I have been through so much in the past week or so, that I just forgot that I had such great friends in my life. This song is dedicated to all of you.' I said and started playing the Piano Man by Billy Joel.

The starting got me applause from my very private audience.

'La la la didi dah, sing us a song you're the piano man, sing us a song tonight, well we're all in the mood for a melody, and you've got us feeling alright.' I sang the chorus for the song and all three of them clapped for me.

The song ended and Emma got up to kiss me.

'I loved it, why didn't you ever tell us about this?' she said.

'Just didn't get enough time, now I do, so I did this for you.' I said and she kissed me again.

Then I played some other songs for them and they liked each and every one of them.

'Dude, you are good. You should play in your college.' Ritwik suggested.

'Yes you have to, you guys will have a fresher's party right? Play in that party, play the Piano Man, they will love it your voice Deven.' Shelly said.

'Ok, I will try, now can we guys have breakfast?' I said and then we had a debate on where should we go to have breakfast.

Between all that was happening with me and Emma, I totally forgot about Harshaali, I still lovd her, I still wanted to talk to her, I still wanted to meet her but now I knew what I had done, I knew that I couldn't face her, I didn't want her to know about this at all. But somewhere inside I knew I had to let her go, that was going to be the best thing for her, to leave me behind and move on with her life.

I never had any idea that I would be the worst thing in her life, never wanted to hurt her, never wanted her to think bad about me, but that was going to be difficult now that I had cheated on her.

'What are you thinking?' Emma asked.

'Nothing, I just had a friend in India, I was thinking about her.' I said.

'A girlfriend?' she asked and Ritwik looked at me.

'No, just a friend.' I said and looked down at the floor; I was actually ashamed of myself in that moment.

'Ammm is she Ok?' she asked.

'We should go to that new place across the street, I have heard that its chicken and other dishes are all really great.' Ritwik interrupted.

'I guess that's a nice idea.' I said.

We all got up and started walking outside, when suddenly I realised that I wasn't carrying my phone with me.

'You guys go, I will meet you guys at that place.' I said.

'What happened?' Emma asked.

'I have to call home.' I said.

'Ohh, ok.' She said and they walked outside the apartment. I locked the door after they left. I gathered up the strength and went inside my room to call Harshaali.

'Hello?' I said.

'Where the fuck have you been Dev?! Do you have any fucking idea how tensed I was, you have been avoiding me from last week? What is the matter with you? Do you have another girlfriend over there? Tell me the truth, what's going on with you over there?' she started yelling at me the moment I picked up. I had tears in my eyes as I had heard her voice after such a long time.

'Hmmm, I was a little busy.' I said.

'Busy with what? Or should I say busy with whom?' she yelled again, she was angry, so angry that she didn't have any idea what she was saying, but whatever she thought, it was all true, it had all happened. So I had no other option.

'With Emma, I have been busy with Emma.' I said and she stopped talking, then I heard her weeping.

'What did I do wrong Dev?' she asked, her question made me cry too. 'I trusted you, loved you with all my heart, and this is what I get? You are leaving me for a girl you have for less than a month?' she said.

'I am sorry Harshaali, but this is over now, you will be happier without me I know. Believe me, you have to move on.' I said.

'Is it that fucking easy for you to say? Alright, I will move on, don't ever try to contact me again.' She said and disconnected the call.

I looked at myself in the mirror and slapped myself several times, not because I cheated on her, but because I made her cry, because I did everything that I never wanted to do. I left my phone on the bed and went out to get some breakfast with others.

CHAPTER 18

A FRIEND WHO LOVED ME MORE THAN A FRIEND

AFTER BREAKING UP WITH HARSHAALI, all I was left with was my friends in New York, Ritwik, Shelly and the one girl who stood by me all the time, Emma. We started dating after a few days, but I always remembered harshaali, she was all that I thought about, she was all that mattered in my life, but I had to let her go. I knew that I couldn't give her the love and the life she deserved, I was a cheat. She deserved far better. After a few days I started going to college regularly, I wanted my life to get back on track.

'What do you keep thinking about?' Emma asked, we were sitting in the canteen.

'Nothing, I was just thinking about the songs I would sing for the college on our fresher's party.' I said, although I was thinking about her.

'Oh, I thought you were singing Piano Man, any other songs in mind?' she asked.

'I don't know, I am just a little tensed, what if they don't like it? What if they don't like me?' I asked her.

'Hey, everybody would love your voice, trust me, I have heard it myself.' She said and gave me a kiss on my cheek, I smiled at her.

'You have to listen to a song that I prepared a long time ago, it is a Hindi song, but I will explain it to you later. I love it.' I said.

'Ok, I will stay with you tonight,' she said.

We had been together since the first night we spent together. I liked her and she liked me too, we were really comfortable together. After college we took a cab back home.

'Ritwik would be there, right?' she asked.

'Yeah, why?' i said.

'Nothing, stop the car.' She said and went outside instantly.

She came back after a few minutes, empty handed.

'Why did you do that?' I asked her.

'What? Do what?' she asked me back with a confused expression.

'Nothing, let's go, sir.' I said and the cabbie started the car again.

We reached our building a few minutes later.

'Go check if Ritwik is home, if he isn't, call Me.' she said.

I was confused but still I said OK.

I opened the door to my apartment and saw that the apartment was empty, so I called Emma.

'Nobody is here baby, come upstairs.' I said.

'Turn around.' She said, and I did.

As soon as I turned around, she kissed me; I didn't know how long she had been standing there, just waiting for me to look at her. She pushed me on to the sofa and I sat in it, taking her with me.

'Check my back pocket.' She said while kissing me.

I took my hands off her breasts and touched her butt, or her back pocket to be precise. I felt something inside, I pulled it out and realised that it was a condom.

'So this is what you stepped out pf the car for?' I asked.

'Yeah, this and I called Ritwik to leave the apartment empty for us tonight.' She said and looked at me, biting her lip, her heavy breathing told me that she wanted me to hold her tight, but tonight it was going to be different, tonight I wanted her to lead.

'You know what? I want you to do stuff for me today; I won't even move a little bit, you do all the work.' I said and she laughed.

'You want me to do it all?' she said, laughing.

'Yeah, I think you will be really great.' I said and pulled her closer to kiss, but she pulled herself back.

'You want me to do stuff to you right? Then stop moving.' She instructed me and I followed.

'Ok.' That was all I could say before she kissed me with all her passion and wildness.

She stripped off every inch of cloth on her body and sat in my lap, rubbing her hot body againg my clothes, kissing me and rubbing her pussy against the tent in my pants. I could already notice the wet patches on my pants, from her pussy. I tried to control my hands as much as possible but it was too much. She kept rubbing herself on my hard on, until she decided to take my pants off, she took them off in her own seductive style, pulling them all the way down, taking her time.

Then she started doing the thing she was really very good at, she started using her hands to take it to a whole new level. She started licking it up and down to the whole length, and then she sucked it, so hard that I was actually left breathless, she enjoyed the way she did it, so she continued with that crazy blowjob for a bit longer. Then she took the packed condom from my hands and tore away the packing, wrapped it on my penis and looked at me.

'This is going to be the best ride ever.' she said and jumped on the couch, making her way towards my her desires, she kissed me until it dug deep inside her soaked pussy, she moaned. After that she just started bouncing on it, it was heaven, the way she did all that, she was the goddess of seduction, the whole time she bounced on my dick, she looked straight into my eyes, as if she wanted more.

'Oh fuck, Ok, my turn now.' I said and picked her up in my arms, threw her back on the sofa and got into my own position. I started with licking her pussy and using my fingers to give her different rounds of pleasure at the same time, she was enjoying each and every second of it. And then I gave her what she actually craved, we did it for more than half an hour, in which we changed several positions and she had too many orgasms.

'That was AWESOME.' She screamed.

'I know it was.' I said as I got up from the couch and walked towards the kitchen to get the bottle of Whisky, I needed some.

'Why do you always drink after sex?' she asked.

'I don't know, post-coital requirement I guess.' I told her and laughed.

'This is not funny Deven; this just shows how much you rely on it.' She said.

'Do you know the reason I drink?' I asked her.

'You never told me, you never talk to me. I want to know the reason behind this, after you came back from India, you started drinking so much, why is that?' she asked, I made a big glass for myself and drank it before answering that question.

'There was a tragedy back home, when I had to rush back.' I said.

'You need to talk about it, it's eating you inside.' She said as she got dressed again.

'Hmmm, I know.' I said and made another glass for myself, but before I could drink it up, Emma took away the glass.

'Drink this after you tell me everything,' she said, actually she ordered.

'I had a brother, he died in a car accident, his car fell from a cliff, his girlfriend was with him at that time, she survived and I lost him forever. We have filed a case against that bitch. If it was in my hands I could have killed her on my own.' I said and took the glass from her hand. She released it instantly.

I was looking at her and she was staring at me, I didn't want anything else, just sit there and have my drinks.

'I am so sorry.' She said, her voice cracking up.

'You don't have to be. It's not your fault.' I said.

'You are dealing with all this alone? Why are you doing this to yourself Deven?' she asked, taking my hand in hers.

'I have sort of made my peace with this thing. But even today, I feel helpless when I think about the things Saman must have gone through, what he must have thought about in his last moments. I am telling you the truth Emma, if we had any idea that he was lying there all by himself injured and bleeding, both me and Naman would have jumped into that forest to bring him out alive. We would have done anything and everything in our power to save him, but we couldn't.' I said as tears came pouring down my eyes, a few drops in the whisky and a few on Emma's hands.

'Deven, please don't cry, I am here for you baby, I am so sorry I brought this up, please calm down, everything will be fine.' She said and pulled me closer to hug me.

'I feel like this all the time Emma, all the fucking time, I can't sleep, I don't eat, I don't talk much, I only keep thinking about this. I don't want to live like this, I want this to end.' I said and cried.

'Shhh.. Come; let's go inside, you need rest.' She said as she took the glass from my hand and helped me get up.

Everything seemed to be my fault, my brother's death, my breakup with Harshaali, the situation my family was in, everything. But there was still one person who wanted to be with me all the time, it was Emma. To be frank, I was also attached to her now, but not as much as I was to Harshaali. I always looked at my phone hoping that maybe she would call, but she never did after we broke up. I knew she missed me, I knew she still loved and I knew it was all my fault, but I was ready to let her go, because I knew I was damaged goods now, I couldn't see her getting hurt because of me all the time. Yes I loved her that much. I didn't want to become the reason for her "Sweet_Sorrow", and for me, all that mattered was Harshaali's happiness and her smile, she couldn't be happy with me anymore. I knew she had to move on without me and I told her the same thing, I was ready to accept her hatred towards me for life then to become her worst nightmare. I just wish I had the guts to tell her about Saman, but I knew she would have stayed if she knew what I was going through, that's the reason I didn't tell her.

Sometimes you just find the right person in the most unusual places, it might be a basketball match, it might even be a bar or it might be a desk in front of you in your own class. I found mine, she sat in front of me and I hated her at first, but today, when I think about her, all I see is images of the best five years of my life, I just wish her happiness in whatever she does and wherever she lives. All I wanted my whole life was to be her "Number One", I just didn't realize how hard it could be, I just wasn't right for that girl, I broke her trust and I cannot forgive myself my whole life, because she never did. But whatever, I was fortunate enough to have her by my side for five long years and I will always cherish that time of my life. I know I wasn't "The One" for her, but that girl was always "The One" for me, and she always will be.